frequency

CHRISTOPHER KROVATIN

Entangled Publishing, LLC
2614 South Timberline Road
Suite 105, PMB 159
Fort Collins, CO 80525
rights@entangledpublishing.com

Entangled Teen is an imprint of Entangled Publishing, LLC.

Visit our website at www.entangledpublishing.com.

Edited by Stacy Abrams
Cover design by
Mayhem Cover Creations
Heather Howland
Liz Pelletier
Cover images by
D-Keine/iStock
MATJAZ SLANIC/iStock
liulolo/iStock
Interior design by Toni Kerr

ISBN: 978-1-64063-181-6
Ebook ISBN: 978-1-64063-182-3

Manufactured in the United States of America

First Edition October 2018

10 9 8 7 6 5 4 3 2 1

This book is dedicated to the memory of Nick Harris, my collaborator and fellow storyteller. Without him, none of this would be possible. Even when we butted heads, Nick never gave up on me, or this story. It hurts that he never got to see it get finished.

Here it is, man.

chapter 1

The crunch of tires on gravel grew in the distance. Oncoming headlights turned the tree line buttery yellow at its edges. They cut across the asphalt, illuminating a faded Sunkist-orange sign featuring a ruddy cluster of grapes and the cursive words

Hamm Winery
Spend a beautiful day in a beautiful place.
Exit 14 off State Road 217.

Behind a nearby tree, Fiona Jones, nine years old, squinted and hunkered down close to her bike. She'd overheard the men correctly. They'd brought him here.

Edgar Hokes's blue pickup truck shuddered to a halt by the side of the road no more than twenty feet away from her. Her father, Robert, hopped out of the passenger seat and purposefully strode to the back of the vehicle. Edgar himself, tall and unflappable, with deep lines in his face, calmly stepped out from behind the wheel. Darren Fiddler—*Caroline's dad*, Fiona thought, *so nice during sleepovers*—was seated in the bed of the truck. She'd known these three men her whole life, but the hard looks on their faces made them unrecognizable to her.

Edgar Hokes opened the back door, and he and Robert Jones carried the boy out of the back, their arms hooked at his elbows. Fiona's stomach clenched in terror—his hands were bound with duct tape, his feet similarly so. They dumped him facedown on the grass at the foot of the road sign like a sack of garbage.

Edgar Hokes knelt behind him and pulled a deadly-looking knife from his boot. For a moment, Fiona thought her heart might explode, but then Edgar dug in with the blade and the boy's hands and feet came free.

The boy got to his knees. He removed a rag from his mouth and a blindfold from his face. His army jacket was torn and bloody; a back patch with a strange symbol on it curled up at one corner like the lid of a half-opened can. The hood of his black sweatshirt was pulled over his head, obscuring him but for a few dangling strands of stringy hair.

Fiona couldn't take her eyes off him.

"A few things you ought to know," said her father in a tone she had never heard before, cold and slimy as a stone at the bottom of Winston Pond.

"The next time I see you," said the boy, "I'm going to stand on your neck."

Edgar's knee pulled up, and in a flash, his boot struck the back of the boy's skull, smashing his forehead into the support post of the winery sign with a *thunk*. Fiona gasped without meaning to, tears springing to her eyes. The boy fell forward but managed to stay on his hands and knees. The sound of his blood dribbling into the grass made her head spin.

"First thing is, you stay away from here," continued her father as though nothing had happened. "I'm not just talking about our town. I mean the county, the region, the whole state. Got it?"

The boy spat.

"He asked you a question, you little shit!" yelped Darren Fiddler, a shaking leaf where there should've been a man. Fiona's dad held up a hand, and Darren quieted down.

The hooded figure coughed. "My equipment," he mumbled, "my laptop, my records—"

"Gone. Forget about them. Those are the least of your concerns," said her father. "Your laptop? Son, you're lucky we didn't take your teeth."

Tears ran down Fiona's cheeks, hot and quick. She didn't know why, but taking his music and equipment felt like they were desecrating him, ripping out his soul.

"Second. I'm sure you have plenty of friends from the city who think they're real tough. Real gangsters. But I promise you, if any of your degenerate pals roll through here, they ain't leaving. Which leads me to our third and final word of warning." He leaned in close, his voice barely audible. "If we ever see one of these kids you got rid of wandering around our streets again, we're going to take it as an attack. We *will* find you, and we'll hold you personally responsible. Got it?"

A pause, the night full of electricity.

And then the boy shook as a dark, throaty laugh wheezed out of him.

"Something funny?" said Hokes, flicking his thumb on the handle of his knife.

"The...*blindfold*," spat the boy. "My *gangster* friends. You three." His chuckle became a cackle lined with a gurgle. "You think you're a bunch of hard-asses because you beat up some kid in funny clothes? Let's be honest, Mr. Jones, *you couldn't pay me*. You made a deal with the devil, the time came to pony up, and you chumps didn't have a soul among the lot of you."

With a long inhale, the boy rose to his feet, the headlights illuminating the patch that dominated his jacket. Fiona's eyes drank in the design on it—circles within circles, old Latin words, strange figures beckoning to distant planets.

"So here's *my* warning to *you*," said the boy. "Before tonight? You were just another pathetic small town that needed an exterminator. But I promise you, I'll never forget this, or you." His one hand slapped wetly against the sign, leaving a bloody handprint. "Hamm, Ohio. A beautiful day in a beautiful place—"

Her father's fist hit the boy's kidney with an ugly *thud*, sending him back down to his knees. Then Edgar and Darren moved in and kicked him for what felt like hours. Fiona sobbed silently and finally threw her hands over her eyes, unable to watch.

When the sounds of boot on flesh ceased, she parted her fingers and peeked at the scene. The three enforcers stood there in the dark, panting. The strange man who used to be her father nodded, and his cohorts climbed back into the truck. "Last warning, boy," Robert Jones called over his shoulder. "Walk away."

The truck's engine coughed to life. The headlights flared, illuminating Fiona's hiding place for one heart-stopping instant—and then they were gone in a spray of gravel. The night resumed its heavy silence, cut only by the shrill cries of crickets and the bloody coughing of the boy in the dirt.

After a few minutes, Fiona wiped her face on her sleeve and rose from her cramped crouch. The boy had moved only slightly, half collapsed against the post of the sign. What little of his face she could catch in the moonlight looked swollen and shiny with blood. She watched as he wept for just a moment—wracking, full-body sobs that shook him at the waist, reminding to Fiona just how young he really was—before he swallowed hard and went silent.

Somewhere in her core, she knew he was brave. To get

upagain and again, to not fold under their threats, to *talk back to her father*...those weren't the actions of a coward. There was no way he was the simple villain her town feared.

He was so strange, like an alien or an angel, a creature from a place she'd never known. She wanted desperately to help him. Her hands dug into her backpack, searching around for something, anything, to show him that he wasn't alone out there.

She later considered how weird it must have looked to him—here he was, lying beaten and bloodied a good eight and a half miles from anywhere, and out of the trees comes this skinny, little girl with an overbite and a ponytail, the girl from the town council meeting, holding out an apple and a bottle of water.

It must have been frightening, surreal. But he didn't even flinch when she approached him. As she put the food down a good three feet away from him—because who knew? Maybe he *was* dangerous—he didn't budge. He just followed her with his eyes.

What did he see in her? she wondered. What was there *to* see?

"Thank you," he whispered, his eyes shining like stars. "What's your name?"

Her heart leaped, her lungs failed her, and she ran. She was on her bike in seconds, pedaling her butt off down the back paths through the woods. In one final glance over her shoulder, she saw him pushing himself up to his knees and reaching for the water.

chapter
2

Like all small suburban towns, Hamm, Ohio, had two faces. By the end of every evening—because there wasn't really a *nightlife* in Hamm, just a couple of bars that catered to locals with bad reputations and reluctantly returning college students—the town and its people were disorganized and messy. Black garbage bags were dragged out into the street; sweaty aprons and work shirts were tossed into hampers with relief. Petty arguments were whispered between couples or shouted between kids and parents. But in the morning, with the dew undisturbed on the lawns of its identical houses and the chairs resting silently on the tabletops of the cafés and restaurants downtown, Hamm was pure, as innocent as a newborn fawn getting its first footing.

One thing was certain: both faces were incredibly lame. The evening's issues were all first-world problems, and the quiet mornings were too sugared-cereal, paper-route *adorable*. There was nothing even slightly rock-and-roll about Hamm; it had no teeth whatsoever.

For the first time in years, Fiona Jones, eighteen years old, gave no fucks about that. All that mattered was how good his hoodie smelled.

As she coasted down South Burgundy Street on her beat-up bike, the Scorpions blasting hot sonic love through her headphones, she hoped the scent of his hoodie followed her like a cartoon vapor trail. It smelled like his hair, mostly, from what she could gather with her deep sniffs—a heady mixture of natural oils and something else, something personal. There were equal parts BO and deodorant, both of which were a little gross but familiar and comforting, and a tang of spices she couldn't identify from his parents' restaurant. There was a hint of weed, too, an odor she used to associate with huddled hippies and creepy vans, but which now just made her think of his carefree grin. They all rolled up into a smell she could only call *Boy*.

What did it matter that the sweatshirt was ripped along one sleeve and had no doubt spent time stuffed between couch cushions? It was black, had a giant tarantula with hypodermic needles for fangs on the back, and belonged to him. As the breeze billowed her upraised hood, she wanted everyone to see her wearing it. *Behold, Hamm, you silly American relic, behold this hoodie, and know that I am Spoken For. There's no way he left it by accident.*

Hamm rolled past her, and she smiled despite herself. It was everything she dreamed of escaping, dollhouse pretty on the outside but loaded with secrets and people trying to be normal and failing miserably. Mr. Fredericks sipping coffee on his lawn in a black silk robe with Chinese dragons on it like some kind of suburban Hugh Hefner. Natalie Charrest jogging in full spandex—that she had no business wearing, dear God, woman—with her German shepherd, Genghis. The Tarters in their gaudy Italian business wear, pecking each other twice on each cheek before heading to their separate cars. They all tried too hard to pretend like everything was *fine*, which meant *boring*, *dull*, *unrealistic*, and really, just *uncool*.

But today, it didn't matter. Maybe things were gritty and real in places like New York and L.A. and all those big cities with cobblestones and tiny punk venues. Maybe the people there didn't lie to themselves about alcoholism and divorce and apathy. She'd get there eventually. But Hamm had Horace. Horace had her, and she had him. To hell with the rest of the world.

As the matching houses gave way to an empty country road lined with sparse woods, she sensed the vibrations of other people on the street. Looking over her shoulder, she saw Rita, dark and doe-eyed in a vintage dress and knee-high socks, biking behind her, and Caroline, lanky and glistening with sweat in her gym clothes, her ponytail bobbing up and down as she jogged alongside them.

"How long have you been creeping on me?" Fiona asked, pulling off her headphones.

"We've been calling your name for, like, three minutes," said Rita, folding her arms. How she could bike without hands, Fiona would never know.

"You know biking with your headphones in is super dangerous, right?" said Caroline, half breathless. "You're going to turn into the path of a car and get killed, and then we'll have to have a candlelight vigil and shit."

"Let me get run over," said Fiona. "I can die happy."

Her friends shared a glance, raising eyebrows.

"Someone's feeling sassy," said Caroline, speeding up and turning around to face Fiona. Hearing new gossip was more important than seeing where she was going; the world would get out of her way. "What's going on? What's behind this crazy glow you've got about you?"

"I'm fine," declared Fiona, smirking back. "It's just a beautiful day in Hamm."

"*Wait* a hot second," said Rita, speeding up to flank her friends. Fiona felt Rita's gaze scanning her, taking notes. Suddenly, the girl's eyes went wide, and her vintage Schwinn stopped with a sharp scrape of tire on asphalt. "You trollop! *Finally!*"

Fiona slowed but never stopped. She felt her cheeks burn and her grin spread wide.

"What's up?" panted Caroline, jogging in place next to Rita.

"Caroline, look at what she's wearing."

"Oh, hey, that's…" Fiona heard Caroline gasp. "*Daaamn*, girl!"

Suddenly, they were at her side again, eyes bugging and mouths agape. Fiona laughed, recklessly, mischievously.

"Really!" cried Rita, looking impressed.

"Yes, *really*," said Fiona, almost offended. "A *good friend of mine* told me six months was long enough." Rita rolled her eyes and gave her neckline an exaggerated Even-White-Boys-Got-to-Shout tug.

"Tell me you washed that," said Caroline, shaking her head as she ran faster. "You're going to get sick from wearing that thing. You realize it's probably soaked in bong water and jizz."

"Even you cannot ruin my morning with your grossness," said Fiona, beaming straight ahead while Rita cackled at Caroline's remark. "It is a wonderful September day, and I am having a wonderful morning."

"Good job getting laid, weirdo," said Rita. "Took you long enough."

"It was!" Fiona proudly told the morning, the silver roadside barricade, the silhouette of their school growing in the distance. "It *was* a good job!"

"I swear," Caroline called over her shoulder, her ponytail still bouncing as she pulled ahead of them. "All this over Horace Palmada."

Horace Palmada. Cue the click count, the bass drop, feedback, distortion. Horace Palmada. The name sounded like the boy himself, lanky and quick, moving among people with an intense kind of glee, like the world was a beautiful joke. It spoke of him physically, too: thick lashes, that bit of hair over the ears and forehead, a perpetually guilty smile on those caramel lips. Horace Palmada, who said that it always sounded better on vinyl, that Spotify cheapened the listening experience. Who rolled around with one of those boxes for his records, the kind with a lock and a handle and slots for each LP. Who had a keyboard that he talked about turning into a keytar. Who knew how to match beats and could spin a decent set of some bomb-ass shit.

She'd made Horace Palmada wait. If she was going to open up that can of worms, she wanted to be 100 percent sure. *Like with a tattoo*, she'd said, and he'd laughed, but he'd waited. And given how he'd acted last night, it was damn well worth the wait.

Horace Palmada seemed to call out to her as she and her friends arrived at school—through chaining up her bike and heading to her locker, there he was, a frequency that only she could hear, drawing her to the source. Loading up on her books for American Lit II felt like an obvious precursor to seeing him, and as she walked to class with her bag clutched to her chest, Fiona could feel the distance between them shortening, step by step, until *bam*, there he was, loping down the stairs in front of Ms. Larimer's classroom.

They made eye contact, and her heart seized up like a fist. What if the past six months were all a lie, a game played by an extremely patient creep? What if leaving the hoodie *had* been an accident, a bleary-eyed mistake made by a typical boy scared of getting his ass kicked by *Mr. Jones*? What if he called her "bae," or "shorty," or "boo," or something else equally The Worst? What if he was with that stoner friend of his who he called "Swordfish" and tried to act cool by giving her a nod or some greasy wink? It would kill her. It would blow her to smithereens. She would physically murder him—

And then he shot her a lopsided grin, and she felt her insides turn into hot chocolate. Flashbacks of last night—his neck between her teeth, the rhythm of their pressed bodies, that same smile appearing on him as they finally caught their breath and held each other in the dark—crossed her mind as he approached, making her feel light-headed. They closed in on each other, and as they passed, he reached out and put his hands on her hips.

Hands on her hips, in front of everyone. Not shoulders or elbows, her hips, her waist. She tried to keep from biting her lip and smiling like a fangirl, but she couldn't help it.

He nodded at her headphones. "What were you listening to?"

Unf. It was always the first thing he asked when he saw her, and it got her every time. "The Scorpions."

His grin expanded, and he gave her an ironic set of devil horns. "Killer. Rock on, girl. I have calc now, and then gym, but lunch?"

"You bet," she said.

"Awesome." He kissed her once, quickly but not dryly. A full kiss, not the peck they'd shared in the halls when he'd dared to kiss her at school in the past.

"That hoodie looks good on you," he said and darted off.

She spent English half awake, exploring this new feeling rushing over her again and again. *Killer. Awesome.*

The worst had been avoided. After last night, things had only gotten better. The hoodie was left with her in mind. It looked good on her.

Two periods later, he was waiting for her by the back doors with his record case strapped over his shoulder. He took her hand and led her out to the back patio and through the gauntlet of curious stares at the outdoor tables. Some of Horace's stoner buddies gave them a lewd passing "*Ooooh,*" but he just rolled his eyes and shook his head. "Virgins," he mumbled.

Once they were out on the bleachers, he and Fiona did a perimeter check—no teachers around, no dumb-ass jocks playing Frisbee—and then their eyes met, and animal instinct kicked in. She grabbed him and yanked his face to hers, their lips colliding, her hands on his face and neck. His hands clamped onto her hips and pulled her against him, then snaked around her waist and squeezed her until she could barely breathe. They were being sloppy, she knew, but it was as though they'd opened the floodgates last night, and now she wanted to be daring and brazen with him.

"What if we went for it again right now?" she whispered. "Right here, on the bleachers?"

"You're crazy, girl," he whispered back. "Maybe if you were wearing a skirt." She cackled, and they resumed making out.

A few minutes later, they separated. She lay back on the bleacher with her head on his lap, and he dug deli sandwiches out of his bag. They ate in satisfied silence.

"What time did you finally leave this morning?" she asked, relishing the decadence of their late-night tryst.

"Around four thirty," he groaned, stretching his arms.

"Good, you got out in time," she said.

"Girl, I'm slick as hell." He leaned over; she sat halfway up, and they kissed in the middle. "Seriously, though, you don't think your dad saw me?"

"He would've said something." She laughed. "He's not great at subtlety. Got any new vinyl?"

"That I do," he said. "Hold on, I'll show you."

They sat up and got down to business. He unlatched his case and removed a short stack of records, mostly electronica, psytrance, and hip-hop, but also a few gems, items he knew were more her speed—a Ramones LP after Infected Mushroom, some Doors next to Deadmau5, and spookier beats like Espectrostatic and Portishead remixes throughout. She knew he'd gotten these records only to impress her, and it actually made his rock-and-roll finds even sweeter. He liked making her smile.

As she flipped through his new offerings, she could tell that something was up. Normally, he went on and on about each record in detail—studio location, production, release year, the whole Wikipedia entry. Instead, he seemed to be waiting—

"Whoa!" she said, revealing a cover festooned with a grinning, ax-wielding zombie whose name she knew—Eddie, Eddie the Head. Iron Maiden's *Killers*, a classic. "This album *rules*. You're super true for having this, you realize."

He grinned. "It was my uncle's. He finally let me go cherry-pick through his collection last week. He also had some Whitesnake, but this seemed more up your alley."

"You've got to spin this as much as possible. Work it into your set."

"That'll be hard when it's at your place."

It took her a second to parse what he was saying. When her eyes finally met his, she saw the sparkle in them. Her heart bent in the middle, and a look of disbelief crossed her face. "No, no, wait, this was your uncle's, you can't just give it to me—"

"It's yours," he said, shaking his head and looking down at his hands. "You know I'm not huge into the heavy stuff. I'm just glad you like it."

She felt choked up. It was too much; *he* was too much. He kept surprising her. She remembered the night before, when her hands had shaken as she'd told him about Harry Suggs at that party the year before they'd started dating. Keeping it from him was a mistake. She'd told herself that she had no reason *not* to tell him; she was her own woman and could do whatever the hell she liked, and if it upset him, well, screw him…but for some reason, it worried her, and she'd choked at the last minute and hid it from him. When she blurted out the truth, that she'd rushed to lose her virginity, she played out a mental soap opera of him calling her a lying whore and storming off in a huff. But Horace had just shrugged and said he didn't care, that was then and this was now, and she'd felt that wave of safety pass over her, like there wasn't a problem in the world that could touch them.

She was about to jump on him again when another record caught her eye.

It was like the world stopped spinning on its axis. Like all sound faded into a single deep note.

The record's sleeve was a hard green, with a patch of shiny lines at its center—no, not lines. Scales. The green of the background was the exact same shade as the snake coiled at the center of the album cover. The longer she stared, the more she could discern—the glittering body, the striped, diamond-shaped head, the forked tongue, the beady, orange eyes hanging over gaping, black nostrils. And there, floating above the bunched mass of venomous muscle, were two words in an industrial font:

PIT VIPER

"Where'd you get this?" she asked, finding her mouth dry. She felt a head rush as the memories came rocketing back to her, turning her giddiness into confusion and fear.

It couldn't be.

"Oh, man, this guy's *amazing*," Horace said. "I found it at that shop on Main Street. He's a DJ and programmer whose stuff has this sick heavy-bass sound but does these soaring things on top of them that sound like, I dunno, like fire in Heaven or something." He eyed her for a moment, wary of her fascination. "Sorry if that sounds crazy. Have you heard of him?"

"Actually, yeah," she said numbly, "yeah, I have."

chapter
3

She made a slew of excuses—a family obligation for Caroline, a need for some alone time and a promise of later for Horace—and rode her bike out on the back paths, away from school, home, Hamm proper, and through the woods that bordered town to the north. The trails became rocky and narrow, but she kept her bike steady.

Unlike that night, when you almost crashed a million times, she thought.

The autumn breeze whipped the hood off her head, like it was trying to push her away from the winery sign. She was on autopilot, navigating from memory. Nothing mattered but the neon-green snake from the album cover that seemed to coil and slither in her stomach, hissing the same terrifying message over and over like a scratched record:

He's back.

The sparse trees gave way to the stretch of highway Fiona had dreamt about most of her life. She slowed to a halt, asphalt crunching under her wheels, and took it in. The grass along the roadside was overgrown, and the sign for the

Hamm Winery looked more washed-out and decrepit than ever, its promise of *a beautiful day in a beautiful place* coming off like a mean-spirited joke. The winery itself was a carefully preserved fossil, bankrupted in the crash of '08 and not yet spoiled by the town's drunk teens, but the sign was disgusting— its orange had faded into a horrible pus color, and its face was splattered with what looked like dirt and the occasional neon blast from a paintball gun. An empty cardboard case of Miller Lite sat next to it, along with a grease-stained pizza box. Fiona thought of the sign as Dorian Gray's painting in the attic—while Hamm had cleaned up and stayed respectable, the sign had taken on all its ugliness.

There, at its base, was a brown handprint.

His blood. His mark.

The night replayed in her head as clearly as if it had happened yesterday—the truck, her father, the kneeling boy with his scratchy voice and bloody hair.

Sometimes she told herself it had never happened, that it had just been a realistic nightmare. But she'd avoided coming this way for years, knowing that the sight of the winery sign would make it real again.

And here she was.

It all stemmed from this, she knew. It sickened her, it was so obvious. When she rolled her eyes at her hometown, when she refused to believe a promise made by her dad, she told herself she was rebelling against authority, the system, her simple upbringing…but it was because of that night. That night had made her realize that the small town of Hamm was just a lie that a bunch of adults told themselves to feel safe and secure. This morning, she'd seen her hometown as the place that created Horace, but underneath all that, she knew it was still the suburban fortress that had damned the other boy.

The Pit Viper, who'd saved Hamm from itself. Had it really been nine years?

Nine years, but it felt longer. What was it her cousin Jake had said that one time over spring break? "High school years are like dog years. You got so much *doing* to do in them, they take forever."

It felt like forever. Before the Pit Viper, it had been a different place altogether, a town from an alternate dimension.

By the time she'd turned nine and had really begun to understand what was happening, the Goring Steel Mill hadn't been just a place to party, it had been a nightlife destination. Every Saturday evening, after gymnastics—her burden until she was twelve, dear God—her mother would walk her down Main Street, tightly clutching her hand as the partiers swarmed around them, teenagers and twenty-somethings rocking silver jackets and skintight jeans and glow-in-the-dark beads in their dreadlocks. They had blasted tooth-shattering break beats out of their cars as they crowded every stoop and parking lot. Rude, loud, in everyone's way, never from here, quick to laugh at the dumb small-town folks. And when the sun went down, they would flock to the ramshackle cathedral of the mill and rage until dawn.

Fiona had overheard complaints from her dad and other members of the Hamm town council: passed-out club rats huddled on every inch of the train station platform, puddles of vomit dotting Oak Avenue, not a single bottle of Benadryl or NoDoz for miles. Some of her father's friends on the town council had thought of the partiers as "the bad element" and would cross their arms and grumble about these kids transforming their town into a drug-addled freak show. But a lot of locals hadn't seen the problem, and her father, head of the council himself, had admitted that he wasn't worried about it. Sure, these club kids were a little obnoxious and funny looking, but who wasn't when they were young? Besides, they were bringing money to local businesses and publicity to their little burg. After the economy had died on its feet in 2008 and killed the winery, the town's tourism trade had been officially nonexistent. They needed to bring in any funds they could, and the media coverage about the mill was helping. Did anyone see that Hamm got mentioned in a *Vice* article?

From the back of the council meetings in the church basement, Fiona had heard both sides of the argument, never fully understanding either one. At nine years old, she'd actually enjoyed seeing the town flooded with new faces once a week. Their clothes had been cool in a weird way, so different from everyone else's. They were always smiling and saying hi to her. A girl with blue hair had once drawn a heart on her arm in highlighter. These were just people having fun.

Like a tidal wave, it had crashed down hard.

Two local kids, Geraldine Brookham and Jake Anderson—Fiona's cousin—had overdosed on GHB one night at the mill. Geraldine had been found a mile away from the mill, huddled in a drainage pipe.

Jake had been found *in* the mill, not fifty feet from the dance floor. The coroner had estimated that his heart had stopped beating *during* the party. If anyone had noticed, no one had done anything about it.

Jake had fallen in with the club rats, much to the displeasure of Fiona's Aunt Emily, but he'd always made curfew and had managed to stay sunny and sweet even when he'd obviously been wasted the night before. Fiona remembered him as a laid- back guy who would blast Hendrix and The String Cheese Incident out of his mom's sedan, who'd worn embroidered jeans and been able to recite Poe's "The Conqueror Worm" from memory. He would carry her on his shoulders during family get-togethers and let her braid his huge, frizzy head of hair. She'd considered him the coolest guy in the world.

The police report had said he'd choked on his own tongue.

Just like that, there'd been no more debate about the club rats. Everyone had agreed. Something had to be done.

But the cops had barely lifted a finger. Someone from the city, Fiona's dad had surmised, had been greasing their palms. When her aunt and uncle had contacted the mill's owner—some company that had relocated but still held on to the real estate, in the event an offer came along—they'd received death threats from several people, including one man who'd left a voice message describing Aunt Emily's personal appearance, where she shopped, and how sad it would be if even further tragedy were to befall her family.

Fiona's father had fought to help them but could do nothing. Robert Jones, head of the Hamm town council, had been at the end of his rope.

Then, one night, an impromptu meeting had been called. Her dad had been frantic. In the living room, unaware of his daughter lying on her belly at the top of the stairs, he'd whispered to Fiona's mom that he'd found someone who could help. On the phone with the other council members, he'd been short, barking orders, insisting they tell no one.

He'd only said the name once: "They call him the Pit Viper."

Fiona had *had* to know what this was all about.

But that night, after she'd helped her father set up the

folding chairs and coffee in the church basement, she'd been, for the first time in her life, banished to the Children's Room, a stuffy, foul-smelling closet space filled with building blocks and Golden Books. It had been a slap in the face—she'd always been allowed to sit in on meetings before, not banished to the nursery like some baby. The minute she'd overheard her father's big-announcement voice, she'd snuck out of her dusty prison, crept down the hallway, and watched the meeting through the thin crack between the double doors.

At first, she hadn't realized that the skinny boy with the patchwork coat and the bright eyes was supposed to be the savior she'd heard her father speaking about. She'd expected someone older, an outlaw, broad-chested and powerful, who cracked his knuckles as he talked. The teenager she'd seen looked more like one of the club rats they'd been trying to drive out of Hamm, all green army jacket, black hoodie, skinny jeans, huge high-top sneakers.

He'd been handsome, she gave him that; even at nine years old, she'd seen something alluring in his bright eyes and perpetual smirk. But the more she'd watched, the more she'd seen something special in him. The crowd had been rapt as he'd spoken. There'd been tension in the room, more powerful than the day Chad Wokley had brought a gun to a meeting. The teenage boy had gotten their attention just by being there.

"Here's how it's going to go down," the Pit Viper had announced. "Next weekend, I'm going to DJ a rave at your mill."

"Are you out of your goddamn mind?" Edgar Hokes had bellowed amid a rumble of confusion. "I thought you were here to *fix* our delinquency problem, not add to it—"

"You need to shut up and let me finish," the DJ had replied. Fiona had been stunned—no one talked to Edgar Hokes that way, especially not a kid. "I am going to spin a party at your mill. I will make sure everyone's there. Under *no circumstance* are any of your children or your friends' children to attend. Chain them down if you have to, break their legs, I don't give a shit. But they *cannot* be there. The next morning, your problem will be solved, and one week later, you will pay me one hundred thousand dollars."

Another murmur of anger and confusion at the gall of this punk kid.

"What are you getting at?" Bart Sciezowski had asked in his fat, throaty voice.

The Pit Viper had waved a hand in their faces. "You don't need to know, and you don't want to know. Saturday night, you keep your kids at home, and Sunday morning, your 'problem' will be solved. Then, one week from Sunday, I come back and you give me one hundred large, cash. Got it?"

Fiona had tried to read the council's faces through the crack in the door. Most of them had looked suspicious, but many of them had seemed resigned. Even she had been reassured by the tone of his voice. He'd obviously meant business.

"And what if it…what if whatever you're planning doesn't work?" Aunt Emily had said in a soft, shaking voice. "What if our town is stuck with these…people?"

The DJ had turned to her, paused, said, "You're the dead boy's mom, aren't you?"

The council had cried out as one. Fiona herself had felt a sting of rage, knowing the *dead boy* was her cousin. "*Hey*," her dad had said, taking a step forward.

The DJ had raised his palm to Robert Jones. Fiona had expected her dad to barrel through it, but he'd stopped, looking as confused by his compliance as Fiona had felt.

"I am terribly sorry for your loss," the Pit Viper had said calmly. "That's why I'm here, ma'am. I'm an exterminator. My methods are unorthodox, but I get results. And you can ask my previous clients in Bergen, Kansas, and Pompeii, North Dakota. They'll tell you I scrubbed their towns clean." His shoulders had lowered slightly; his voice had softened. "You stick with me and your son won't have died in vain. But you'll have to let me do my job."

Tears had welled in Fiona's eyes, both for Aunt Emily and for Jake, for his curly hair and big smile that had filled every photo they'd placed around the funeral home.

A pause, without murmur, without interruption. Then, Aunt Emily, her face lowered, had said, "Do whatever you have to do."

"A hundred grand, one week from Sunday," he'd said, striding down the aisle between the chairs. "Keep your kids locked up Saturday night. Don't try to find me; I'll find you."

He'd moved toward her, and before Fiona had realized what was happening, he'd been at the door.

She'd pressed her back to the wall and hidden behind the door as it had opened, hoping he would walk down the hallway without looking back. But then it had swung closed and there he'd been, a stylish scarecrow with hard stones for eyes, staring down at her. Her breath had caught in her throat.

The Pit Viper had glanced between Fiona and the door. He'd knelt and peered into the crack she'd been using to watch the meeting. Then he'd stood up and given her a smile that had made Fiona realize why he was named after a snake.

"Nice work," he'd said as he'd headed down the hall, his sneakers squeaking on the floor. "But you ain't seen nothing yet."

And just like that, they'd been gone.

No one knew where they'd gone, and no one had asked.

The police had towed their Volvos and Jeeps with Burning Man bumper stickers and had left them to rot in the impound. The local businesses had found their Sunday morning devoid of hungover club rats, their sidewalks puke free. The streets had been safe again; the next Friday, Fiona and her parents had gone out to dinner and had seen a live classic-rock cover band made up of local oldsters (her dad had danced with her to "Jumpin' Jack Flash"—it was the last time she'd danced with him). And though everyone enjoying downtown Hamm had worn the skittish, confused faces of people waiting for the other shoe to drop, there'd been an understanding that had filled the streets, an unspoken agreement that had been passed around like a note in class: the problem children were gone. Hamm belonged to its citizens once more.

She'd never heard her father speak of the money again; whether they'd even tried to gather it was a mystery. But she'd listened in on his phone conversation with Edgar Hokes on Sunday afternoon and had felt a sickening cold spread through her as her dad had told Hokes to bring rope or duct tape, and to be ready for a fight.

"He'll be at the church at eight," he'd said softly. "We'll be waiting for him. I was thinking out by the winery sign... Yeah. Exactly."

Fiona grimaced. Her breath was coming out in short, sharp bursts.

Over the years, her memory of that night had diminished in volume like an echo, but it had never gone away entirely. These days, it was a constant soft undercurrent in her mind, telling her that purity was a myth and it was best to rebel.

Normally, she just chalked it up to being punk rock, but she knew it stemmed from that awful night.

And now, the record in Horace's box. That green, glittering snake, ready to strike. It felt like it had been foretold by the bleeding DJ facedown in the dirt. What was the word— *prophetic*.

She hopped back on her bike and pedaled down the smooth pavement of the country road rather than taking another jostling ride over the back paths. She was too emotional for an uneven ride, too engulfed by sadness and nostalgia and dread.

She needed to check herself. She needed Betty.

chapter
4

The windows of her house were lit up as she glided into the garage next to her father's car, Ruby The Hatchet blaring over her headphones. From inside, she could hear the rumbling of voices—her mom, her dad, and someone else, someone with a deeper register. A glance into the street confirmed her fear—the Hokeses' hideous maroon SUV was parked across from their house. At least it wasn't Edgar's truck, traded in years ago. That would've been too on the nose.

She entered through the front door and was hit by a wall of hot air and the smell of stew coming from the kitchen. She hoped to get to her room before anyone else could see her, but no dice—Janelle Hokes emerged from the hall bathroom and nimbly intercepted her.

"Fi*ona*," declared Janelle, throwing her arms wide and yanking Fiona into a bear hug that made something in her back pop. Damn, the woman was strong.

"Hey, Janelle," she said, doing her best to inch away. "How are you? How's the store?"

"Ah, you know," she said, "mismanaged by the idiot men

in my life." She held Fiona out at arm's length and smiled at her. "Sweetheart, you are too pretty. We've got to find you a man. If only Calvin were right for you. We should get that boy a tattoo or something."

Fiona did her best to laugh sweetly, but inside she shuddered. The Hokes twins, Calvin and William, were polar opposites—William was huge, loud, boorish, while Calvin was clean-cut, polite, boring. Each of them sucked in their own special way: Will was the guffawing jock, Cal the prudish square. At least she could blow off Will's shallowness as pigheaded male posturing, but Cal stared at Fiona's boobs like it was his job. If there was ever a living metaphor for the dark side beneath Hamm's polite face, it was Cal Hokes, the nice guy with the creepy gaze.

There wasn't a tattoo in the world cool enough to make Fiona like him.

"Fiona?" Her dad came into the front hall, a scowl on his face. "You're late. You knew I was making stew tonight."

Anger flared up in her, and she did her best to swallow it. She knew the visit to the winery sign was making her more emotional than she should be. But still, Robert Jones's need for order, routine, and things to operate according to his standard always infuriated her. As a little girl, she'd seen him as strict; as a teenager, she realized how narrow-minded he was. Like not setting the table for stew was some symptom of *moral degradation* in her.

"I'll be down in a minute," she said. "I just need to change."

"All right, but hurry up," he said and cocked an eyebrow. "Wow, where'd you get that ratty sweatshirt? That design on the back is hideous."

Thankfully, before Fiona could fire back at her dad, Janelle's bossiness intervened. "Robert, stop it. Lord knows what we wore back then. Edgar had this pair of acid-washed jeans..." Fiona used the distraction to duck away and bolt upstairs, Betty on her mind.

Her room was full of slept-in blanket smells and had comforting shadows in every corner. The walls were papered with posters, stickers, flyers, and scotch-taped pinups from various magazines—*Spin*, *Revolver*, *Juxtapoz*, *Decibel*, *Rue Morgue*, and of course *Guitar World*. Memories of Horace from the previous night were scattered throughout—the tangle of blankets, a hair on her pillow, the faint sneaker smudge on her windowsill from where he'd climbed in after her parents had gone to bed.

But she had more important needs right now. The record sleeve and the trip to the winery sign had left her unsettled. She knelt down, reached under her bed, and pulled out an oblong, black leather box. It was beaten and flaking at the corners and peppered with band stickers—cool beyond any possible description.

Fiona unlatched the buckles on the side and opened the lid.

"Hey, Betty," she said.

Betty stared up at her: black face, white pickguard, two DiMarzio humbuckers, rosewood fingerboard, pure mahogany, an ebony Gibson Les Paul Standard named after the grandmother Fiona had never met, a woman her father referred to as "that tough broad."

Betty had been a stray, near death when Fiona had spotted her in the back of the thrift shop—only two strings left, one of her tuning knobs rusted beyond repair, her finish scratched and her paint coming off on the far end. Aunt Emily dutifully reminded her that they could buy *three* beginner's guitars down at the Target for the asking price—a fact that Robert Jones had repeated when Fiona had come home carrying the leather case—but Fiona was insistent, and Emily had quieted

Robert simply and sadly: "I think Jake would've liked this one." Then she'd gotten teary, and Fiona's dad had backed off. It had taken time and effort, but Fiona had been patient. She'd spent every cent of babysitting, dog-walking, and gutter-cleaning money she'd ever made on nursing Betty back to health; while the rest of her friends saved up for down payments on their own cars, Fiona chose to ride a bike and instead dropped big bucks on new pickups and a real Marshall amp that had once been played by Pantera. And as Fiona gave her new life, Betty had responded by being Fiona's emotional conduit through her many ups and downs—the first crush, the failed tests, the brief period where Fiona was obsessed with A Day to Remember for some reason. They'd grown up together and knew each other inside and out.

Carefully, Fiona lifted Betty out of her velvet bed and plugged her into her amp. She tuned her for a bit and then let her fingers walk up and down the scales. Once she had warmed Betty up, she closed her eyes and began strumming out chords, letting the sound fill the air and work its way into her body, heart, mind, and soul. With each note, the emotional clutter in her brain uncoiled like a pair of tangled earbuds in patient hands.

The Pit Viper was back. That meant something, and it frightened her. The events surrounding the DJ, from poor Jake and the council meeting all the way to Horace handing her the record, felt like a string of mystery that had been plucked nine years ago, the vibrations only reaching her today, like a radio broadcast in space.

The chords Fiona played turned darker, projecting storm clouds and doom in her mind. She felt her brow furrow as Betty tapped into her heart. Why now? This morning, she'd been in love with Hamm and Horace and her boring, dishonest, small-town life. Now even last night with Horace felt like a part of it, their first time together a stepping-stone toward something else. What did it mean? For her, her family, her town?

The final note, melancholy and discordant, hung in the air, and she let it fade into a soft whine of feedback that felt like a cold washcloth on her neck as it dissolved into the buzz of her amp.

Her eyes opened, and the sanctuary of her room, the bits of Horace's presence strewn everywhere, greeted her like a reliable friend. Free of chaotic emotion, the world came to her with clarity. Downstairs, her mother's laugh made its own sort of music, and the savory smell of stew seeped through the floorboards and into her nostrils. She was back in her head and ready to face life again.

"Thanks," she told Betty. As usual, the guitar was silent as a sphinx, but Fiona couldn't help but feel like the instrument gave her a nod. *You're welcome. Any time.*

"Fiona!" came her father's voice. "Dinner!"

"Coming!" Fiona placed Betty in her case, slid the box under her bed, and headed back out into everyone else's world.

As always, her dad's stew was great, served piping hot on top of a pile of buttery egg noodles, and after having burned off the day's frustration with Betty, the conversation wasn't as bad as she'd dreaded. Janelle Hokes was kind of a fun guest, loud and in your face. Edgar was a little unnerving to talk to, but that had been the case since long before Fiona had seen him put a boot to someone's skull. Hokes was a huge man with a slab of a face whose sense of humor was buried deep inside him. Something about Fiona's dad brought it out—over dinner, he chuckled and called Robert on his exaggerations—but when Fiona spoke, Edgar looked at her like he was humoring her by letting her talk.

Midway through dinner, Fiona's phone buzzed in her pocket. Horace was texting her — *doughnut tonight?* She had to bite her lip to keep from grinning, but her joy must have been obvious, because her mother rapped a knuckle on the table near Fiona's plate.

"No texting at dinner," said Kim Jones, all short red hair and turtleneck.

"Sorry," said Fiona.

"Oh, let her answer it, Kim," said Janelle, taking a sip from glass of wine number seven (*seven!* Dear God, Fiona would be singing show tunes on the floor! How did the woman do it?). "It's not her fault she's so popular."

"It's rude," said her mother calmly. "Besides, these kids spend too much of their lives on screens. They need a break from it."

Janelle rolled her eyes. "Bunch of squares, Fiona. Don't listen to them."

"It's all right," replied Fiona, picking at a soft chunk of carrot and hoping that the conversation would end there.

No dice. "Who's texting you?" asked her dad. "One of the girls? You should tell them to come over. How's Rita, anyway?"

"It's no one," said Fiona.

Robert raised his eyebrows. "Is it that boy?"

"Robert, he has a name," said her mother. "He's been her boyfriend for a long time now."

Robert squinted suspiciously. "Then he's that *patient* boy."

"Dad."

"I know all about teens these days," said Robert, shooting Edgar a wiseacre smile. "With their *dubsteps* and their *random hookups*! I read the Tumblrs! I'm hip to the major hashtags!"

"You are the lamest person I know," said Fiona, shaking her head and rolling her eyes.

"The Palmada kid?" asked Edgar Hokes.

"That's him," said Kim. "Cesar and Helena Palmada's boy, Horace. He and Fiona have been dating a while now. He's very sweet."

"Right, right," said Edgar. "Calvin told me he and Fiona are very friendly. A shame his parents never sat in on a town council meeting, but I guess not everyone feels the need to participate."

Fiona's cheeks burned. Of course Calvin would have mentioned it. Of *course* he was reporting back to his dad, dreaming of his own role on the town council.

Her father seemed to sense Edgar's weird tension and interjected. "Cesar and Helena's restaurant has always done great stuff for the street-fair fundraisers, haven't they?" Edgar shrugged, but Janelle and Kim nodded profusely, and Fiona mentally thanked them. "Good for them. Is he coming over later?"

She could tell by his tone that her dad was in a good mood (stew had a way of doing that to him), and for a moment she even considered inviting Horace over for yet another terse conversation with her father. But she didn't want to subject him to Edgar Hokes, and besides, she needed to get out of this house ASAP.

"We're going out to Chance's later for a doughnut," she said.

Robert smiled. "A Hamm institution," he said. "Those doughnuts sure are good."

Fiona couldn't help but smile back. Sometimes, for a brief moment, her dad would say something like that, and she could forget who he really was.

Edgar said nothing but leveled a stare at Fiona that left her severely skeeved. Like Calvin, he also viewed her as an object to be manipulated, but it was obvious that his intentions were different from his son's. It was the same way he'd stared at the Pit Viper, as though Fiona were a nuisance that might need to be dealt with at a moment's notice.

chapter 5

For me, it's the production that's the best part," said Caroline as she pulled her mom's sedan onto the highway.

Fiona glanced up from fiddling with the radio, making sure to drench her stare in a healthy coating of *You're kidding me. Right?* "What do you mean? He's just a DJ. Production doesn't factor into it."

"There's no way he's *just a DJ*. With the sounds he's making, he's got to be doing something special. Adding keyboards, altering the bass and the balance... I don't know." She caught Fiona's expression and elbowed her lightly, laughing. "Fuck you, I can think things about an album's production! You don't have the monopoly on feelings about music!"

"How compressed does the bass sound?" asked Fiona. "Can you hear the *space in the studio*? Does he have more of a Timbaland recording style, or was it like the time you worked with Phil Spector?"

Caroline smirked haughtily. "Tell me about all the studio time *you've* logged, Ms. Jones. You know, with *your* band."

"Oof, wounded." Fiona grinned, but she definitely felt the

comment's sting. It was a running joke among her friends—
Fiona, the guitarist with no band. She'd tried, of course, over
and over. She'd jammed in practically every garage in Hamm,
with cover band members in their early forties, rap metal
thirteen-year-olds, and even for a few days with the Hamm
First Church of Jesus Christ of Latter-day Saints band (it had
all gone south when she asked if they could cover a Black
Sabbath song). But it never worked. She hated the confines
of playing easily labeled material and always secretly wished
she was home pouring her heart out through Betty. That, or
she went off on three-minute self-indulgent solos that resulted
in a lot of foot tapping from the remaining members. During
those jam seshes, Fiona always got an irritated vibe from Betty,
like her guitar felt offended at being forced to plunk through
yet another rendition of "Drops of Jupiter."

"All I'm saying is, there's something special about that
record," said Caroline. "This Pit Viper isn't your typical hands-
in-the-air type. He has a true sense of musicianship."

Fiona bit the inside of her cheek. Caroline's opinion was
popular; more and more, she was hearing the Pit Viper's
music booming out of cars and worming through the cracks
between her headphones and her ears.

But the worst part was that it felt like the album was
following her and her alone. Every morning, as she checked
the usual indie-music blogs and web forums, she expected to
see a thread pop up hailing the DJ's self-titled debut as genius,
or dissing it as derivative…but there was nothing. No mixtapes
or parties he'd curated, no SoundCloud or Bandcamp where
his music was available to stream or download, no merch
portal. The only mentions she'd seen of the Pit Viper on the
internet were in social media posts from other kids from
Hamm.

"You're certainly talking him up enough," said Fiona.

"Careful, watch that truck."

"It's just nice to get into an album that doesn't sound like everything else."

"No comment," said Fiona. Caroline loved whatever was on the radio. Fiona had suffered through too many Justin-Bieber-fueled study sessions (Rita was too distracting to do homework with—they just ended up talking). So, what had her branching out into spooky electronica? Who'd tipped her off? "Did Horace give you the record?"

"I think I found it posted on Jared Vanderway's Facebook," said Caroline. She raised an eyebrow at Fiona. "Why? Worried Horace and I might be—dare I say it—*sharing Spotify playlists*?"

"No!" said Fiona, laughing. "God, is it weird that that's on par with cheating for me?"

"I bet if you found out he made a playlist for another girl, you'd be furious," said Caroline.

"I would fucking murder her," said Fiona.

They settled on Fleetwood Mac—not Fiona's *personal* favorite, but at least she and Caroline could agree on it. As she stared out the window and watched the highway roll past, something nagged at her. Was it the Horace comment? Caroline was always a self-aggrandizing smart-ass—it was what Fiona loved about her—but she herself got super jealous when it came to boyfriends, so she made it a point not to goad anyone in the same position. Maybe now that she and Horace had finally slept together, Fiona was just becoming a territorial psycho.

But there was something else.

Production?

Caroline liked songs you could shake your ass to; the only music she and Fiona ever agreed on were sexy artists like Prince. Caroline didn't know anything about production, or bass, or balance; usually she declared Fiona "a hipster" for trying to explain those things to her. But here she was, going into detail over the impressive sounds of the Pit Viper, the ghost from Fiona's past who was suddenly back and inundating her group of friends like it was no big deal.

The way the DJ's music had infiltrated her social sphere was only part of it—Fiona also didn't care for the music itself, even though everyone else around her adored it. Caroline was right, there was more to the Pit Viper's music than just break beats and samples, and whatever instruments he used or pitch he played at turned Fiona's stomach. She'd listened to one or two more songs last night at Horace's request, but she could only take a minute or so of each before she turned them off. The other day, he'd tried to put it on before they had sex; it had made her skin crawl, and he'd seemed genuinely upset when she'd asked him to turn it off. It had always been that way with Fiona and music, ever since she'd bought her first Important Albums (*Machine Head* by Deep Purple and *Version 2.0* by Garbage, both of which she'd discovered in a mall bargain bin just weeks after the night at the winery sign). She'd heard those albums and *known*, deep in her gut. Her gut feeling had only ever done her right, and even when it alienated her from her friends, she'd trusted it.

She trusted it now. Something was off.

Her face screwed up. Ridiculous. So what if the Pit Viper's music had made its way to Hamm? So what if she didn't like it? Even if he'd sent promos there on purpose, it was no more than a middle finger to the people who had pissed him off... right?

The city rose in the distance, a series of towering gray blocks and mirrored, knifelike skyscrapers. Soon they passed through the cramped residential areas and pulled off the highway just short of downtown, outside of a beige cube of a building with barred windows that served as a community center. Their dads were waiting outside and gave them big smiles and waves as they got out of the car.

Fiona forced a smile at Caroline's dad as she approached. The night at the winery sign wasn't the only thing that made Fiona feel weird around Darren Fiddler. He seemed as angry and fed up as Edgar Hokes, but he always came off as weak and powerless about it. He let Caroline and her mother walk all over him, but not without the occasional sneer of rage crossing his face. Still, he was a council member and a friend of her father's, so nothing could be said about it in Fiona's household. The thought made her smile falter. In Hamm, all you had to do was be friends with Robert Jones and everyone would overlook the fact that you were a goon.

Inside, the remaining eleven council families were bustling around a yellowed basement room, getting the cafeteria space ready for breakfast. Chairs and tables were unfolded; coolers of coffee and tea were dragged to their proper stations, plastic bins piled high with onions and peppers were carted to the kitchen. The Joneses knew the drill—within seconds, Fiona was wearing gloves, an apron, and a sailor-esque paper hat.

She thanked God that Rita's family wasn't on the council. It was one thing for these kids to see her in this getup, but her fashionable, vintage-clad friend would never let her live it down. And if Horace ever saw her in it…

She smiled wickedly. Maybe he'd like it. Maybe he'd ask her to keep the hat on.

"Any idea where we are today?" she asked Caroline.

"Extra bread and wipe-down," she responded, pouring Fiona a cup of coffee. "I can't believe we still have to do this. Weekends are for sleeping late and catching up on Netflix, if you ask me."

"It's our civic duty," said Fiona, mimicking her dad's voice.

"Yeah, okay," said Caroline. "At least your dad's a goofball. Mine's just, *Be there at nine. No excuses.*"

"Could be worse." Filip Moss grunted as he hauled a cooler of tea onto a folding table. His much-whispered-about biceps tattoo—H.P. Lovecraft's Cthulhu chowing down on the planet earth—flexed when he lifted the heavy plastic container. "My dad has an air horn."

The girls laughed. Filip was something that perplexed everyone: a functional weirdo. The fact that he was a handsome six-two defensive tackle for the Hamm High Razorbacks was made immediately dubious by his Toxic Holocaust shirt and how high he always was. When Fiona became guitar crazy, her parents assumed she and Filip would be an item, but they'd gone on one semi-date that went nowhere—she needed more presence, and he needed more drama. She vaguely remembered hearing that his current girlfriend had a neck tattoo and was named Lilith or something.

"And how do you deal with losing your Saturday, Filip?" asked Fiona. "Hot tea and meditation?"

"*Hot tea* is certainly a name for it," said the boy with a stoned grin. "The Black Dahlia Murder and high-grade sativa dominant."

"How did you even get this baked between waking up and coming here?" asked Caroline, peering into the boy's bloodshot eyes.

"Blazed in the shower," he said. "It takes some maneuvering."

Once everything was set up, Fiona's dad stood on a chair and waved his arms in the air. The whole room went quiet at once, hanging on Robert Jones's every word. His command over these people, Fiona noted, was incredible.

"All right, guys, this is three of our seven-breakfast pledge for the soup kitchen," he said. "I feel like we've got a good rhythm going, so let's keep it up. Remember: be informative and polite. Not everyone's as lucky as us. Least we can do is show them some dignity."

Just like that, everyone hustled to his or her station with looks of righteous determination. As she and Caroline headed to a table loaded with bagels and croissants, Fiona's mind burned with the green album cover, the coiled snake, the DJ's name in letters as black as the reptile's eyes.

Everyone in Hamm sure was lucky. And people got beaten up to keep it that way.

The morning proceeded slowly. Caroline was over-caffeinated too early in the game, and her banter soon became a steady rhythmic hum of mumbled complaints and narrating what she was doing. Fiona just focused on the job at hand, tossing rolls and snacks into wax paper bags and handing them out to the steady line of soup-kitchen regulars. She took a moment to make eye contact and say, "You're welcome" to any thanks she got.

It felt corny, because this was her Saturday morning and she knew she should resent it, but her dad was right, she loved this—giving people what they needed, the rush of warmth she felt every time she handed someone their daily bread. And even though Hamm's fakeness and shady history bothered her, she sometimes wondered if kids from the city grew up too cynical and desensitized to appreciate a moment like this. She yearned to break free from her small town, but at least it had taught her that all people were people.

She didn't notice Will Hokes until he was leaning on his broom in front of her, peeling back his lips to reveal a gum-heavy smile. Fiona thought he looked like a 'roided-out orangutan.

"Yo, Jones," he said, scratching his belly through his polo shirt. "Yo, Fiddler, butter me up some *toast*, girl."

"Fuck you, Hokes," said Caroline genuinely.

"Jones, you're looking smashable today," said Will. "Why are you wasting all that on Horace Palmada, girl?"

Now it was Fiona's turn. "Because he's not a piece of shit like you, Hokes."

"Is it true he's DJing Tess Baron's party?" asked Will. "Pretty impressive. I didn't realize you guys were in with that crowd."

Fiona felt her brow knit despite herself. That couldn't be true, could it? Horace hadn't said anything, and Tess Baron was a self-important hipster insect.

Still, she couldn't give Will Hokes any satisfaction. "Horace can do what he likes, you fucking mouth breather."

"Oooh, defensive, I dig it," chuckled Will. A small line of newcomers waiting for bread was forming behind him, but the huge boy seemed to ignore them. "Does he show you his burrito, *si*? His spicy Palmada *enchilada, eh, chica*?"

Fiona opened her mouth to unload a torrent of rage, when: "The Palmadas are Peruvian. Enchiladas are Mexican."

All heads turned to Calvin, bright-eyed and lanky, standing at his twin's side. He smiled politely, though his eyes flickered to Fiona's chest every few seconds.

"Oh, who *cares*, Cal," said Will, rolling his eyes. "Whatever *Peruuuvians* eat instead of rice and beans and shit."

"Actually, Peruvians *do* eat rice and beans," said Cal.

Will shook his head. "My brother, everyone. Give him a hand."

Fiona couldn't take it. A Hokes brother was hard to deal with on his own, but both of them at once threatened to ruin her charitable mood. "Guys, you're clogging my station. Get out of here."

Will did a poor imitation—"Clogging my station, meh meh meeeeh"—but wandered off to sweep between tables.

Calvin hung around for a moment, like he wanted to say something, but then just mumbled, "Welp," and turned back to the basement.

Fiona decided that as long as she had an aggressive spark going, she should blow on it. "Calvin, hold up." The boy turned, his eyes wide with excitement at hearing Fiona Jones of all people say his name. *Well*, thought Fiona, *too bad*. "Next time you feel like telling your family who I'm dating, go ahead and *don't*."

He blinked rapidly, looking surprised. Next to Fiona, Caroline whistled.

"Sorry?"

"You heard me. Your dad had dinner at my place the other night, and he said you were telling him about Horace and me. Next time, mind your own business, okay?"

"I didn't realize it was a secret," he said, his cheeks flushing red.

"Who I'm dating doesn't concern you." It was difficult staying angry at such a square, but she kept it going. "Just keep my name out of your mouth."

Calvin nodded, a hangdog expression falling over his saltine face, and then turned and slowly sauntered off. Fiona and Caroline handed out bread in silence for a few moments. Fiona felt her righteous anger disappear, leaving a gross, cold spot in its place.

"That was mean, wasn't it?" she mumbled to Caroline.

Caroline shrugged. "Yeah, kind of. I mean, it is none of his business, but Cal isn't a jerk like his brother, just super in love with you. You could let him have his little crush."

Fiona sighed, guilt slowly overwhelming her. "Ugh. I just don't like how he looks at me, you know? Blecch. And great, now I feel shitty."

"Okay, it's break time for Fiona," said Caroline, giving her a slap on the back. "Go take a lap, splash some water on your face. I'll hold down the fort."

Fiona weaved between the tables of homeless diners, smiling and waving at the repeat visitors. She beelined for the back hallway where the administrative bathrooms were. The morning had been emotionally taxing—if it wasn't worrying about the Pit Viper, it was feeling guilty about telling Cal Hokes what he should already know.

She reached the linoleum corridor and was about to turn a corner when her father's voice stopped her dead in her tracks.

"You think it could be him?"

Fiona's breath caught. Her dad wasn't speaking in the tone of voice he'd used this morning to instill order into the town council. Instead, he sounded like the man she'd watched from the side of the road nine years ago.

"You know anyone else who goes by that name, Bob?" said Edgar Hokes.

She peeked around the corner. The two men stood with their backs to her, hunched over a square in Robert Jones's hand—a green CD case. She couldn't read the writing on it, but she had an idea of what it said.

"Could be someone else," grumbled her dad. "Bands reuse names all the time. Kids today aren't too original."

"You willing to take that risk?" asked Edgar.

Robert tapped his thumb on the cover. "Calvin had this?"

"William. I found it while looking around his room."

"What were you doing looking around his room?"

"What do you care?" A pause. "I'm worried he's smoking. Point is, I found it."

Robert nodded. "He know anything about it?"

"About...him? Of course not." A pause. "You ever told your... Fiona?"

"No," said Robert. They stared at the cover for some time.

"Okay. Talk to Darren, keep your eyes peeled. If you hear anything from the boys that could prove that it's him, you come to me."

"What do we do if it is him?" asked Edgar.

"Well, what did we say we'd do?"

Fiona turned and headed back the way she'd come as silently as possible, her feeling of weary accomplishment replaced by disgust and fear.

chapter

6

"Look, there they are," said Caroline, palming the wheel.

She pulled the sedan to the side of the road by Maple Hill, and they all piled out. Fiona cracked her neck and went to get Betty from the trunk while Caroline rubbed her butt awake; as a rule, when her post-charity caffeine rush dropped, she lost feeling quickly.

Rita, Keller, Horace, and Penny Kim waved to them from atop the hill, shaded by the huge maple that overlooked the old graveyard. Penny was the new girl from North Carolina, and upon the gang's approval of her, Rita had decided that she needed the grand tour of Hamm (*Meaning maybe five places*, thought Fiona with a smile, *including this hill*). Horace and Rita had played tour guide while the others were busy—Caroline and Fiona at the soup kitchen, Keller at SAT prep—but they'd promised to swing by for the picnic at the end. Fiona brought Betty and a Tupperware of leftover fried chicken while Caroline hauled pillows and sodas.

As they climbed the hill, she heard Horace in animated conversation with Keller. For every part of Horace that was sharp and spicy, Doug Keller was round and sweet; he had big cheeks that got chapped in the winter and wore a ratty army jacket around his chubby frame. He glanced up at Fiona and waved her over as she approached.

"Fiona, you're a good judge of character," he said. "Please talk Horace out of this party he's going to spin."

"This Tess Baron's party?" asked Fiona, plopping down next to Horace and giving him a peck on the cheek. "That I had to hear about from Will Hokes today?"

Keller put up his palms. Horace sighed. "It is. Sorry, she only asked me yesterday. Guess word got around. But it could be cool, right?"

"I mean…it's cool that people are talking about your DJing skills," said Fiona.

"But!" chimed Keller.

"But…Tess Baron?" she said.

"It's not like I'm getting offers left and right! And besides, Tess has a lot of connections who…" He caught Fiona's cocked eyebrow and deflated with a sigh and a smile. "Okay, yeah, she's the worst. You're right."

"Whoa, *she's* right?" cried Keller.

"I say do it anyway, though," said Fiona, breaking Betty out of her case. "Who cares who's throwing the party? It'll be great exposure."

"I'd harangue you for encouraging him," said Keller, "but you look too cool with that guitar for me to give you any shit."

They dug into the chicken and sodas. Horace had brought some empanadas and ocopa sauce from the restaurant, much to everyone's delight. Caroline recounted Fiona's freak-out at Calvin Hokes, which made Fiona blush and Horace hug her a little tighter. The sheer amount of rage she'd vented on Cal made her feel like a high-maintenance psychopath, so she turned attention away from that morning and asked Penny what she thought about Hamm.

"Oh, it's an awesome town!" responded Penny. "Winston Pond is really pretty. It has so much *character*." Everyone glanced at Rita, who'd no doubt used that word earlier. "Oh my gosh, you have a guitar? Totally rad." Fiona nodded, swallowing a laugh. Okay, so Penny was a little overeager. She just needed time.

And Rita was a good teacher. As her friend flattened her skirt, dished out food, and poured soda into jam jars, Fiona found herself deep in admiration of Rita's style. Maybe she preferred her bands in ill-fitting tuxedo pieces and untied Doc Martens rather than Fiona's full-on leather pants and skull belts, but Rita was pure rock and roll. Everyone else was always so *thirsty*, chomping at the bit for whatever was newer, better, *more*; Rita was content to show the new girl around and throw a picnic overlooking a defunct cemetery.

Fiona hoped Rita got out of Hamm. She had noticed that sometimes her other friends played at an edginess that Rita did for real. That wasn't an insult, but simply one of those facts that carried a hint of sadness with it. As everyone ate and recounted local legends to Penny—the night Keller's older brother drove his car into the Lidells' pool, that time the entire town got sick from Old Lady Bierstock's brisket at the fair, the Great Halloween Fail of three years ago— Fiona recognized that most of her crew would stick around and grow into the small-town lives that had colored them as people, and Hamm would be a better place for it. Keller would take over his dad's firm and become perhaps the only contractor in the world who could belch a Shelley poem. Horace would run the best Peruvian restaurant in small-town Ohio. Caroline would eventually place her long-distance track trophies on a shelf at the bank or in her own local law firm. And even after they traded their ripped vintage clothes and vulgar bumper stickers for comfortable shoes and dad jokes, they would be strong, earnest, beautiful, and happy.

But Rita had a fire in her, a flame of glamour and mystique that would burn her alive if she tried to smother it with the compromise that was necessary to living here. Fiona didn't want that for Rita. She wanted Rita to be cool until the day she died, surrounded by her lovers and pugs in a Paris loft.

And her? Fiona gulped, feeling suddenly alone among her friends. Graduation was in May, then the year off that she'd fought so hard to convince her parents to allow her, a year making money and experiencing new things while figuring out college...and then what? What if everything went wrong, and no schools accepted her, and she was alone without a plan? Would she end up back here in Hamm, teaching music?

Would Fiona Jones be the head of the town council?

Would it someday be her crouching in the dark, threatening a boy's life if he ever showed his face in Hamm again?

"What's that building over there?" asked Penny, pointing.

All eyes turned to the distant structure, blurry in the afternoon light. Even by day, it seemed cloaked in mist, as though perpetually cooling off. Fiona hadn't even noticed it, but now that Penny had pointed it out, it dominated the landscape in her eyes.

Rita made a point of chewing and swallowing before she answered. "That's the old Goring Steel Mill. We don't go there."

"Why not?" asked Penny.

For a second, everyone seemed to be asking themselves the same question, digging through their memories for why exactly the mill was off-limits.

"It used to be an illegal venue," said Fiona.

"Oh yeah!" said Horace. "They threw insane raves there back in the day, right?"

"Exactly," said Rita. "If you can believe it, this was a rough town for a little bit. The mill was a hot party spot for the area, but it brought in some shady characters."

"Define 'shady character,'" said Keller.

"You," said Caroline.

"Burn," said Horace.

"Like, drug dealers, gangbangers...the usual rough crowd," said Rita. "Don't get me wrong, this is all kind of hazy. We were, what, nine back then? It was right after the winery went under, and the town was going through serious changes. I just remember my folks being freaked out by the graffiti on the walls and drug vials on the ground."

"So, what happened?" asked Penny.

Fiona held her breath. Rita had an incredible mind for news and gossip—did she remember? Had she heard rumors about the night the Pit Viper had wiped Hamm clean?

Rita popped a piece of empanada in her mouth and said, "There was a tragedy, and everyone stopped coming."

"Didn't some kids OD or something?" asked Caroline.

Fiona felt a minor chord in her heart and decided she might as well get in front of the bad news. "My cousin."

Rita nodded with an apologetic smile. "Jake," she said. "I remember him."

"Right," said Caroline, face-palming with an audible *smack*. "Sorry, Fiona. Totally forgot. I'm an idiot." The gang all echoed the apology. Keller reached out and patted her elbow; Horace put his face in her hair.

"It's okay," she said, waving them back. "It was a long time ago. Anyway"—it was a perfect transition, a chance to steer away from the truth—"that's why they shut it down and the town got cleaned up."

"Well, obviously," said Keller a little too quickly, pointing a chicken wing at the distant mill. "Some people tolerate that kind of shit, but our nutty suburban parents? That's like

Fiona in a band right there—not gonna happen." He gave her a slight nod; she gave him the finger. "The minute their kids get messed with, they take action. Like a mother bear."

"Yeah, but...still, you gotta wonder," said Horace.

"About?" asked Caroline.

"Well, obviously, that—what happened with your cousin, that was horrible," he said, "and it's good they shut the place down. But..."

"Horace," warned Rita, "I'd watch these next few words."

Penny laughed nervously. Horace glanced at Fiona, and she looked back at him expectantly, hoping he didn't put his foot in his mouth.

"Just that the folks in this town can be a little white-bread and closed-minded," said Horace with a shrug. "And obviously, whoever messed with your cousin, hon, he deserved to be run off. But what about the chill kids? Maybe some of them were just having too good a time, or they dressed a little weird, and they got chased away by the xenophobic town council."

"Ex*cuse* me?" said Caroline, rearing her head back. Fiona felt tension move through the gathered crowd. The calm heat of the autumn day was suddenly irritating. She plucked out a sour-sounding note on Betty.

"No offense!" countered Horace. He squeezed Fiona's arm. "Sorry, was that out of line? My bad. I'm a dumb-ass."

"You should pay more attention to your girlfriend's feelings," snapped Caroline.

"Okay, Caroline," said Fiona.

"No, come on, Fiona!" It was obvious Caroline was more upset about Horace taking a shot at the council than she was at his treading heavily on Jake's memory. "You know our dads are on that 'xenophobic' council, right? You think they just chased off some kids because they wore bright colors? That was Mr. Jones's nephew who died in there. The Hamm town council isn't the fucking Klan."

"Let's keep this party polite," said Rita firmly.

"I didn't say anything about the Klan," cried Horace. Fiona felt him pull back from her, and she hated it. Being caught at the center of an argument bothered her. At least the sadness she'd felt at their earlier conversations was sweet in a way, like a Johnny Cash song; this was just a combination of embarrassment and anger.

"I mean, I can understand what you're saying," said Fiona, trying to help Horace out of the hole he was digging. "I know there were some cool parties there."

"You don't need to do that, Fiona," said Caroline.

"No, really. There was something…special about it, even if it did get ugly." She scrambled, and before she knew what she was doing, it came out of her mouth: "The Pit Viper performed there once."

Everyone's attention turned toward Fiona, backed by a general outcry.

Oh crap, thought Fiona, *oh crap, crap, crap.*

"*Really,*" said Rita, incredulous.

"Oh my God, have you heard the album?" chimed in Penny. "It's so insane. So fun and danceable, but *deep,* too."

The news rippled over the gathering of her friends. They pressed in around her, asking her questions. She immediately backtracked, freaked out by this very unexpected type of attention. "It's just a rumor I heard. Not a big deal."

"*Kind* of a big deal, honestly," said Keller. "I mean, that album is *huge.* I don't know anyone who isn't obsessed with it."

"Did anyone bring some speakers?" asked Caroline. "We should listen to it now!"

As the gang pulled out their phones and began searching for the album, Fiona stared off at the mill. It wasn't like she could tell them the truth—that the Pit Viper had somehow shut down the mill with a party, that her and Caroline's fathers had beaten him up and driven him out. They'd be heartbroken, and who knows—maybe word would get back to her and Caroline's dads. Maybe they'd go looking for him.

But it wasn't just that. The Pit Viper was her story, the thing that had changed her into somebody special, somebody who wanted to get out of Hamm. She selfishly didn't want that to be just another part of the breaking trend.

Caroline put on the album and dropped her phone into an empty jar, creating an impromptu speaker. As the breeze was filled with throbbing electronica and her friends' heads began to bob, Horace leaned in close to Fiona's ear. "You never told me that before."

"I didn't think it was important," she lied.

chapter
7

Tess Baron's party snuck up on Fiona, a testament to how little Fiona cared about being in the popularity loop. She felt overwhelmed, partly by getting ready for the kind of party where you had to consider anything other than what band's T-shirt you were going to wear, but mostly by straight-up sexual frustration. Horace had taken her exposure comment to heart, and with him holed up in his room perfecting his set every night, she was left with nothing more than suggestive texts. Betty helped her vent the sighs and snarls, but just barely.

Finally, Friday night arrived, and she spent the evening getting her doll face on—her ripped skinny jeans, her heaviest eyeshadow, her pointed black boots, and hell, black lipstick and a faded Twisted Sister T-shirt. Let them gawk in private; just because this was a jock/hipster party didn't mean she was going to sell out.

She groaned at herself in the mirror. A jock/hipster party. She would do her best not to vomit all over the first girl she saw in an ironic Ramones shirt.

As she pulled Horace's hoodie on in the front hallway,

her father came out of the living room and caught her. "You heading off to play the Hammersmith in that outfit?"

Despite herself, Fiona raised her eyebrows and laughed. "Solid reference!"

"You forget I lived through the eighties," he said. "Remember that you got your love of Van Halen from me."

"You always seemed like more of a Culture Club type to me," she said.

"Oh, you're killing me!" Her dad jabbed an imaginary knife in his chest and made a pained look, and Fiona giggled. When the laugh died down, they were left silent, nodding and staring anywhere but at each other. Fiona bristled at these moments of dead air that always came after they'd had a good talk, reminders that once upon a time it had been chummy and sweet between them, that they were so much alike. That he wasn't *just* the man she'd watched kick the shit out of an innocent boy.

Outside, Keller honked.

"Bye, Dad," she said.

He almost went for the hug, but then looked away and formed a tight smile. "Have fun, kiddo. Back by curfew."

During the ride over, they listened to Queens of the Stone Age and cracked jokes about who would be on the most coke by the time they got there. Keller took the main roads through the richer developments of Hamm until they finally reached the Barons' house. The place was huge, the kind of house owned by a family who were happy to feel like big fish in a small pond but too self-centered to join the town council (Fiona's dad had urged Dave Baron to get onboard over and over, but the man obviously didn't want to give up his Saturday afternoon tee time to help out poor people).

Fiona eyed the McMansion with contempt. Her father ran the town council and they lived in a normal house, but he had spent his life chasing out ravers and beating up DJs to "save" Hamm for *these* people? Gross.

Only a half hour after the evite said the party started, and the lawn was a veritable mosh pit, with groups of howling teens barreling toward the lit-up house from which emanated a thick, steady beat. Fiona, Rita, and Keller weaved between the small circles of Solo-cup-clutching meatheads and bitching prepsters that dotted the lawn, Keller scowling in disgust and Rita clucking and laughing at some of the fashion choices.

They were almost through the front door when a huge hand clapped onto Keller's chest. Horace's friend Vince, aka Swordfish, blocked the door, a blank expression on his golem's face. Guffawing next to Horace, the guy always seemed like just another snickering pothead, but this close, Fiona realized how tall and broad-chested he was.

"And you guys are?" he asked.

"I'm Keller. Horace's friend?" said Keller, sounding more than a little offended. "We've met before. Swordfish, right?"

The boy remained stone-faced as he looked over his shoulder and barked, "Yo, Tess!"

Tess Baron appeared, dressed in what Fiona would describe as Brooklyn Trust Fund (dear God, the girl's shawl budget must be out of control). She continued typing on her phone in silence for a few minutes before finally looking up and scanning the crew with her perpetually bored gaze. Her eyes settled on Fiona, and after a squint, she nodded.

"...Fiona, right?"

"Yeah, hi, Tess," said Fiona, waving. "Horace's girlfriend."

"Riiight, right right," she said, going back to her phone. "It's cool, Vince, they're fine."

Fiona broke out in a sneer—*way to hire your classmate to bounce your high school house party, Baron*—but she quickly replaced it with a smile. "Thanks, Tess."

"No problem," mumbled Tess, immersed in her phone. "You guys should head out back. He's spinning right now." "What?" asked Fiona, shocked. According to his last text, Horace's set wasn't supposed to kick off until mid-party. Swordfish removed his paw from Keller, and Fiona pushed past her friends, surging through one opulent room after another until she reached the backyard.

The front lawn was just the beginning—the deck out back was a seething mass of athletic dudes, stick-thin fashionistas, and wily indie rockers huddling around Beirut tables and bobbing their heads in the cool night air. The crowd was definitely not what Fiona was used to—no council kids except for Caroline, whose tipsy laugh could be heard from somewhere among the throng. The occasional reedy, black-clad artist or faux-rockabilly chick from the city lounged in a plastic lawn chair, obvious imports for a party being thrown by Tess, whose edgy outside-of-school relationships were the stuff of Hamm High legend.

Off to one side, next to the covered pool, Horace leaned over a pair of turntables, lit from below by the rope lights that outlined his equipment. Fiona flinched when she saw the look of frustration on his face.

Rita appeared next to her, followed her gaze, and mumbled, "Shit" before punching a fist in the air and shouting, "All right, Horace!" One or two Solo cups raised in salute, but not enough. Fiona ran her hands through her hair and swung her hips in front of Horace, in the hopes of reviving his spirits, but it was no use, she was the only one dancing. He was just spinning way too early—everyone was still getting drunk, building up energy, waiting for their friends to arrive. He was background music.

After a few minutes, Tess came up beside him and whispered in his ear. Horace nodded, heaved a sigh, and began packing up his records.

Fiona's heart sank. This party was supposed to get him noticed. That was the only reason he'd taken the gig. But he'd died up there.

She waited while he and Keller disappeared to load Horace's wax into the car, but somehow missed him on the way back. She tried to lose herself in Rita's outfit-bashing—"Look at that one. Honey, your mother needs to have a talk with you about a *lot* of things."—but all she could do was picture Horace's dejected face, over and over.

She heard his voice coming from the kitchen a few minutes later and found him at a counter with Keller. They both tossed back shots of tequila alongside one of Tess's creepy older friends, a stubbled guy in ultra-tight jeans and a salmon-pink shirt.

Fiona came up behind Horace and draped her arms over his shoulders. "Ask me what I was listening to."

He turned to face her, and already she could see the booze unhinging his brain in his half-closed eyes and faint swaying. "Okay, what were you listening to?"

"An awesome set by my amazing boyfriend," she said and kissed him. The flavors of lime, salt, and liquor filled her mouth.

Horace broke off the kiss and shrugged. "Thanks," he said. "Nice of you to say, anyway."

"Aw, Horace, it was fantastic," she said. She moved to kiss him again, but he raised a beery Solo cup to his lips. It burned her to feel him forcing distance between them. She didn't want him to dwell on it. "Come with me, okay?"

She took his hand and led him away to the ridiculous

hoots of Keller and Tess's city friend, Horace letting himself be pulled along. She managed to get him up a staircase, down a hallway, and into an empty bedroom, all of which had been cream-colored and highlighted with cheap silver.

As she closed the door, Horace sat down on the bed, a bitter look spreading across his face. "What's up?" he said.

"I'm sorry I missed the beginning of your set," she said. "What happened?"

He waved a hand in front of his face. "Apparently, there's someone else coming in, some friend of Tess's who wants to… It doesn't matter. Don't want to talk about it."

"Hey, look," she said, sitting down next to him. "It's okay to be upset. That really sucks. I'm so sorry." He went to gulp his beer, and she reached out and held his wrist, stopping him. "But you're drinking really fast. Please take it easy, okay?"

Annoyance crossed his face, but then he considered the cup and nodded, placing it on a bedside table. "You're right. You're totally right. I'm sorry, Fiona, I just…*uuuugh*, I feel like such a *dick*. I worked all week on a set that no one got to hear."

"It happens," she said. "Besides, these assholes wouldn't appreciate your stuff anyway. You're too good for them."

Finally, there it was—a smile. A reluctant one, maybe, but she'd take it.

"*You're* too good for *me*," he said, putting an arm around her. "Thanks, babe, I…needed this. I needed you to talk some sense into me."

"I just want you to be happy," she said, riding the sudden rush of relief.

"I know," he said. "That's why I love you."

Boom.

Her breath caught; her heart jumped. He blinked hard, as though he never expected to say it out loud. There it was, six months in, out in the open. She'd thought about this, had expected to say it right back, but now that it was here, she was speechless.

"I'm so sorry," he said immediately.

"No," she whispered, praying he wasn't sorry, *anything* but sorry. "Say it again."

His eyes met hers. He licked his lips, readying himself. "Fiona," he said, "I—"

"*Yo!*"

A hard knock at the door, yanking them back to reality. Both their heads snapped up to see Keller peering in, his face a mixture of joy and panic.

"Horace, get down here *now*," he said.

"What's wrong?" asked Horace.

"Nothing's wrong," he cackled, "but it's—"

"He's here!" shrieked Caroline, barreling in behind Keller and grabbing Horace's hand. "He's here, right now! You have to come downstairs!"

"What the fuck are you talking about?" said Horace, his face a mask of concern.

"The Pit Viper!" she screamed. *"He's here!"*

Oh my God, thought Fiona.

"Oh my *God*," said Horace, leaping off the bed and rushing after his friends. Fiona followed him, the bottom of her stomach sinking deeper with every wide-eyed partier she passed.

"Holy shit, this is insane," screamed Horace as they blasted out into the night air. Fiona was inclined to agree—the party had lost its collective mind. Gone were the drunk conversations and bopping couples; instead, the entire backyard was moving to the sultry, grinding rhythms that permeated the air. People swayed, stomped, caressed, spasmed, grinded (ground?), popped, locked, leaped, and screamed. A haze of steam rose from the writhing masses, sweaty and overactive as they were.

Fiona spotted Rita, eyes half open and hair mussed, moving her body sinuously against Dave Hettenberg, a lacrosse player whose hands clutched her wantonly.

As they pushed through the throng, Caroline pointed, ecstatic. "There he is!"

Fiona froze. The crowds disappeared. The music faded away.

There he was.

He'd changed. No patch-covered jacket, no stringy hair, no puckish smile—the boy who'd knelt bleeding by the winery sign was now a man, tall and muscular. He wore an immaculately white hoodie with the sleeves cut off, revealing arms covered in weaving tattoos. He stood over the turntables, legs shoulder-width apart, hands flying between records and knobs, fingers splayed and crooked like those of a harp player. With his hood up, his eyes were invisible, and given how much older he looked now, Fiona wondered if maybe it was a different DJ with the same name, like her father had suggested in the church...

As the beat swelled, crescendoed, and then dropped with a punch to the guts, the crowd cried out in unison. The night exploded.

The Pit Viper raised his head, and Fiona saw his eyes, bright and lively, shine out from the shadows of his hood... and look directly at her. The stunned look that she felt on her own face instantly echoed on his.

It couldn't be anyone else.

"Holy shit, I can't believe he's here!" screamed Horace, bouncing on his feet and punching his fist in the air.

Fiona couldn't reply. The Pit Viper's gaze pinned her to the spot.

She believed it.

chapter
8

On Monday morning, all anyone could talk about was the party. Even the kids who hadn't been there had heard about the mysterious DJ's impromptu performance. Rumors spread about an entourage ushering him back into his Hummer after the set. Everyone was dying to know his real name—who knew? Maybe he'd graduated from Hamm High. Tess Baron was being hailed as the most in-the-know girl in Hamm, connected to all the major players in the city. And bit by bit, that album cover, the image of the coiled green serpent, was doing heavy rotation in Hamm High—on stickers in lockers, on iPhone screens, even on a shirt Chris Caprizi was rocking in English.

Fiona felt like she had maggots under her skin the whole time.

The fallout from the party had been harmless enough—Keller had gotten home late, visibly stoned, and had been grounded; Caroline had woken up hungover and had been unable to attend Saturday's town council function (not a terribly uncommon occurrence, hangover or not); Rita had eventually hooked up with Dave Hettenberg, who was now texting her constantly, much to her embarrassment (she said it was "like kissing a golden retriever")—but they were all enamored of the Pit Viper, now more than ever. Even Keller had decided to "open his mind" to electronic music.

Only Fiona could see what had really gone down—*he'd gotten in.* He'd shown up in town without any resistance, played the biggest party Hamm High had seen in years, and then vanished like it was nothing. If Robert Jones and Edgar Hokes were willing to tie up this boy and drag him away, they were willing to do worse if he came back—but the Pit Viper had just waited until he was ready, and had come back to Hamm with all the bluster and fanfare of a reunion tour.

And he'd looked right at her.

The memory stopped her dead in her tracks again, this time as she walked between classes. Most of the time, Fiona felt in control of her life, but when his eyes had locked with hers, she'd felt naked and vulnerable, like nine years of bottled-up secrets and fears had suddenly been made flesh and shown to the world. They'd stayed staring at each other for not that much longer, but for long enough that Fiona knew it meant something. The party had gone on; more had happened, but she had no clear memory of anything after the Pit Viper, his eyes, how shaken they'd made her feel.

Even now, in the stark light of school, her stomach felt frosted over and her knees unsteady. She ran a papery tongue over shivering lips. It was a scary feeling, but every time it hit her, it was less and less unpleasant. Maybe that's why she'd been thinking about it all day...

Fiona's eyes focused, and she realized she was standing frozen and dazed between surges of people going to class. Her cheeks burned with embarrassment as she picked up the pace and went stomping off among them. What was she doing?

The hell she was in control. She had daydreamed through an entire American Lit class without absorbing anything. She'd entirely avoided Horace all morning because of, what, some coughed-up childhood emotions? Nuh-uh. She needed to get it together, sit with Betty, and burn all the weirdness out of her. Of course, home was still four hours away. For now, she'd let Lemmy Kilmister drown it out and cranked Motörhead's *Iron Fist* over her headphones in an attempt to tamp down her obsession.

A hand landed on her shoulder, and Fiona whirled, ready to swat whatever idiot thought sneaking up on her when she had her headphones on was a good idea.

"Easy," said Vince, aka Swordfish, putting up his hands in defense.

Fiona took a deep breath and forced herself to calm down. This guy didn't deserve the brunt of her worries, even if he was somewhat of a goon.

She plucked off her headphones. "Yeah?"

"Motörhead, huh? Nice. My brother liked that band."

"What do you want, Swordfish?"

Fiona noticed a momentary flash of distaste cross the boy's face. "Don't call me that. You can call me Vince or Vincent."

"Horace calls you 'Swordfish' all the time."

"Yeah, Horace knows me. We've hung out a lot. I ain't never hung out with you, so you don't know shit about me. My name is Vince."

Fiona raised her eyebrows. The reprimand felt harsh, but it was also fair—she'd never said more than three words to the guy. "Sorry. Vince. What's up?"

"So I take it you saw the Pit Viper at Tess Baron's party the other night," he said.

"Yeah," she sighed. "It was a big deal; everyone's talking about it."

"And apparently, you said he spun Hamm once before, at the old mill. That true?"

His words caught Fiona off guard. She clenched her fist. "Who told you that?"

"Who else? Your boyfriend," said Vince. "Was I not supposed to know?"

"Where is he?" she said.

"Horace? He's out at the far tables talking to some of the guys," he said. "But wait, is it true? Do you know anything about—"

She power-walked through the murmuring hordes in the cafeteria, out of the double doors that led to the back patio, off to the far picnic tables that lay around the side of school. Class was forgotten; adrenaline filled her entirely.

The smell of weed drew her to the last table, where Horace sat across from, of all people, Calvin Hokes. The bright-eyed boy nodded and scribbled in a notebook while Horace ranted at him, his commentary punctuated by a lot of frantic hand motions.

"Horace," she said.

Horace did a double take: first a sidelong glance, then a joyfully stoned grin.

"Babe!" he yelled. "We were just talking about you. Come here. Sorry, what are you listening to?"

"Can we talk?" she said, trying to remain calm.

Horace glanced between her and Calvin, mouth hanging open. "…We're sort of in the middle of a thing."

"Actually, I have some questions for you," said Calvin.

Fiona glared at him, and something sharp, the kind of thing that Betty would normally have siphoned off, passed between them. If she didn't know better, she'd say she actually shot lightning out of her eyes. Calvin was gone in seconds, leaving Horace, whose bloodshot eyes were wide with surprise.

"Are you okay?" asked Horace.

"What was Calvin Hokes doing here?" she asked.

"He's helping us plan this event," said Horace. "He's really good with graphic design, actually. That's what we wanted to talk—"

"Are you telling everyone I know the Pit Viper?" she asked, getting to the point.

"N-No!" he stammered. "Just that you knew he spun a show at the old steel mill once before, back when it was a thing—"

"Horace, what are you thinking?" she cried. "You *know* how popular he is after Tess's party. That was among friends, but this? Now I have a rumor dogging me. Now everyone wants to know what I know, and they're bothering me about it."

He nodded slowly. "No, you're right, I totally didn't think that through. This kind of shit always gets around. Who's bugged you about it?"

"Your friend Vince just stopped me in the hall."

Horace leaned back and guffawed. "Oh, babe, that's nothing! I'm sorry, Swordfish isn't much for tact. I asked him to find you because we wanted to talk to you. He *just* left here."

She felt relieved that there weren't school-wide rumors about her—the idea of every idiot who wanted to know about the Pit Viper approaching her in the halls made her want to breathe radioactive fire and melt faces—but Horace's laughter felt mean. "This isn't funny."

"Here's the thing," said Horace. "The Viper is spinning this party in the city next week, and a bunch of us are going. We were talking about trying to meet him after the show. We just wanted to double-check that he's the same guy who spun here back in the day. Friday night, you said he looked different, and Pit Viper's a cool enough DJ name that we figured it might have been some other dude."

She sighed. Horace couldn't possibly grasp what she was feeling—he just wanted an in with this cool new musician. "Yeah. Yeah, I think it was him. Why?"

"We were going to have him do a big reopening of the mill."

The words echoed in her head like a gunshot, silencing everything else.

"What?" she whispered, praying she'd misunderstood her boyfriend.

"Think about it," said Horace, holding up his hands like a visionary director. "We clean that place up, bring it back to its former glory, and have a *massive* dance party to celebrate. We can do it up ultra-industrial and stylized, and have flyers, and—"

"That's...the place where my cousin died," she said, astounded.

Horace froze mid-sentence, a look of utter stupidity forming on his face. "Right."

"Are you really trying to organize a party there?" she said. "You don't think that place was closed for a reason?"

"Well, like I said, you have to admit, this town is kind of fucked in the head," said Horace. "I mean, it's not just you and Caroline's dad and all the nice white people—my parents, too, are super conservative."

In a lot of ways, Fiona agreed with him—oh, if only he knew—but Horace's callousness in the face of Jake's death was too much for her to handle. "Two people our age *died*," she seethed.

"And that's terrible," said Horace, doing his best to keep up with her. "But maybe if Hamm had worked with the kids who ran those mill parties and helped make the place safer by providing security instead of just kicking everyone out..."

The concept of people dancing in the spot where Jake

had passed away threw gasoline on the fire inside her. She felt like an electric chair, charged and deadly. "You think it's *just terrible* that they found my cousin curled up in a corner with his face turned black?" she snapped.

He wasn't ready for that one. "Jesus, Fiona."

"Find me when you're not too stoned to think," she said, heading back to the cafeteria doors. Calvin Hokes was on the patio and tried to say something to her, but she shoved him aside. He called after her, but the blood rushing in her ears drowned him out, louder than any riff she could possibly blare.

Fiona cut her last class; she was acing French anyway, and Ms. Traubert probably wouldn't notice. She scrabbled for her headphones in her jacket pocket but couldn't find them anywhere, which only made her more frustrated. She biked home at top speed, Betty on the brain.

Fiona's mom stood in the living room as she entered the house, and a look of surprise crossed her face. She opened her mouth, and Fiona knew it was to comment that Fiona was home surprisingly early. She rushed upstairs, knowing that having to explain a cut class would just make her break down in the living room.

Fiona closed the door hard, cracked out Betty, and cut loose.

This was not the laid-back poetry she and the guitar normally shared. This was an outcry. She cranked the volume as loud as she could and let the ax wail for her, snarling, pounding, shrieking at the top of her lungs in hard, gasping sobs of distorted anguish and tremolo-picked rage. She sped up and soloed, tapping out a blistering chatter of disappointment and heartache that climbed the neck until it broke off in a loud groan of resigned frustration.

Fiona paused, panting, and heard a light knock at her door.

"Sweetie? The wineglasses are shaking in the standing cupboard. Maybe go with Buddy Holly over Mötley Crüe for a little bit, okay?"

She nodded, suddenly aware of her own wild, angry behavior. "Sorry, Mom, long day," she called through the door. It didn't matter; she was spent anyway. She sat on her bed and let her fingers pluck a soft, repetitive melody on Betty, the last trickles of blood ebbing out of the wound Horace's carelessness had left in her heart.

"Fiona, you have a guest."

Fiona got up from her homework and went downstairs. Her dad had the door open and was chatting animatedly, with the straight-backed pose of the man of the house. Calvin Hokes stood in front of him, speaking in the sort of formal voice reserved for the head of the town council; in his khakis, polo shirt, and polite smile, he reminded Fiona of a baby chick rather than a teenage boy.

"I'm sure your dad would be proud to have you take over the store," said Fiona's dad.

"Oh, of course, and I'd be proud to do it," said Calvin. "It's just that Will's always been more of the hands-on guy when it comes to hardware, and I'm better with finances and planning. Figure a degree in business could help with that."

"You're positive?" asked her dad. "There are things you could learn on the town council that they don't teach in college, you know. And..." His volume lowered, not all the way to a whisper but enough to suggest thoughts of conspiracy. "You know, Fiona's taking a year off, and with all her friends gone to school she'll be lonely—"

"Dad," said Fiona.

The men looked up at her, caught. Calvin blushed and lowered his gaze, but Robert Jones just smirked, proud of his not-so-secret agenda. Fiona knew she could stare all the daggers in the world at her dad and it wouldn't do a damn thing—he was happy to let her know how much he'd like to have his way.

"Well, it was great seeing you, Cal," he said, slapping the boy on the arm. "Say hi to your dad for me. And come over for dinner sometime." With that, her dad headed back to his seat in front of the TV.

"He's one hell of a character, isn't he?" said Calvin, nodding after her dad. Fiona didn't respond. Calvin nodded, acutely aware of her displeasure. He yanked off his backpack, dug through the front pocket, and held up her headphones. "You dropped these earlier at school."

"Oh." She finished descending the stairs and took them from him. "Thanks. Sorry for shoving you."

He shrugged. "You were angry. It happens. I just figured… these look crappy enough that, if you hadn't gotten new ones, maybe they were, uh, *vintage*?" He said the last word like he was tasting it for the first time. "SO I figured you'd want them back."

She sighed, the plug pulled on her distaste for him. Calvin being nice was almost worse than him ogling her. He was spot-on—they were her ratty cheap headphones that she'd had since she was fourteen, all scotch-taped together. It would've broken her heart to discover them missing. "Right. Thanks, Calvin."

"Sure," he said. "And, ah…I talked to my dad. Told him

to leave you alone, to mind his own business."

"That wasn't the problem," said Fiona. "The real issue was *you* telling him about my business at all." She huffed, remembering the guilt she'd felt when she'd last exploded at Calvin. "I'm sorry about being a jerk at the soup kitchen the other morning. I just don't like being gossiped about."

"No, I get that," said Calvin. "It's not an excuse. I'm just…" He squinted and rubbed his chin. Fiona could tell he was having a hard time doing this, but she forced herself not to help him by finishing his sentence or cutting off the awkwardness. Maybe Calvin Hokes was more than a pervy square, but if Fiona was going to acknowledge that, she needed to see him make an effort. She'd rebuilt a broken guitar; Calvin could fight through his insecurity. "Sometimes, it's like that's the only way I can make him happy. Like, he smiles if I tell him about people, like I'm the council spy or something. Fucked up, right?" He shrugged. "But that's not cool, I know. I'll keep my mouth shut. Sorry."

She nodded. "Well, okay. Thanks for the headphones."

"One last thing," said Calvin. "I talked to Horace, and I wanted you to know the mill was my idea. I thought it was cool and poetic, but I'd forgotten about what happened with those, uh, with your cousin. Horace…he's a really good guy. He felt terrible when we talked later."

"He can tell me that," said Fiona.

"He's too proud," said Calvin. "That's his problem, of course. But I just wanted to tell you, I'm the one who messed that up."

"Okay," said Fiona, a little softer this time.

"Right," said Calvin. "Anyway, I oughta leave. Have a nice, you know. A good. Uh. Right." Calvin shuffled out the door and got into the Hokeses' SUV. As Fiona watched him go, her mother poked her head out of the kitchen.

"Calvin joining us for dinner?" she asked.

"No," said Fiona.

"Too bad," her mom said. "I know you might not think so right now, but he's one nice young man."

Though it killed her inside to admit it, Fiona couldn't help but agree with her mom. "Well, I've been wrong about people before."

"I'm going to quote you on that," laughed her mom.

Fiona went to her room and thought about what Cal had said, about Horace's pride. Horace would never be the one to blink first. Before, it had been sexy having a boyfriend who was stubborn about what he believed. Now, it felt like an obligation, forcing her to extend the olive branch.

She couldn't just let him off the hook. Today had really hurt, whether the fault was Calvin's or not. Maybe there was a middle ground.

F: Ready to tell me you're an idiot and that you can't live without me? she texted him.

Thirty seconds later, she got a reply:

H: babe ive been ready to tell you since you left.

She sighed. It was a start.

chapter 9

"And your phone is charged."

"Yes."

"You have the money your mother gave you."

"I'll bring back change."

"No taking drugs from strangers."

Eye roll. "Or candy, right?"

Her dad was not amused. "Is 'candy' a slang word you guys use for painkillers? Opioids?"

"Dad."

"Remind me of the name of the band you're seeing tonight?"

"Ultradrool." She swallowed a laugh. No even-remotely-savvy rock and roller would believe there was a band called that. But as she'd guessed, the fake name sounded *just* audacious and repulsive enough to convince her father that it was real. He tightened his grip on the steering wheel and grimaced, but said nothing.

They stopped in a parking space outside the train station. Fiona could see a small gathering of her friends up on the platform, dressed to kill; she herself wore her tightest black jeans, her most torn-up T-shirt — she'd gone with Nine Inch Nails, given the night's electronic flavor — and an often-unworn pair of red Doc Martens, along with the obligatory slather of eyeliner and lipstick. But it was the studded collar around her neck that her dad eyed warily as he turned to her in the car.

"I really wouldn't mind waiting outside the club," he repeated for maybe the sixth time.

"Everyone else is taking the train together," she said. "It's sort of a thing."

"I could give them a ride, too," he said. "You guys don't know how dangerous — "

"Dad," she said.

He squeezed his eyes shut and sat back in his seat, sighing. "Right, right, independence, rebellion, I get it. Just please, *please* be careful, okay? The city isn't as safe as Hamm."

"I'm well aware," she said, opening the door. "I'll text you when I'm on the train home. If we have any problems, I'll call." He nodded and didn't say anything, so she climbed out into the crisp autumn night.

Once she had her ticket in hand and was on the platform, it became increasingly apparent to her that the teenagers of Hamm were out in full force, and that very few of them knew how to actually dress for a club. Kids from her school mulled about everywhere, wearing all manner of crazy gear constructed from what was available at home or the mall — glow stick necklaces, drawn-on highlighter tattoos, sleeveless bargain-mart T-shirts that left the guys shivering, tiny shorts and skirts that the girls tugged at endlessly.

Her own crew looked full-on zany — Keller was wearing a black turtleneck like some kind of German poet, while Caroline had neon-green fishnets coming out from beneath her cutoffs. Horace's stoner friends were all baggy jeans and boxy, voluminous hoodies. Only Horace and Rita looked great, seeing as Horace hadn't dressed up at all and Rita wore a solid vintage LBD and combat boots.

As Fiona approached them, her friends crowed excitedly. Horace ran up to her with a childlike grin on his face. "Tonight!" he said. "Babe, tonight. Pit Viper, one night only. That night? Tonight!"

"Save some of that energy for later," she said, putting her hands on his shoulders and leaning in close to him.

"Hmm? Oh, right," he said and gave her a peck before glancing around nervously. "Shouldn't the train be here by now? Yo, Keller, didn't you say seven fifteen? What time is it?"

She tried not to show the sting of his slight, but inside Fiona blistered. Here she was, dressed to the nines for a show by a DJ whose music she didn't even like, and Horace treated her as if she were just another distraction. Even after he'd apologized profusely for trying to arrange a party at the mill, Horace had stumbled over her feelings, never on the same towering level as before but in little ways that left her upset. He didn't even ask her what she was listening to anymore—all that mattered was that she *wasn't* listening to the Pit Viper. Where was the guy she'd been so crazy for, the single-minded dude ready to trade records with her the morning after sneaking through her window?

Simmer down, ho, she thought. *He's just stoked for a party. Don't be needy—he can't fawn over you all the time.*

They hung around and talked for a few minutes—Caroline described Fiona as "sex in jeans," which gave Fiona a little validation—before the train pulled up with a groan and a hiss. They waited impatiently while the tired-eyed evening commuters disembarked (including Keller's mother, Janice, who shook her head and mumbled, "Jesus Christ," at her son's tight black ensemble), and then they piled on the train, gaining scowls and eye rolls from the businesspeople hiding behind their tablets and newspapers.

Fiona leaned her head against Horace's shoulder, feeling the pounding of his heart beneath his skin. "This is going to be fun," she said, mostly trying to convince herself.

"What? Yeah, definitely," mumbled Horace, his eyes focused out the window.

Central Station was a madhouse of commuters, but Keller and Ben Willis, a junior Fiona knew through Rita, led the way, used to visiting relatives in the city and traveling in to see bands or hit up parties. Right out the door, buildings rose on either side of them like monuments to mathematical gods. Puddles reflected liquor-store neon; men in overcoats burst through vent-spewed walls of steam; accented women lounged outside of work and shared much-needed smokes. Life and energy, spilling out of every crack and crevice.

This was what rock and roll was all about, thought Fiona with a twinge of electric excitement, real rock and roll. John Mellencamp may have lived and died in a small town, but Lou Reed and Ace Frehley and Jack White wandered the streets of the city.

The walk to the club, Cacophonie, was long, but their high spirits made it pass quickly, and besides, trying to figure out the bus or subway would have been an absolute disaster. When they were a few blocks away, they stopped at a diner and dominated a large table, chatting loudly. The waitresses shot stink eyes their way, nonplussed at serving a table of small-town kids counting their dollars for plates of cheese fries. Horace ducked out with a few friends and returned reeking of weed. Ben and Rita, ever the sophisticates, broke off to grab sushi somewhere. Fiona grimaced—raw fish. She'd rather eat her Doc Martens.

"How long do you think he'll spin?" asked Caroline.

"Probably two hours," said Horace. "Maybe more, if we bring the energy."

"Is the club the actual venue, or is it just a *map point*?" asked Penny Kim excitedly.

Horace and one or two of the hipper Hamm kids rolled their eyes at Penny, but Vince, aka Swordfish, said, "That's more of a warehouse thing, actually. Map points are really for warehouse gigs where you don't want the cops showing up. This is just a show." Penny nodded as though learning a deep fact, though Fiona felt newbie embarrassment radiating off the girl. At least Vince had let her down easy.

"Think we'll be able to get backstage?" asked Caroline.

Vince nodded firmly. "Hopefully. Tess told me she'd give us a hand."

Horace pulled Fiona close to him but never gave her the kiss she was hoping for. "Would that be okay? It'd be really awesome to meet him. I know your dad's probably being hardcore about you getting home on time tonight, but—"

"Should be fine," she said, cutting off his hyperactive explanation. "As long as we're here, let's hang out."

Horace laughed, and Fiona savored the pleasure of a little rebellion. So she would break curfew a little. Her dad would live.

And maybe Fiona would meet him, too. Maybe. Finally.

Dinner finished, they headed to the club, a faceless gray building with a few velvet ropes leading to a door. A short line had formed, mostly made up of other kids from their school. A lanky, inked-up guy with black, temple-length hair on one side of his head took names and money as they filed toward an equally thin girl with a shaved head who stamped their wrists.

Fiona bit her lip. This was nothing like the concerts she'd been to before, arena shows at the Performing Arts Center outside of Hamm. Those had been huge, gaudy affairs, full of T-shirt hecklers and commemorative soda cups. This was *underground*. If only she were here to see something she liked, something she could brag about, Portland prog or Norwegian black metal or Japanese shoegaze. Instead, she felt nauseous at the very thought of hearing the Pit Viper's music in a crowded room. It was weird—she was truly dreading it, queasy and high-strung at the idea that she'd have to be surrounded by those sounds while packed between sweaty bodies. She didn't like electronica, sure, but even she wondered why she was reacting so strongly to the Pit Viper's album.

She bit the inside of her cheek. Was it the album? Or was it being in his presence again?

No. She stopped herself and nuzzled closer to Horace. Not tonight. Tonight, she would have a good time or die trying. Maybe Horace was acting so distracted because she was lost in her own head.

"Name," said the doorman as they finally arrived at the head of the line.

"Horace Palmada," said Horace. "Tess Baron might have added—"

"You're here," he said with a glance at his clipboard. "Fifteen bucks." Horace wordlessly pulled out the money, while the tattooed ghoul turned to Fiona. "And you?"

"Fiona Jones."

"She might be my plus one," said Horace.

"You're on here," said the man, arching an eyebrow, "and look at that, your door charge has been covered. Get stamped and head on in."

"Wow," said Horace, with what Fiona could tell was a flicker of jealousy. "I wonder how that happened."

"Somebody must like me," she said, her pulse speeding up with apprehension. They got their inner wrists stamped—a black *C* with teeth that was about to devour a musical note—and headed inside.

A dark, pipe-lined hallway that reeked of cigarettes led to a wide-open chamber done up in matte black and tarnished chrome. The ceiling dripped with stage lights, plumbing, and loose wires. Clicky, bare-bones electro beats rattled through the PA, enticing the crowd with music but leaving them hungry for something they could really dance to. The club was divided into three levels—a central dance floor, a stage area with huge speakers surrounding a DJ table, and a balcony section…which, Fiona noticed, contained a full bar, where Tess Baron and one or two of the hipper kids from Hamm sipped cocktails and beers.

"Don't they worry about losing their liquor license?" asked Fiona.

"Guys, hide, someone's mom showed up," said Caroline, rolling her eyes.

Fiona's mouth hung slightly open at Caroline acting like Fiona was some kind of lame-ass. Everyone chuckled; Horace even snorted a laugh and gave Fiona a pat on the shoulder. She winced. It was the kind of gesture you gave a child, or a prude who doesn't get a dirty joke. Bitterness welled up in her, and part of her wished she was home with Betty, using her to tell stories about happiness and sorrow and hope.

The crew sidled up to the bar and ordered drinks. Just to prove she wasn't an utter wet blanket, Fiona got an IPA, its hops-heavy flavor putting Caroline's Bud Light Lime to shame. She sipped it slowly and let the beer take her edge off.

It would be fine, right? Totally fine. She'd watch him spin, and he would look right past her, and then they'd never see each other again. It was probably somebody else who'd put her on the list and paid for her entrance fee. Tess Baron, maybe. Sometimes weird things happened in life. It didn't mean they were all connected, or that the past nine years had all been leading up to this moment.

"Want to get a good spot on the floor?" asked Horace.

"Hell yeah," she said, doing her best to sound enthusiastic. Look at her, being totally fine like a normal person. "Let's move right up front!"

"All right, Fiona!" said Keller, clapping her on the shoulder. "Time to get nuts!"

The dance floor was already a sardined hodgepodge of kids, some from Hamm, others obviously from the city, all shifting their weight and staring expectantly at the stage. She and Horace found a pocket of space up front and elbowed their way in. The sweaty crowd around her made her feel oddly at ease. She was just an audience member—one face among many.

The crowd parted at Fiona's side, and a stick-thin form appeared—the guy from Tess's party, with the salmon shirt. He nodded at Horace. "Dude! Glad you made it out."

"Better believe it," Horace said, slapping the guy five. "Fiona, this is PM."

"PM," she repeated, hoping it would sound less ridiculous from her own lips. No dice.

"My name's Perry, but I'm so boring I put people to sleep," he said, looking over his glasses at her and trying to get a laugh. Horace guffawed. "Oh, speaking of knocking motherfuckers out, you tried this, man? Orbitin." He held up an orange pharmacy bottle between his thin fingers and shook it lightly, making the pills inside rattle.

"What is it?" asked Horace.

"Mood enhancer, two degrees more down than up, more left than right. Bathes your brain in all the best shit, really makes the music pop. Took it last time I saw the Viper, and I just..." He put a hand next to his head and then splayed the fingers with a *poof!* noise. "Mind. Blown. You'll enjoy, I promise."

There was a pause, and Fiona felt it—a wedge forming between them. Horace wanted to get fucked-up on pills, and his desire to do so put him at odds with her complete lack thereof. She kept her gaze locked on the neon-orange bottle, hoping Horace would do the right thing without her having to make kitten eyes at him.

He squeezed her shoulder. "What do you think, babe?"

Ugh. Now he was playing that game, like he didn't know her response. She remembered how stupid she'd thought her father had sounded earlier—*No taking drugs from strangers*—as though anyone would ever do that. *God dammit, Horace...*

"Nah," she said, shaking her head. "No pills. I don't fuck with that."

"Do you mind if I..."

There it was, thrown out into the air. It was like he was asking her for a threesome, like this might be that *one time*. Now, her options were either be a bummer on their big night in the city or let Horace become a glassy-eyed pill casualty, the kind of creep who always had a cigarette dangling from his lip—

Listen to her. *Guys, hide, someone's mom showed up.*

"Do whatever you want," she said.

"Cool," he said, not even risking his chances with a third and final *Are you sure?* Perry smiled and tapped out two pills, cylindrical, purple, into Horace's palm.

"Don't worry," said Perry, holding up a bottle of water. "A few hours of dancing, he'll sweat it all out." Horace tossed the Orbitin back with a swig.

"I take it *the first taste is always free*," said Fiona in the most accusatory tone she could muster.

"Hell no," said Perry, holding out a spidery hand. "Twenty bucks."

"I'll be good," said Horace, kissing her on the head and slapping a twenty into PM's palm. "Don't worry, I've done shit like this before. I can handle it."

"You took some Vicodin when you had a tooth pulled," she snapped. "Orbitin? Do you even know what's in that stuff?"

"I'm assuming it's mostly Molly," he said with a relaxed smile. "I'll rub myself, sweat a bunch, and whisper sweet nothings in your ear on the train back home. I promise, Fiona, I'll be okay."

Fifteen minutes later, the background music went down, and then so did the lights. In the darkness, everyone cheered.

"Here it comes!" squealed Caroline.

There was a hiss from the speakers, like a needle touching an old record or wax tube. The sound grew louder and louder… and then a voice, calm but fierce, as deep and murky as a lake of blood, spoke:

"There is a voice," said the voice.

"A sound spoken by swimmers in a serene sea. We are aware of it, have always been, will always be. It echoes loudly throughout the ages, broadcasting truths understood by the sages. It is a voice that we've been taught to ignore. And yet we hear it. And we want more.

"So when your patience reaches its limit, ask yourself: Whose voice is it? Whose voice speaks for the unholy and divine? Is it theirs? Is it his?

"Is it mine?"

The stage lights blared. The crowd roared. There, in perfect white, stood the Pit Viper, arms spread like Christ.

Behind him loomed a ten-foot-tall banner of the snake on his album cover, only this serpent was not coiled and waiting. Its head was raised, its mouth open and showing off curved fangs protruding from pink reptilian flesh, ready to strike and envenom.

Fiona gasped at the sight of him, of his wiry arms, his sharp chin, and dominant smile, his eyes beaming out from under his hood like spotlights. He was so much more than the boy she'd seen ages ago, in so many ways. Her skin prickled. Forgetting her makeup, she licked her lips.

"Yes!" screamed Horace. "Fuck *YES*!"

The Pit Viper extended a finger, lowered it to his turntable, and the beat dropped.

Fiona's frozen gaze was broken by the crowd's oceanic shift, the partiers around her rippling and pulsating to the thick and chilly rhythm. She watched her friends twist and move to the music in sensual ecstasy. Caroline's hands slid over her body, nails scratching at her skin. Keller had his fists in the air, his mouth open in a scream Fiona couldn't hear. And Horace at her side was entirely lost in the music, his dilated pupils focused only on the Pit Viper. She tried to dance toward him, to press against him and take part in the party, but the surging crowd only pulled them farther apart, and Horace didn't seem to care.

She did her best to play along and move to the rhythm, looking to Caroline and Rita and trying to imitate their sexy gyrations, but her heart wasn't in it. No, not her heart—her gut. The music didn't feel right; the vibrations bored into her head and ignited a splitting migraine. There was nothing organic about the sounds filling the room and shaking the floor; it was all a bunch of plastic when what she wanted was…a soul. There was no soul to this music, only sounds, beating and crushing her, shoving her away.

"Horace!" she screamed, reaching out for him, pushing harder into the sweat-drenched crowd.

A hand landed on her shoulder, and she turned to see Will Hokes, his pupils huge and his mouth full of a candy necklace. "ARE YOU HEARING THIS, JONES? *ARE YOU HEARING THIS—*"

She elbowed past him and fought her way up to the raised bar section, but even that was loaded with moving bodies. For a split second, she stared out at the crowd, trying to find her friends, but everybody looked the same. The only distinguishable figure was the Pit Viper standing over them like an electric superhero, his hands moving from one knob to the next in a calculated frenzy.

The room grew hot, reeking of armpits and smoke. People around her kept putting their hands on her, making her feel soiled. The music churned the beer she'd downed too quickly. Overwhelmed and alienated, Fiona pushed her way toward the door.

chapter
10

She was almost back to her old self when she heard someone call out, "Gotta say, I'm surprised."

Fiona turned, her back scraping lightly against the vibrating brick wall. Inside the club, the music thrummed for its third uninterrupted hour; out back, in the alley, she was doing her best to not feel nauseated by the stench rising from a nearby dumpster.

Filip Moss leaned against the wall next to her. He wore ripped jeans and an Aura Noir shirt, but had a security laminate dangling from his neck. He lit a cigarette, offered her one, didn't seem to care when she refused.

"What," she said, "that I'm not in there raging?"

"That you came to this thing at all," he said. "Girl who listens to High Spirits and Damone hitting up an EDM show? Seems a little silly, even if you're not a true metalhead."

She laughed. "I'm sorry that all my favorite bands don't come from Sweden and worship the devil."

He shrugged and said, "Nobody's perfect." They shared a laugh; she needed it, and relished it. Sometimes she wished that Filip was her type in the slightest, but there was no way.

"Real talk, though, Fiona. Why *are* you here?"

"I came with Horace," she said. "He's big into the Pit Viper. You're working, I take it?"

"Yeah, but pretend like we just met if anyone asks," he said. "They find out I'm a minor, I get fired." He sighed, shaking his head. "The Pit Viper. Everyone *loves* the Pit Viper these days."

"Seems like he's tapped into something people really enjoy," she said.

"Seems like he's tapped into a lot of things," grumbled Filip.

"What's that mean?" she asked.

He shook his head. "Never mind. Just kind of off-putting to see everyone going crazy for this guy. He has a history."

The tone of his voice told her he was hiding something, and the thought that he knew, possibly about *everything*, pinched her with excitement. "A history in Hamm?"

"Yeah," he said, suddenly peering at her, curious and testing the waters, just like Fiona. "Yeah, exactly. Do you know? You know, don't you? Robert Jones's daughter, of course you know."

"About the mill," she said.

"About the last party that was ever had there," he said, going the extra mile.

"Yeah, I know." Fiona had always hoped that finding out she wasn't alone in knowing the Pit Viper's sordid story would be a relief. Instead, she felt ashamed, as though admitting they'd both witnessed the same murder and never said anything. "And after?"

"After?" he said. "What happened after?"

Ah. So, he didn't know everything. "I was asking. That's what I've been trying to find out. He performed there, the mill closed, and then what?"

"Fuck if I know," said Filip, taking a deep drag from his smoke. "Seems like everyone just forgot about the Pit Viper."

"I know," said Fiona. "Everyone else is clueless. They're acting like he's this totally new phenomenon — "

"Maybe that's because you can't find information about it anywhere," said Filip. "Not in old newspaper archives online, and they go back to the Sixties. It's nowhere on the internet. It's like that night doesn't exist."

She digested the idea, knowing it was heavier than it seemed on the surface. "Wasn't that the point of the place? It was super underground. You had to be in the know."

Filip sneered. "Yeah, that works in theory," he said, "but given the pressure it brought on the town? On your dad and my mom? The mill was a *thing*. Huge parties, freaky-looking chemheads all over the fucking place, kids OD'ing — " He gave her a sympathetic glance and a nod, silently telling her he remembered about Jake. "And there's not a sentence about it online?"

He was right, there was something way off about that. But something else about Filip's big reveal struck her as odd. "You must be pretty interested in the Pit Viper," she said, "to be looking so deeply into him."

Filip gave her a hard stare and opened his mouth to reply, but just then the pounding rhythm of the music stopped, and was replaced by a roar of applause. "A topic for another time," he said. "You meeting people out front?"

"They don't really know I left," she confessed, feeling a twinge of guilt at blowing off the wild night her friends had so eagerly planned. "And I think they're trying to get backstage after the set."

Filip nodded, took one last puff, and flicked his smoke. "Okay, come on. I'll take you in through the service entrance."

He opened a nondescript metal door in the side of the

building and waved her through, giving a curt "She's cool" to the huge barbacks inside. He led Fiona through a narrow alley of shelves stocked with boxes of liquor, crates of limes and olives, and broken stage lights, until they came out into a hallway covered in zigzagging pipes. Scattered around them were hangers-on and off-hours bartenders, all skinny and model-hot, checking their phones or tipping back beers. One or two gave a nod to Filip as he passed.

"There are your people," said Filip, pointing. "You know that one dude, right?"

At the end of the hall, Tess Baron and Vince, aka Swordfish, stood in front of a lit doorway. They were flanked by PM and another nameless guy, massive and dressed in a tracksuit, his face a galaxy of acne. Vince talked quietly but animatedly, gesturing with his hands a lot; Tess looked mortified, her one fist pressed to her mouth.

"Vince!" called Fiona as she neared him.

Vince glanced at her. "One second, Fiona, in the middle of something here—"

"It's you."

Fiona froze. That voice.

She turned to the door, to the light.

In a dressing room illuminated by mirror lamps, he sat on a folding chair, hunched forward. The white pants were still on, but the hoodie had been tossed to the floor, revealing a taut physique more knotted together than chiseled, slick and shiny with sweat. He was absolutely covered in tattoos of looping concentric circles and ancient runic characters. His hair hung damp and dripping in his face. But for all the new muscles, new outfit, new location, and the new way he made her feel when she looked at him, the Pit Viper's eyes were the same shimmering orbs that had watched Fiona as she'd approached him with an apple in her hand that night.

"It is you," he said, his voice dark and smooth, like a black diamond, "isn't it?"

Fiona wanted to play it cool, to pretend like she barely remembered him, but that was impossible. Her heart raced. Her head spun.

"Yes," she said, her eyes locked on his. "Of course it is."

A smile crept across the Pit Viper's face. "I knew it was you," he said. "At the party. I recognized you."

She nodded. "And I recognized you."

His smile spread wider. "I was worried you might have forgotten me."

She bit her lip. Whatever he was making her feel, awe or excitement or *whatever*, she knew he was feeling the same. "How could I possibly have forgotten you?"

For a brief moment, they were silent, entirely lost in the energy flowing between them—and then Fiona realized, in a blast of cheek-burning embarrassment, that all eyes were on her.

"Sorry, do you two know each other?" asked Tess, sounding both surprised and envious.

"I was just going to ask the same thing, boss," said PM to the Pit Viper.

The DJ's eyes never left Fiona, and he showed no sign of self-consciousness. "The apple, Perry," he said. "It was her."

PM's eyes darted to Fiona, now wide with surprise. "Holy shit."

"So, anyway," said Vince, trying to shoehorn his way back into the conversation, "as I was saying—"

"Where's Horace?" asked Fiona. She had to stay focused on the situation, anything but those tattooed muscles and those eyes burning into her, making her feel both light-headed and comforted.

Vince inhaled sharply, glaring straight ahead like it took all his willpower not to choke Fiona. "He's out there somewhere," he said. "I tried to get him to come back here with me, but he's rolling pretty hard."

Fiona glared at PM, who held up his palms. "Not my fault the dude can't hold his drugs," he said.

"What'd you give him?" asked the Viper.

"Orbitin," said PM. "Sorry, boss, if I'd known who she was—"

"I need to go," said Fiona. "I have to find Horace."

"You do that," said Vince.

She forced herself to meet the Pit Viper's gaze again, trying to match his pressence with her own, and feeling, momentarily, like she did so.

What could she possibly say to him?

"It was nice to see you."

Dear God, Fiona, really?

"You never answered my question," said the Pit Viper.

She wanted to play coy. *What question*? But what other question was there? And anyway, he knew the answer. He'd put her on the list tonight. He'd paid her cover charge. Who else could have?

But he wanted to hear her say it, finally. And she wanted to tell him herself.

"Fiona," she said.

His face softened, and he was the boy again, entirely. For a moment, she thought he might cry.

"Music to my ears," he said. "Good night, Fiona. I'll see you soon."

"Good night," she said and hurried away from the brightly lit room, intent on finding her boyfriend and stopping her trembling.

• • •

The club was close to empty when Fiona reentered, so she followed the last few stragglers outside. Her eyes scanned the block for her friends, and she was beginning to lose hope when she spotted Rita standing down the street.

She trotted over, but as she got closer to them, she saw the extent of the scene, and the excitement of rejoining her crew vanished.

Horace was bent at the waist, both hands up against a wall. His head dangled between his shoulders, dripping long strings of drool. Between his feet spread a splatter pattern of watery vomit that made Fiona's nostrils burn. Rita rubbed his back and looked apologetically at Fiona. Keller and Caroline stood nearby, faces pale and pupils dilated.

"Did you see, when he raised his hands up," moaned Keller, "like this?"

"Oh my *God*," cried Caroline, raking her nails down her collarbone and chest. "It was so beautiful. I wept, Doug, I fucking *wept*."

"Horace?" said Fiona, putting a hand on his shoulder. "Horace, are you all right?"

"He'll be fine," said Rita, swaying tipsily. "Just needs to get all the bad stuff out, and he'll be good."

"Fiona?" moaned Horace. He belched, and his body shook. "Fiona, I heard it. The voice? It spoke to me. It was beautiful, Fiona. They're all beautiful."

"And the drug thoughts," laughed Rita. "The drug thoughts need to get out, too. He'll be okay, though."

Ben Willis trotted over with a bottle of water and some napkins from a deli, and together they made Horace swish and spit and wipe his mouth. When he tried to stand, he had to cling to Fiona for balance.

As they walked back to Central Station, Fiona did her best to coo and smile and listen to Horace's incessant babbling about gorgeous voices and what the sky sounded like, but every so often she would glance at the boy holding on to her for dear life and feel pissed off. Horace had represented joy and vibrancy to her. He had been what could be cool about growing up in Hamm. This guy, his face grayish-pale and sheened with sweat, his voice shaky and insane and carrying the scent of bile—this was not the boy she'd thought she loved.

On the train home, after Horace, Keller, and Caroline had gibbered themselves to sleep, the anger Fiona had been holding back hit her like a slap in the face, and she snarled at her reflection in the window. Tomorrow, she and Horace would talk it out, and he'd apologize profusely and make vows of sobriety, but the simple truth was, he had failed her. He knew they were on unstable ground, he knew he was supposed to be making it up to her for trying to have a party at the mill, and instead he'd acted like the kind of guy she'd always told herself she'd never date, a wannabe rock star who preferred wasted oblivion to her.

Inevitably, her mind kept wandering back to her exchange with the Pit Viper.

He'd remembered her. He'd told others her story; he had waited for years and years to hear the answer to the question he'd asked her on a dark, bloody night long ago, even though he'd somehow found it out on his own (Tess? Probably). His eyes had touched something deep in her heart, a sensation that she felt both giddy and guilty for having.

Thinking about him now brought up familiar feelings. Not the dread of his return, but the excitement of his initial arrival.

And other feelings, too. Feelings Fiona didn't want to admit to herself while sitting next to her boyfriend. She thought about the way he'd looked at her. Her toes curled in her boots.

As they stepped off the train back in Hamm, Horace

hooked an arm around her shoulder, shuffling along with bleary slow-blinking eyes and a glistening slick of saliva down his chin.

Fiona shook her head, wondering how things could get much worse, and then looked up to see her father waiting by his car.

chapter
11

"Breakfast!" shouted her mom.

Fiona rubbed her eyes and groaned. There was no more terrifying word in existence for her right now. Somewhere in Hamm, she knew, Horace was shivering off a final sweat, and Caroline was probably retching out the bottom of her stomach while her mom held her hair, but as far as Fiona was concerned, they had it easy. They had not sat in the back of that car after dropping off Horace, hadn't endured the hunched silence of her father's *I told you so* disappointment as they rolled through the streets of Hamm. Now, the trouble she was in waited for her downstairs, and there wasn't even time to get in a few minutes with Betty before she had to face it.

She put on her pajamas and left the fortress of her room, hoping she was ready. Every step down the stairs was exponentially more nerve-racking than the last, but felt inevitable, like a walk to the gallows.

Robert Jones sat in their well-lit kitchen with his coffee mug to his mouth, his wrinkled brow aimed directly at her.

Her mom, looking displeased but far less vengeful, heated up butter for eggs.

Fiona fixed herself some cereal and poured her coffee, doing her best to act natural. But she was sitting at the table for less than five seconds before her father went on the offensive:

"I hope you're not planning to go anywhere today."

She shrugged. "Nope. Was just going to take today easy. If that's okay with you."

Her mother gave her an over-the-shoulder glance — *Don't push it* — while her cavalier response only made her father's nostrils flare.

"And I hope you won't be seeing that boy anymore," he said.

She sighed dejectedly. "Well, I have school with him tomorrow," she said. "But I'm happy not to go if that's what you'd prefer."

"Is this funny to you?" snapped her dad. "That boy is a bad influence. I don't want you spending time with him."

"He has a name. Horace. Remember? At dinner the other night you were talking about all the good things his family does for the town —"

"That was before he made my car smell like a sick ward," said her father, setting down his mug and linking his hands together.

She made a mental note to kick Horace in the shin for putting her in this position. "He had a bad night," she said calmly. "I'm sorry, I know, it wasn't a good look, but come on, Dad, it happens to everyone. You never got wasted in high school and threw up?"

"Don't talk to me like I was born yesterday," he said, his voice suddenly so loud that even he felt surprised. Fiona's mom froze mid-whisk. "That boy didn't have one beer too many or smoke a doobie when he shouldn't have—"

"Doobie? Really?"

"He was all fucked-up on something dangerous," said her dad, slapping a hand down on the table. The salt and pepper shakers rattled together.

Fiona was dumbfounded. Robert Jones did not drop f-bombs at breakfast. She was in serious trouble.

"Robert," said her mother, "don't be ridiculous about this."

"You're making a big deal out of nothing," said Fiona, trying to sound like she was bored by the conversation already. "He's probably super embarrassed and is going to give me flowers or something at school tomorrow. Calm down."

"You think you have *any* idea what boys like him are up to?" said her dad, his expression aggressively pitying. "Well, you don't. I may be an old man to you, kiddo, but I've seen things that would make your hair turn white. And I've seen what happens to kids like *that*."

If only she'd had some time with Betty before breakfast, she thought, she might have taken this castigation a little better. Today, though, she was still carrying a lot of her own anger at Horace's behavior last night, and it smoldered the edges of her composure.

"Oh, do tell, all-knowing Council Fuhrer," she shouted. "What happens to boys like my boyfriend?"

"They end up like your cousin Jake," spat her father.

She gasped involuntarily; her mother did, too. Robert Jones snorted, as though he felt angry that he had been forced to touch on such a dark subject.

"Oh my God," was all Fiona could come up with.

"Yeah," said Robert. "Suddenly it's not so *fine*, is it? So, the next time you want to hang out with junkies and hoods, picture them huddled in a corner dying while you and your friends dance around them—"

Fiona was out of the kitchen and up the stairs in seconds, tears welling up in her eyes. She slammed the door viciously, but her rage was all angst, and fell apart the minute she was alone. She collapsed on her bed and sobbed until her throat burned and her back hurt, too overwhelmed to even play guitar.

"Jesus Christ," said Caroline through a bite of sandwich at lunch the next day.

"Seriously," said Rita, putting a hand on Fiona's shoulder.

Fiona shook her head. "I don't know," she said. "He's scared, I guess. And I know he's just looking out for me, but still…"

"But still, that's maybe the *creepiest* thing you could say to someone?" countered Caroline. "Fiona, girl, don't feel the need to justify your dad's bullshit."

"Easy there," said Rita, but then she turned to Fiona. "Caroline has a point, though. Your dad's upset, yeah, but that doesn't mean you were wrong. And it was unfair of him to say something that cruel. Unfair to you, and to your cousin's memory."

"And if your dad had been there and had seen what we saw, maybe he would have a better perspective on it."

Fiona glanced up at Caroline; suddenly, she felt unsure they were talking about the same thing. "What do you mean?"

"I mean the Pit Viper!" she said, grinning. "I know I was flying on that Orbitin stuff and all, but wasn't that amazing? I keep going back to that set in my head and just feeling… *freer*!" She grinned at Rita. "Back me up here."

"To be fair, I was just a little drunk," said Rita with a guilty smirk, "but yeah, that show was beyond incredible. I've never danced that hard in my life."

"It was like midway through the set, the music and the drugs and the dancing all sort of came together in this perfect moment, you know?" Before Fiona's eyes, Caroline became engrossed in her own little world. "It kind of changed everything. Like, I'm looking at school, and track, and my dad, and all the town council bullshit, and realizing, it's just so repressed, you know? Like, I'm sitting in class, listening to Traubert babble on, and I'm like, wait, compared to how I felt Saturday night, how do I feel now? And the answer's *shitty*! Why do things need to be so shitty…"

Fiona frowned. What was going on? This wasn't Caroline. Yes, she was always a smart-ass, but she was driven and intelligent about it. She didn't buy into some talk about ecstasy and life being a drag. Fiona looked to Rita for vindication, but Rita was caught up in Caroline's rant. Her eyes had glazed over as she absently stirred her rice bowl, her mind lost in memories of Saturday night.

Fiona winced. One minute, her dad was making her and her friends out to be monsters; the next, her friends were acting like the type of blind hedonists that Robert Jones was scared of. Why was everything going so crazy all of a sudden?

"Anyway," said Caroline, snapping back to the present, "you should tell your dad to go fuck himself. What Horace does on a Saturday is none of his business."

"I'm not going to tell my dad to go fuck himself," said Fiona with a laugh.

Caroline shrugged. "That's what I'd do. Just saying."

Horace was a ghost all afternoon. At one point, Vince tried to stop her in the hall—he wanted to talk about the Pit Viper, again with the damn Pit Viper—and she asked him about Horace. When the boy shrugged, she stormed off. She didn't have the time for gossip. Her boyfriend owed her an apology.

Finally, at the end of the day, there was AP Chemistry, the class they had together (she noted the irony, given her last interaction with Horace). She showed up early and watched the door, ZZ Top chugging away on her headphones, until Mr. Chanesh arrived and started class.

Five minutes after the lesson began, Horace tiptoed in, a smile on his face. He plopped down in the seat next to Fiona, leaned over, whispered, "Hey, babe," and pecked her on the cheek.

"Ms. Jones, Mr. Palmada," said Mr. Chanesh, folding his arms across his chest. "Are we disturbing your canoodling?"

Fiona felt her face blaze and opened her mouth to say sorry, but before she could, Horace said, "Actually, if you could give us a few minutes, that'd be great."

The room rippled with laughter. Mr. Chanesh shook his head. "Strike two," he said and turned back to the whiteboard. The rest of the period, Fiona sat silently, trying to focus on her work and doing her best to avoid eye contact with her classmates. Twice, Horace reached for her hand under the table; both times she pulled it away.

When class was over, she hurried outside and waited for Horace a little ways down the hall. He sauntered toward her a few minutes later, his brow furrowed.

"So," said Horace, "that seemed a little weird back there."

"What the fuck are you doing?" Fiona hissed.

"Whoa, easy, babe," he said. "Are you all right?"

"Horace, the last time I saw you, you were shirtless and drooling all over me in the back of my dad's car," she said. "And today, you roll into class acting like a jerk-off for no reason. No phone call, no email, just showing up like nothing happened."

"Wow, you are *not* all right," he said, blinking in surprise. "Fiona, I spent yesterday having the worst hangover of my life, plus I was super embarrassed about how things went down in front of your dad. I wanted to see you today. I'm sorry I didn't call."

"No, instead, you waited to get to class late and try to hold hands with me under the table like all is forgiven."

"What is this?" He laughed, throwing his arms up. "I roll into class late *all the time*! I've rolled into *this* class late so many times, and we always held hands and shit!"

"Well, maybe Saturday night changed things," she said, riding her anger. The more he spoke, the more she realized he was right, she was being emotional, paranoid, pissy, but... where were her flowers? Where was her big apology? "That was not a good look for you. It was not fun dragging you to the train and having my dad see you rolling your face off."

"First of all, I was definitely *tripping*, not rolling."

"Don't be an asshole."

A snarky grin spread across his face. "And *second*, you got chewed out by your dad, didn't you? I can practically smell it on you."

She froze, mouth open, caught off guard by how silly she felt hearing the truth out loud. "Back off. This isn't about my dad, it's about you behaving like a supreme dickhead."

"Which I said I wanted to apologize for!" he yelled, letting his arms flop down to show how *exhausted* he was by this conversation. "Would you prefer I came to class on my knees, hanging my head? Yeesh, your pops really put the screws to you, huh?"

"Why, because he doesn't want to see me with someone blacking out on pills?" she said, feeling suddenly defensive of her father, the man who only yesterday had sent her storming up to her room in tears.

"Look, Fiona, I was having a great time, and I made a dumb choice," he groaned. "Teenagers get trashed and vomit and learn very painful lessons about it in the morning. If your dad is gonna hate me because of that, then he's overreacting as much as you are, and that's *his* problem."

She hated him then. She'd tried defending him to her father, and now here she was forced to defend her dad to Horace. How dare he make this about her life, when he had behaved like such an inconsiderate putz on Saturday night?

Maybe she was freaking out. Maybe she should just admit that her dad had chewed her out and fall into his arms. They could go over to the bleachers and make out and talk about his newest vinyl, and it would be...

"Bullshit," she blurted.

Horace blinked. "What? What's bullshit?"

"What about the pills, Horace?" she said. "You knew I didn't want you to take those things, and you popped them anyway. Why was getting high more important than us having a night together?"

Horace shook his head and laughed. "Listen to this Hugs Not Drugs nonsense! Man, all the black concert shirts and loud rock music might fool you for a second, ladies and gentlemen, but she's still just Fiona Jones, small-town daddy's girl..."

"Don't even try that," said Fiona. She felt empowered. Her heart pounded a death march in her chest. "I'm just *right*, and you know it. And guess what, I'm *done* tolerating this kind of behavior." She couldn't believe what she was saying, but it felt delicious. Her gut told her to go for it. "Saturday night was *disgusting*, and instead of apologizing to me, you insulted me. I'm not interested in a relationship with someone like that."

His smile collapsed as the confidence drained from his face. "Sorry, what?"

"You heard me," she said. "Right now, it feels like you're not ready to be in a serious relationship. And if I'm going to be with someone, he needs to be serious about me."

"Wait, wait," he said, eyes filling with panic. "Okay. So that escalated pretty fast. Let's rewind. What I meant was—"

"Too little, too late," she snapped back. In her head, she screamed, *Are you crazy? This is Horace Palmada! You've never felt this way about a boy before!* But it was drowned out by the grinding noise of her anger. "For six months, you were so good to me, but now it's like I'm the love of your life until it's inconvenient. Until you get upset that your DJ set got cut short and you start drinking like a fish. Until having the party at the old mill is too cool to pass up because, what, because I have some stupid hang-up with my *cousin dying there*, right?"

"It's an awesome venue!" he cried.

"You selfish dick!" she shouted. "Go fuck yourself, Horace Palmada." And then, even though she knew it was too much, she went over the edge: "Never mind, go have the party at the mill. Maybe you can die there, see if it's cool."

Horace stepped back as though he'd been slapped, and Fiona herself was surprised that she had said such a thing. She was choking on the emotions she normally exorcised with Betty, and they were spilling out of her uncontrollably, like she was Carrie wrecking prom night. Part of her wanted to try that, to lift Horace off the ground with her mind like Darth Vader and watch him gag as she closed an invisible hand around his throat—

She shook her head, casting off the murderous thoughts, and left. He didn't even call out after her.

• • •

She made it halfway through her bike ride home before the tears began fluttering out of the corners of her eyes, the wind blowing them back into her ears. Storming through the house, she was only flustered and shaking, but seconds after entering her room she crumbled outright. It had been a long day, and she was overdue for a serious cry.

Once the initial wave of sobs gave way to quieter, sniffling sadness, she dragged Betty out from under her bed. She closed the blinds, locked the door, went to turn off her phone—

A notification glowed on her screen.

One new email.

Sender: PV.

Her crying stopped in a gasp of disbelief. She tentatively opened the message and read it.

Tess gave me this address. I hope it's yours.
If it is you, I want to see you, soon. We have a lot to talk about.
I've thought about you every day.

-Pit Viper

She blinked, absorbing the message.

Carefully, Fiona pulled Betty from her case. Her fingers found their way to Betty's strings, and together they spoke.

But the message from the Pit Viper had pivoted her mood. This wasn't the minor-chord heartache and eighth-note angst that she'd planned to unleash, but a twanging sense of possibility and apprehension and heat. As it built, it slowed to a humid, stomping Southern-rock riff that spoke of something primal, old, and wise.

She closed her eyes. The slouching, laughing image of Horace hung in her mind for a second, and then it vanished and was replaced by a a lithe figure humming with power, his skin marked with sigil and star, body hard and burning with a distant, cold light like the sun off snow. As the notes from her guitar outlined him in her mind, they all came together in the roar of his eyes, two distant lights in space, hungry as the gaze of a snake. He reached out to her, and without hesitation she put her hand in his, and they pulled each other close...

She swayed with the music. The room grew dim in her vision, the air cool against her skin. A bead of sweat formed at her brow, ran down her face, dropped off her chin.

I've thought about you every day.

She pulled Betty off her and flopped back onto her bed, her temples pounding as he raced through her mind. The halo of power and confidence around him made her head spin, until it was as though she was drunk on the very thought of him.

chapter
12

Horace tried to contact her three times that night, but each time she let his call go to voicemail. He left two apologetic messages with a loud, angry one sandwiched between them. She wasn't sure anything she might say to him would be fair or productive. Besides, she was too conflicted to listen to his apologies quite yet.

She responded to the Pit Viper's email.

That week at school, she was surrounded by Pit Viper fever. The DJ's renown had spread like wildfire. You couldn't walk anywhere without seeing a Pit Viper shirt or sticker. The name was scribbled in every bathroom stall, carved into multiple desks. Online profiles featured Pit Viper logos and links. A rumor had gone around that Scott Driscoll, a friend of Tess Baron's, had gotten a Pit Viper tattoo; it turned out to be false, but the fact that people were so ready to believe the lie spoke to the devotion that was being fostered.

She didn't hear anything more about it from the town council, but she knew her father was aware of what was going on. On Thursday night, she was looking around the house for some glue to fix the handle on Betty's case and found a copy of the Pit Viper's CD tucked away in one of her dad's drawers in the garage, next to some tax papers and an old watch he'd gotten as a present. The sight of the green snake in her home bothered her, and explained why her dad was acting so distracted lately. Who knew what he might do next? Had he listened to the album? Had he noticed its deafening rhythms blaring out of cars and bedrooms all over town?

Fiona still couldn't stand the music itself, try as she might. After she'd gotten the email from the Pit Viper, she'd attempted to listen to the album one more time and feel the attraction, but once again the music just drove a nail in her brain. She supposed she understood the draw—cold, insect-like, polished to perfection, deeply efficient. Even if the album wasn't Fiona's cup of tea, there was definitely something there that could excite someone.

She'd hoped to keep her secret to herself all week, but no dice. Unsurprisingly, it was Rita who finally confronted her.

"I don't know what's going on with you, but you have to talk to Horace," she said over coffee Thursday evening. There were two cafés in Hamm, family-owned Finnerdee's and hippie-run Powerdrive, and they sat at a carved table near the wide front windows of the latter. Rita knew the dreadlocked owner, Weber, pretty well; though the place was often packed, he always found a table for her.

"Horace can talk to me when he wants to," said Fiona, nipping at her latte.

"Yeah, except he's been trying to," said Rita, cocking an eyebrow at her. "And you're doing that thing where you don't answer, and that's supposed to *be* an answer. That's not fair."

Fiona responded with a shrug. "I don't have to be fair. I'm taking the time I need to make sure that this is what I want. You should've heard him on Monday, Rita. He was a real ass."

"And I get that," she said. "Look, Horace and I have been friends *almost* as long as you and I have, and I'm well aware that the dude is a complete idiot who cares *way* too much about being cool. But he's freaking out about you cutting him off."

"Define freaking out."

"He's officially transitioned from *She won't talk to me because she's a bitch* to *She won't talk to me because I'm the biggest jerk in the world*," said Rita. "He's super down on himself. He's smoking way too much weed."

"But that's just it," said Fiona. "Horace wants to celebrate, he gets wasted. He's feeling depressed, he gets wasted. It's the same childish reaction, every time."

"Well, sure," Rita said. "But since when has *not* telling someone that helped? He's a lovable guy, but still about as smart as an elbow. Spell it out for him." Rita exhaled hard. "And it's not just that. Other people have noticed something's up with you this week. It's like you're in your own little world."

"I don't know what to tell you," said Fiona. "Maybe the fight with Horace let me see things in a different light, you know? I'm learning to live without him."

Rita rolled her eyes beneath her perfect bangs. "I give up. Who is he, Fiona?"

"Horace? Like, on a personal level?"

"No, and don't be cute. Who's the guy who's making it so easy to ignore Horace?"

Fiona kept her face motionless, though she felt overwhelmingly caught. "What makes you think—"

"A month ago, you rocked Horace's hoodie like it gave you superpowers," said Rita plainly. "But Monday, you break up with him in an ugly, public way, and now you're just *fine with it*? I know you, dude. You're too emotional to be suffering a tectonic life shift this well if there wasn't something else on your mind." She squinted. "And it's a 'he.' Obviously. When you've grown up with the level of small-town gossip that *we* have, you know it when you see it."

Fiona gulped. For a moment, she considered spilling the story—the whole story, from the winery sign right up to the email—but she managed to swallow it. "It's complicated," she said, unable to answer with an entire lie. "Extremely complicated. I'll give you the details when it's over."

"Got it," said Rita. "Just don't think I'll pull some Caroline shit and be super-opinionated about everything, or fawn over you like Keller does. You know you can be really honest with me, right?"

Fiona nodded, her heart swelling. This was why they would leave Hamm behind someday, why Rita was destined to carve her own path. "I do. Thanks, Rita."

Rita smiled and shrugged. "No problem. Life's hard, even in a place like this stupid town. Just figure your shit out and get back to me before you go running off with this mystery man."

"I sincerely doubt that will happen," said Fiona.

Fiona spent the entire bike ride home planning out how she'd do it. Plane tickets, passports. New names, new places, new lives.

Getting off the train at Central Station felt less electric and ceremonial this time around, with shafts of daylight pouring through the windows and no giggling friends at Fiona's side. She texted her parents to let them know she'd arrived safe and sound and would be back in a few hours; even though she'd biked to the train station, her father had made her spell out her plans in perfect detail and requested that she text them along the way. Obviously, they didn't really know.

She made her way to the right bus and took it to the neighborhood he'd mentioned in his follow-up email. He'd offered to get her at the train station, but she'd refused. She felt like it was a power play for him, to lead her around like a tourist or a kid. She wanted him to know she was capable of handling herself.

The restaurant he'd suggested was a ramen house called Hageshi, the inside decorated in equal parts ancient Japanese art and modern-day pop culture; behind the bartender stood a three-foot-tall plastic Gundam, and beneath the plastic inlay of her table was an image of the Colossal Titan peeking over a stone wall. As she ordered a green tea, she couldn't help but be slightly tickled by the whole experience. She was used to the small-town trio: diners, cafés, and pastry stands. He obviously wanted to impress her with ethnic food at a restaurant straight out of *Blade Runner*.

She was flip-flopping between drunken noodles and spicy stew when a chair scraped the floor and her table shuddered. She glanced up from her menu and was met by a focused gaze that caught her off guard even though she'd been waiting all day to see it.

"I'm surprised you showed," said the Pit Viper in his smooth baritone. She was speechless for a brief second—foolishly, she realized, she'd imagined him appearing shirtless and sweaty, like he'd been at the club (the way, she considered guiltily, that she'd been picturing him since). Instead, he wore a T-shirt and a peacoat. This close, she could study his face thoroughly. His cheeks were tight, his chin strong. Over his left eye, between strands of straw-colored hair, was an inch-long scar, no doubt from where his head had collided with the winery sign. There might be more under his shirt...

Then she snapped back to reality, mentally reminding herself that she had to meet him as an equal. "I said I would, didn't I?"

"Yeah, but people often flake at the last second. Nerves, guilt, all those man-made constructs." He nodded at the menu. "What are you having? The fish is really good here."

She smirked. "Wow, the fish is really good at a Japanese restaurant? You must be a regular here."

A smile spread across his face, making him look sweet. For a moment, he was the boy at the town council meeting again.

"Guess that's what I get for trying to show off."

"Guess so."

He got a bowl of simple tofu ramen and some cold sake, while she went with the stew (it was chilly enough for it, she decided). The waitress didn't even blink when he ordered the booze, and Fiona wondered just how old he actually was. He'd been a teenager then, when Fiona had watched him take a beating nine years ago. His eyes were boyish and bright, but his face was lined with experience, putting him somewhere between twenty and five hundred. The idea of having lunch with an *older guy* felt a touch gross, but he had none of the velvet perviness and poorly masked hunger of a creep prowling for young girls. He was like a living statue, somehow both crisp and ancient.

The waitress came back with his drink, and for a while, he sipped his clear wine in silence and then, much to her relief, avoided more small talk and dove right into it.

"Were you surprised to see me back in Hamm?" he asked.

"A little," she said. "If those men on the town council who tied you up and carted you off—"

"One of whom is your father," he said calmly, holding up a palm. "Let's just establish that I know this before we go any further, so it doesn't have to be some sort of reveal."

"If they caught you again," continued Fiona, "they'd probably mess your life up pretty badly. Might even kill you."

He nodded. "They said as much. For the record, how much of that night did you witness?"

A cold pang ran through her. Not "see," *witness*. Like a crime.

"Everything that happened at the winery sign," she said calmly. It felt like a seal being broken. The floodgates opened: "And I was at the town council meeting where you first showed up. Do you remember me from then, too?"

"Later, I did. But the apple made more of an impression." He raised his eyebrows and sighed. "Wow, so you were around for the whole sordid affair."

"Yes," she said. Then she spat out what she'd wanted to say for nine years: "I'm sorry they did that to you. It wasn't right."

He half shrugged. "What I do isn't a nice business. Sometimes, these things happen. Besides, that was a long time ago. I was weak then."

When the food came, they fell into silence. He was slow and careful in the consumption of his noodles, sucking them down without slurping. His eyes darted to her occasionally, watching her but not too closely. Not like Calvin Hokes did. She sensed courtesy in his behavior, like he was trying to see what she thought of him. He was being polite.

"How have the last nine years been?" he finally asked.

"Good," she said. "I grew up."

"I noticed that," he said. "Man, and I thought *I* was young then. It was crazy how quickly I recognized you, because in my mind you were just the girl with the apple. Must have been something about the eyes, that way you were looking at me." He glanced at her quickly, then looked away. "Or maybe something deeper. I don't know."

"That's how I recognized you," she said. "It wasn't on sight, because you look so different. It was something about you."

"Interesting," he said. "Guess my appearance has changed dramatically since we last met."

"You've filled out," she said.

He chuckled. "Right. And I'm not, you know, bleeding everywhere."

"Do you have a real name now?"

"Pit Viper's not real enough for you?"

"Aw, who's a cryptic guy?" she said, though inside she was dying to know. "Did your mom just name you Pit Viper, or did she go full DJ Pit Viper on the day of your birth?"

"You know, I've always hated that," he said, frowning and stirring his ramen. "The DJ honorific. It immediately evokes this image of a guy in front of a spring-break crowd in Ibiza, throwing glow sticks at people. I'm more than that. I work harder than that. Besides, if you're a good DJ, why do you have to let everyone know you're a DJ?"

Fiona bit her lip and watched his eyes spin like 45s as they followed his noodles. It was as perfect an answer as she could imagine, and it had just come out of him, effortlessly. Any moment she felt like she was matching him, he did something that made her feel hugely out of her league. The worst part was, it didn't seem like he meant to. He wasn't bragging. It was just *him*.

"Well, what else do you play?" she asked.

"A little keyboards, some bass and guitar, and then some digital manipulation programs," he said, "though, okay, to be fair, a lot of it *is* just work with a turntable—"

"So how are you *not* a DJ?" she asked.

"Because…I don't spin together pop hits," he said, sitting back in his seat. "I don't remix Cardi B. I merge and manipulate sound to create new music."

"So, you're not *even* a DJ," she said with a smile, going

for the throat. "You're just a samples engineer. Like the sea urchin dude in Slipknot."

He laughed back at her daring, which made her blush all over her body.

"And what do you play?" he asked. "No, wait, let me guess. Acoustic guitar. Ani DiFranco covers, mostly."

"Screw you!" she laughed, feeling as though both of their mad crescent-moon grins were officially matching. "Electric guitar. Classic rock, biker chug, acrobatic solos. No mercy."

He smirked and rolled his eyes. "Ah, yes, because distorted guitar has been so unexplored in music thus far. You're really breaking new ground."

"The old ways are the best, dude," she said. He said "Ah" with a blasé snarkiness that made her feel like a know-nothing kid, like Penny Kim talking about *map points* because she'd watched *Groove* one time. Fiona pushed further. "No, I'm serious! Music is best when it regresses to its core. You see it in rock and roll all the time. Prog rock in the seventies got too weird and silly, so punk came along. Punk got too floofy-doo and became New Wave, so metal and hardcore rolled through. Those genres got either superficial or self-important, so grunge and industrial knocked them down. Even dance music is like that—isn't that why dubstep was a thing? Because people wanted to dance to something they could feel in their *bones*? People have been shaking their hips and pumping their fists since the dawn of time. If it ain't broke, don't fix it."

She realized she was basically shouting at him, attracting glances from other tables. She hunched down into her seat with cheeks burning. But he didn't seem bothered. If anything, he looked pleased, even a little refreshed.

"That actually makes a lot of sense," he said, nodding and appraising her with new interest. "That idea has a lot of bearing on how I make my music. That the old ways are always going to be the most powerful." He stared off into space for a moment, then shrugged and shook his head. "Then again, I play the keyboards, which is probably the ultimate fashion instrument. So what do I know?"

She smiled, grateful for the shred of self-deprecation and humility he was offering her. "A little, I guess. Keyboards can be used effectively, though. And there are worse instruments to play."

"The tuba," he said.

"The theremin," she said.

"The harpsichord," he said.

"Yo, *fuck* the harpsichord!" she guffawed, and the two of them snickered like total nerds.

"So, would you say your music has regressed?" she asked, unable to wipe the grin from her face. "Has it gotten back to its core roots?"

His brow furrowed as he considered the idea. "I'd say so. I think back in the day, I wanted to be more of a...maverick. A rock star, really pushing buttons and making waves in an obnoxious way. I wanted my music to change the way people thought. Now I just want it to be effective. Powerful, primal, like you were saying. That's where strength lies, I've decided."

"What changed your mind?" she said.

"Your dad and his friends kicking the shit out of me," he said.

The words struck her with a wave of cold. She dry-swallowed and did her best not to make eye contact with him. "Right. Stupid question."

"It's fine," he said. "Sorry. I don't blame you, obviously. And it was a blessing in disguise, maybe, because it made my music stronger."

"Whatever you're doing now, it's working," she said, doing her best not to feel guilty about the night the Pit Viper had the wonder beaten out of him. "My friends are obsessed with the album. Everyone I know owns it."

"Good," he said. "Then yes. It is working."

"You must be getting big all over the club circuit," she said.

"Not really," he said, and added softly, "just Hamm."

"Really?"

He slowly finished his sake, and said, "Do you want to go for a walk?"

He stood, and she followed. She'd only just pulled her wallet out when he tossed three crisp twenties onto the table and nodded toward the door.

"Okay, so…Van Halen."

"Like, neon on metal," said Fiona. "Neon lights reflecting off a chrome tailpipe. Or fins or something—car fins, not fish fins. No, wait, fish fins. Neon off the fins of a giant chrome dolphin jumping out of a resort pool."

The Pit Viper nodded as he hand rolled a cigarette. They'd been talking about music for a while; every attempt to discuss Hamm was quickly dismissed. Instead, he asked about the rock and roll that Fiona worshipped, which she'd described with all the nervous enthusiasm of the teenage girl she was trying not to act like.

The idea of selective synesthesia had come up—a merging of the senses, flavors as music, music as images—and he'd begun quizzing her. She sensed that for most people, this would be a fun game. For them, true sonic devotees, it was serious business. "The Misfits."

"A spiked bracelet-wrapped hand all sticky with popcorn

butter from a bad zombie double feature," she said after a moment. "And eye makeup."

"That's a good one. Ghost."

"A...haunted castle in a children's coloring book."

"Muse."

"The world's supervillains descending onto a Queen concert."

"I'm not sure you're allowed to reference one band with another band."

"You do if you sound as much like Queen as Muse does."

"But you like Queen."

"And Muse." She folded her arms. "Come on, give me a hard one."

He arched an eyebrow. "FIDLAR."

Fiona bit her lower lip, pleased with him. She hadn't even mentioned them, he'd just known. "The back seat of a really grimy Volvo that's just returned from the beach. Condoms and comic books and beer cans with sand all over them."

He nodded, lighting the smoke and inhaling thoughtfully. "I'm impressed. Thin Lizzy?"

"A sure-statured man firing a Care Bear Stare out of his crotch."

"Absolutely. Bruce Springsteen. AND the E Street Band."

"Just, the most earnest chin you have ever seen."

That one finally got him, and he tilted back his head and cackled. His laughter boomed out through the park, across the river, over the city, over her skin, and along her nerves. She couldn't take her eyes off him; even grinning and laughing like a goofball, he was so gorgeous, so sure in every angle of his face and form.

He offered her a drag from his smoke, and when she shook her head, he didn't make it a big deal, and because of that she said, "Wait" and took it and had a puff. The tobacco wasn't as noxious as the horrible soft-pack lights Caroline and Keller sometimes smoked, but it still made her throat catch and tasted like a burning tire. She felt silly for how much she hoped he was watching her, finding her cosmopolitan and sexy when all she was doing was trying not to cough.

"You don't really like my music, do you?" he asked suddenly.

There was no fishing for compliments in it, and she searched for an answer that was as devoid of bullshit as his question. "Not particularly, no."

"Not a big fan of electronic music in general?" he said, exhaling a seemingly endless cloud of smoke that became little puffs with each word.

"Not really," she said. And then, wanting to meet him even more head-on, she added, "But it's not that. There's something funny about your music. If I listen to it for too long, it actually, physically, nauseates me. I don't know why that is."

He nodded, looking as though he knew a secret he wanted to tell her. She found the expression endlessly handsome. "Fascinating. That's a really good sign, actually."

"What is it, by the way?" she asked, somewhat excited to find out there was a reason behind her response to the album. "Some sort of low frequency? Like the infamous brown note that makes you crap your pants?"

He shook his head. "Close, but not exactly. My music is… more precise."

His words seemed to bring a gust of wind, cold and cutting. As she looked at him in the gray city light, she began to see the hard lines in his sweet face, the cords in his neck. She had been so distracted by their game and her attraction that she had to pass over her mind, and she finally asked him outright: "That *precision*…it's what made all the club rats leave Hamm, isn't it?"

He tapped the tip of his nose. "Well done."

"How did you do it?"

He rose from the bench. "I'll show you."

chapter
13

They wandered winding streets that led out of downtown until they were in a quiet neighborhood. It was the kind of place Fiona's dad would call *industrial* and Edgar Hokes would call a *dump*, made up almost entirely of looming warehouses and garages, where the occasional passersby walked with their head down.

The silence of the maze around her was more unsettling to Fiona than the honks and shouts of the city. She felt like she might get lost and disappear among the buildings without the Pit Viper to guide her through the endless labyrinth of boarded-up windows and corrugated metal gates. But in his own way, the Pit Viper was frightening and foreign. His fearlessness made Fiona see him in a dangerous light, a ghost from her past leading her into an underworld he knew all too well. As she watched his lanky form stride purposefully down the quiet streets, she considered just how little she knew about him. If she had to tell the cops anything about him later—his name and age, his address, the things he'd told her—all she'd be able to point them to was an album with a snake on the cover.

He stopped in front of a green door in the side of one building, with a single word tagged across it in silver spray paint—"SOUNDS". He opened it and waved her inside, but at the last minute she froze. The doorway made her think of the mouth of a grave, and her paranoid parents had read her more than enough news stories about naive girls in big cities.

"What is it?" he asked.

"This is a strange building," she said nervously, kneading the cuffs of her hoodie sleeves. "You're taking an eighteen-year-old girl to a strange warehouse."

"You think I'm going to rape you?" he said in the same careless, blunt tone he'd used to ask if Aunt Emily was *the dead boy's mom* at the town council meeting all those years ago. "Do I really come across as that kind of guy?"

"No," she said, "but my mom didn't raise an idiot."

He nodded. "No, she didn't," he said. "Fiona, I can offer you no assurance other than a solemn promise that I won't harm you. And you know from what I did in your town that I'm a man of my word." She felt her skin crawl when he said it. "But if you want to know how I cleaned up Hamm, you have to trust me. What's it going to be?"

They ascended five musty flights in silence. The Pit Viper took the stairs two at a time. She tried to keep up, but was panting when she reached him. He stopped and yanked a canvas handle, and a wall-size door rolled open.

The room was vast, with enough empty space to smell cold and only faintly like paint dust. Windows on all walls bathed the floor in gray afternoon light. The Pit Viper wandered down an aisle of blocky shapes that stood along the floor. For a moment, Fiona thought they were tombstones, and that he'd taken her to some kind of indoor graveyard, or a portal to a really shitty part of Narnia. But they were speakers—amps, heads, PA wedges, desktop pods, clunky new age living room units and professional studio numbers, broken up by the occasional desktop monitor or keyboard. Some of the husks of listening technology had obvious defects—torn wires, cracked casings, blown-out subwoofers—but others simply stood there gathering dust, preserved like museum pieces. A few of them looked relatively expensive and rare; one amp Fiona had definitely lusted for in the back of an issue of *Guitar World*, and one was covered in Chinese lettering. The Pit Viper didn't give them a second glance.

Sections of freestanding wall cordoned off a corner of the room. As she passed them, Fiona saw that the walls were a quilt of heavy speakers and sturdy shelves that held row upon row of books, some freshly bought and glossy-covered, others old and wrapped in crumbling leather. Only two shelves held records.

"You have less vinyl than I thought you would," she said.

"I used to have more, but a lot of them ended up in a dumpster in your hometown," he responded.

"I'm sorry."

"It's fine, that was a small thing of me to say anyway. Honestly, I hate those DJs who have massive collections but don't really enjoy them. The music is important, not the medium. If you have more records than books, you're doing it wrong."

Fiona savored the last part. *Please be a good dude*, she thought.

She took in the rest of his headquarters—a pile of mattresses and pillows, an overstuffed La-Z-Boy, two DJ tables, a keyboard on a stand, and a desk piled high with paper and refuse electronics. Three laptops sat on his bed, each hooked up to countless cords and wires.

"This is quite a setup," she said, "for a squat. You're not

worried about getting robbed?"

"I own this floor of the building," he said like it was nothing. "But even then, I don't lock my door. No one around here is stupid enough to fuck with me." He flipped a switch on the wall, and a series of dingy lights flickered on.

He flopped down on the bed and began typing on one of his laptops, and Fiona felt her breath catch. Without thinking, she reached up and ran her fingernails along her collarbone, mentally rehearsing for a scenario she'd half-shamefully pictured a number of times. Here she was, in the DJ's inner sanctum. There he was, sprawled out on his bed, every muscular inch of him. No one knew she was here, not Rita or Caroline or Horace. It was the two of them, alone in the big city, close enough to smell each other.

Anything could happen.

"You said you were going to show me something," she said in a husky tone that she quickly tried to hide by clearing her throat.

He nodded, stood, and went to the floor beneath his desk. He removed a key from his pocket, stabbed it into a metal lock, and then opened a trapdoor. From it he dragged a black metal crate with a weighty combination lock holding it shut. He took his time cracking and discarding the heavy steel fail-safe.

Out of the box came a book, huge and old. The cover was bound in some kind of leather, and its pale flaking surface bore a strange symbol down the middle in black paint, a three-bulbed string, a figure eight with one loop too many. As the Pit Viper offered the book and Fiona took it, it seemed to stick to her hands, like she and it were magnetically attracted. "What is *that*?" he asked, pointing to the symbol on the cover.

Fiona swallowed, trying to think critically through a haze of apprehension. This was another test, she knew. She'd seen that symbol before, different than this but recognizable, but she couldn't be sure where. As she stared at it, it was as though the answer traveled through her fingertips and into her mind, unfolding gently but brilliantly.

"It's a chord," said Fiona.

"That's right," said the Pit Viper. "What you're holding is the third edition of the *Codex Canoris*. Approximately three hundred and seventy years old. Very, very important. Take a look inside, but be careful."

She opened the cover and beheld a scribbled depiction of the solar system, each planet marked with a sinister and carefully drawn glyph. As she flipped the yellowed pages, she took in scrawled Latin and diagrams of the planets, human anatomy, and musical theory, more clinical and carefully mapped than lovingly illustrated. As the book went on, the penmanship became more and more unhinged, as though written in a panic. Eventually, everything was replaced by bar after bar of handwritten sheet music, like the words had undergone an ugly werewolf transformation and had become notes.

"What is this, exactly?" she asked.

"It's an instruction manual on the practical use of music," he said. "There once existed a belief that there was music beyond the reaches of the human ear. Music that existed in spiritual dimensions we can't normally understand. People thought that each celestial body emitted a frequency that had power behind it. They called it the *musica universalis*."

A phrase from her cousin Jake's favorite poem popped into her head. "The music of the spheres."

"Exactly," he said, gesturing to the book. "The *Canoris* outlines the way this music affects people, and then it instructs the reader on how to find it. And use it."

She looked up from the book and into his eyes, waiting

for him to shout "*boo!*" or mention that the *Canoris* was some kind of art project he was selling on Etsy. But no such luck—his brow was drawn; his arms were folded.

"You're talking about magic," she said.

"Maybe?" he responded, shrugging. "That word is really loaded. I've never met any fairies or vampires. The *Canoris* isn't a *spell book*. But what I've discovered is that sound energy can control people on a mental level. And that if you have the right internal rhythm to channel that energy, you can be the one doing the controlling. Not everyone has it, but some people are gifted with a frequency of their own."

"So you used this book to control the club rats from the old mill and make them leave," she said.

"Not just the book," said the Pit Viper. He reached back into the crate and removed a second item—a record in a simple white sleeve. When he pulled the black disc out, Fiona saw symbols etched into the wax. They glittered in the thick warehouse light and made her eyes sting. "This record is where I've focused my power. I call it my *master copy*. I had a similar one nine years ago that your dad destroyed. When I play it, most people just hear a single droning note, but there's actually a lot going on here. I loop some digital recordings I've put together over it, and the sound comes alive. You have to merge certain sounds to wield the *Canoris*'s power. There's a hum I recorded on a hill in Croatia during a meteor shower. There's this steady beeping I got from a radiation counter off a piece of unbreakable rock in a museum in Virginia. There's the heartbeat of this old woman in Quebec who says she can read God's mind. All of them match the musical diagrams in the book." He smiled. "And I haven't even been to Asia yet."

She slowly put the book down on his desk and backed away from it. Feedback rang out in her head. It was all too much. She'd expected lots of things, from mob connections to serial murder. Not some kind of mystical DJ from beyond the stars.

"Did you kill all those kids with music?" she asked, trying to piece the story together. "Did you use the power you harnessed to murder them?"

He froze with his mouth half open, the gravity of her question stunting his enthusiasm. "No," he said finally. "That's the point of *musica universalis*. It's bloodless. You don't kill with it, you just bend minds of others, and they follow you."

"Those kids," she snapped impatiently. "What *happened* to them?"

"I sent them away," he said. "I wiped their minds, made them forget all their sins and addictions, and sent them off. They're under the care of someone else now. He's my...let's call him my benefactor."

"Why are you telling me this?" she whispered. "Is this part of your revenge against my dad?"

He returned the record to its sleeve and put it back in its crate before approaching her. "Why don't you like my music?"

"We've been over this," said Fiona, standing firm. "I just don't. It feels wrong."

"You shouldn't be *able* to dislike my music, Fiona," he said. "The way I've programmed it, you should love it despite yourself. Everyone should. But you're not under my sway; you're floating above it. Which means either I'm good enough to control all your friends but not you...or it means you have an internal rhythm that the *Canoris* understands."

"Maybe I'm just not made for raves," she said, trying to find an excuse not to believe him.

"You're a guitarist," said the Pit Viper, "but you've never been in a band, have you? You've always felt better than that, than playing along with the tabs. Like it should just be you and your guitar and no one else."

She shuddered. He was inches in front of her now, staring down at her. She could smell him—dust and sweat, wire and tobacco, nothing like the youthful scent of Horace's hoodie loaded with drugstore deodorant. Fiona's instincts told her to back off. So why didn't she?

"That night, when you gave me the apple, I thought you were just a sweet girl from some small town," he said. "Now I'm wondering if you're more than that. If there was maybe a reason you were the only one who wasn't afraid of me."

She shook her head. No way. This was a game, a lie, a way to get her onto that mattress. She was smarter than that—which was why she was so angry with herself for not following her gut, for not running. For wanting to be near him for however many more seconds she could allow herself.

"Bullshit," she said.

"Fiona," he said.

He reached out for her. She swatted his hand away, then shoved him with her palm against his sternum. He took a step back, and then gently took her hand and pressed it to his chest. The physical contact made her breath hitch. A burning river of energy flowed between them that made her knees shake, made the hair on the back of her neck stand up straight. She felt his heart pounding against her hand like a bass drum.

"You're crazy," she said, her head swimming.

"Tell me I'm wrong," he said.

She yanked her hand away from him—and then, knowing she'd be angrier if she didn't than if she did, seized his face in her hands and pressed her mouth to his. In an instant, she melted into his arms, hanging herself from his frame. She pulled his lower lip between her teeth and bit it, and his breath carried with it something like a growl.

When she released him, the nature of what she was doing—

touching him, having him, after everything that had happened nine years ago—came to her in an embarrassing blast. All she could think of was Rita's concerned gaze from the previous day, judging how easy it had been for her to give in.

She twisted out of his arms and marched down the shadowy aisle through the speaker cemetery before he could say another word and didn't stop until she burst out of the door and onto the cobblestone street. She gulped fresh air and hugged herself, confused by how much she wanted to do exactly what she knew she shouldn't.

As she walked toward downtown, his music came booming out of the warehouse at her back, making her jump as it ripped open the quiet air. Through her panic, she noticed that every garage worker and huddled junkie and bag lady she passed in that forsaken part of the city raised their heads to the sky and turned their ears toward the Pit Viper's den.

She was back at the station, waiting for her train, when she got a text from him.

PV: I'm sorry. I didn't mean to scare you.

F: It's fine. This is just a lot to think about.

PV: Let me know when I can see you again.

Her breath caught in her throat. Was this wrong? Was it nuts?

She closed her eyes and listened to her gut.

F: I'll be back next weekend. I want to know more.

chapter
14

PV: Tell me about the last song you tasted.

F: Dude, I'm in class.

PV: And you're thinking about tasting songs? Terrible. I'll stop texting you.

F: Don't you dare.

Fiona had never liked romantic texting—she'd always made a point not to trade emoji-heavy, cutie-pie texts with Horace—but she spent the whole week with her face planted firmly in her phone. She communicated with her friends in monosyllabic utterances and absolutely refused to talk to anyone about Horace, what had happened, whether they were broken up or not. She wasn't even entirely sure, but at this point, she didn't care.

She ate her lunches alone out on the bleachers, chewing without tasting as she waited for the next text from the Pit Viper.

F: But come on, man, if it doesn't have a distorted guitar, why am I bothering?

PV: I don't play distorted guitar. I'm a DJ.

F: Maybe not in your music. You ARE sort of a distorted guitar.

PV: Best compliment I've ever been paid.

Maybe it was because the Pit Viper's texts were never overly romantic, or that they never devolved into the idiotic sexting that the teenage boys she knew seemed to be so excited about. More than once, she'd had to navigate messages from Horace asking about what she was wearing or what she would do if he were there right now, responding to them with a quick and painless digital wink or eye roll. But though there was a physical hunger behind the Pit Viper's interest in her, he didn't make it an open issue. He wasn't careless or sophomoric. She felt like she was talking to an equal.

They discussed music constantly. It excited her, how passionate he was, how immersed he would get in their conversations. He'd been raised on a mix of grimy crust punk and party-dance DJs, though he'd obviously dedicated himself more to the latter than the former. He confessed that the first record he'd ever grown addicted to was Ace of Base's *The Sign*, and that he'd once considered getting a lyric from "Young and Proud" tattooed on him (**You are the least cool person in the world**, she'd said. **I know**, he'd responded). He'd lived in a squat, though he wouldn't say where it was, before he'd met his benefactor, though he wouldn't say who that was. He had weird OCD preferences that he told her about: Black coffee with nutmeg. Eight hours of sleep every night, no napping. Clear liquor or wine, no beer, occasionally tobacco but never as a habit. Proper spelling and grammar, even in texts and emails; no substituting letters for words. An hour of reading and an hour of practice every day.

F: Come on, I promise I won't tell anyone.

PV: My real name is Pit Viper.

F: Look, it's just really weird to call you that. Help me out here.

PV: You realize it's now just about annoying you.

F: A REAL MAN would tell me.

PV: Nice try.

F: Dammit.

He wouldn't budge on the name issue. *My real name is Pit Viper*, every time. At first, it had infuriated her in a fun way, and she'd made a game of trying to tease it out of him. Now, it was gnawing at her, a burning question she had to answer if only to show she could pull the boy out of the persona, unearth something about him that told her at least some of where he was from—though deep down, she hoped it wasn't anything *too* embarrassing. If she found out he was actually an *Irving*, it would break her heart.

She loved having a personal window into his world, and at times she was worried her own life in Hamm would seem sad and underwhelming to him, but he seemed enthralled by her existence, too, the way one is fascinated by an episode of *Planet Earth*. He loved the quaintness of the local doughnut shop and hippie café, and sounded genuinely tickled by her idea of the city as a huge, edgy wonderland compared to her own town (**I think you'd really like Madrid**, he'd written her, and she had covered her mouth and giggled without wanting to). He was sympathetic when she complained about the false sense of security that ran through Hamm, the sense of everything being fine when it was actually miserable once you considered it honestly.

F: It's like everyone's so nice and proper, but the minute you threaten their little lives, they become hollow inside.

PV: Trust me, I know.

The town council charity breakfast that Saturday felt as endless as a dentist's appointment. They were at the community center again, and this time Fiona and Caroline were serving alongside their dads. Fiona had potatoes; Caroline had scrambled eggs. Fiona did her best to smile and say, "You're welcome" to each person she served from her steel burner tray, but she was perpetually distracted by her post-event escape plan. She checked her phone repeatedly until finally Caroline stopped her steady rambling about school gossip and the Pit Viper.

"Whose text are you waiting for?" asked Caroline.

Fiona blushed and mentally swore. Caught red-handed. She turned back to her potatoes. "No one. Just, Keller told me he'd text me the name of this song I was asking about."

Caroline shot her a withering *Oh, honey* look; even Fiona could hear how ridiculous that sounded. "Has he been texting you about it *all week*?" she asked. "Come on, Fiona, enough's enough. What's actually going on?"

"Let's not do this now," said Fiona.

"Please tell me you're not going to break up with Horace for Doug," said Caroline. Fiona laughed, assuming her friend was being funny, but when she looked up there was a genuinely pissed expression on Caroline's face. "That would cause, like, an atomic blast of drama in our crew, Fiona. Horace would die."

"Both our dads are about ten feet away from us," whispered Fiona. "Ask me later and we can talk, I promise, but any time other than now, okay?" Caroline stayed motionless. "It's *not Keller*, okay?"

"You swear?"

"Council's honor," said Fiona, holding up a hand. Caroline snorted, and Fiona exhaled heavily as she went back to loading plates with home fries.

Finally, as things wrapped up, Fiona went to the bathroom and carefully rehearsed her lines. She was dizzy with adrenaline as she approached her waiting parents. *Please*, she thought, *please let this work.*

"Ready to go?" asked her mom.

"If it's cool with you guys," she said too quickly, teeth buzzing, "I'm actually going to head out around here for a little bit. There's this underground record store I want to check out—"

"What? No way, Fiona." Her father scowled. "What record store? What neighborhood? How long will it take?"

Fiona's mouth flapped. Too many questions she hadn't figured out the answers to, coming at her way too fast. This was her fault. She should've created a complete fiction, like she had with the night at the club (Ultradrool, dear God). "Just...it's a place downtown. I forget the name. It'll be fine—"

"We'll give you a ride and take you home afterward," said her dad. "This is a lousy neighborhood. You can't just be walking around on your own. Do you have an address?"

"I'm all right," said Fiona. She was still mad at him from their argument about Horace, but she did her best to pretend otherwise. Better to swallow her pride than get dragged back home. "I actually want to take a walk, see some of the areas around downtown that I might not know—"

"How many times do we have to go over this?" sighed her dad.

"Robert, let her go," said her mother. "She's just going out shopping."

"Am I supposed to believe that, given the past couple of weeks?" Now he was using that whiny Trump voice, that victim tone that said, *What about me?* "Given the rampant partying with that Palmada *kid*? The lack of respect?"

Fiona wasn't sure if she was going to weep or scream. Her whole week of texting, and now to have it blown off because her stupid, ignorant dad felt disrespected when there was a boy he wasn't allowed to assault—

"Hey, you ready?"

She turned slowly at the unexpected voice. Calvin Hokes smiled at her and waved politely to the Joneses.

"Uh...maybe," she said, looking back at her folks.

"Cal, you're going with her?" asked her father, suddenly deflated, maybe even a little shocked.

"Yeah," said Calvin. "I'm managing Fiona's band. She wanted me to come see them play." He glanced at her nervously. "Oh, man, you haven't told them? Sorry, I didn't mean to blow up your spot."

Fiona winced. Of all the lies Calvin could have told, this was the least believable. But any incredulity on her parents' part seemed overwhelmed by her having a day out with Calvin Hokes. Her mother gave her a saucy look-at-you smile that made the inside of her mouth taste like burnt medicine.

"You never told us you had a...band," said her father with a smirk.

"We just didn't become a band, you know, *officially*, since l-last night," she stammered. "Which is why I made up the record-store lie! And Calvin is really good with PR and crunching numbers, so I figured why not, uh, have him, you know, manage. Us. The band."

"Well, all right," her dad practically cheered, suddenly elated by the concept of Fiona traipsing around the city's grimier neighborhoods. He gave Fiona forty dollars and a slap on the arm. "You guys have a blast. Be home by nine—" Her mother rolled her eyes and elbowed him. Her father took a deep breath and nodded. "Eleven. But call me and let me know you're on your way before then."

She and Calvin walked silently through the halls. They were almost safely out the door when they ran into Will grabbing a mop from the supply closet in the coatroom.

"Cal, where you going—" The other Hokes twin froze, eyes bulging out of his skull. "No way, son! Check out Cal, making a move!"

"I'm going to murder you later," said Calvin, cheeks going purple.

"Jones and Hokes, together at last!" he called after them. "Town council, *what!* My brother, everyone! Give him a hand!"

"You didn't need to do that," said Fiona once they were down the block and she'd regained her composure. Now that she was free of her parents, of obligation and Hamm, her nervous energy was blossoming into a joy for life and its many possibilities. The outside air felt cool and tasted sweet, even though it was full of exhaust and hobo-pee smell.

"Nah, I kind of did," said Calvin, staring down at the sidewalk. "You were dying back there. You really made no effort whatsoever to come up with a believable lie, huh?"

She chuckled. "Not in the slightest. Thank you, Cal. Seriously, I do owe you one for that."

"Ah, whatever," he said with a shrug. "I like walking around the city, anyway. Maybe you were an excuse for me to get away from them as much as I was one for you."

"I feel you," she said, shooting him a sympathetic smile. She couldn't help but pity the guy. It had never occurred to her that Calvin felt trapped in Hamm, too. He was just so clean-cut, so *nice*, that she'd assumed everything was fine with him. But maybe Hamm was casting him in a role that he'd never asked for. She understood that all too well.

"Welp, now I have to come up with a place my fake band

rehearses," she said.

"Ah, just make something up and change it every time," he said. "'We changed again, now we're called Blowhole and we rehearse at the Spot.' They'll never remember details like that. Works on my dad consistently. And the more confused they are by those specifics, the less they'll ask about whatever it is that you're actually doing. Which is pretty obviously something they wouldn't like."

"Was I *that* easy to read back there?" she asked.

"You looked at your phone all morning and sweated your hat off, so I figured…" He laughed.

She laughed back. They came to a halt on a corner. She smiled up at Calvin, not nearly the cretin she'd imagined. He hadn't even pressed her on her actual plans, which was decent of him. He was trying, and he *had* saved her ass back there. That counted for something. She didn't love that he'd noticed her sweating, and she certainly had sensed that walking out there with her was some sort of triumph for him, but he was making an effort, and he was being a good dude about it.

"Well, look, I need to haul," she said. "Thanks again for the help back there."

"No problem," he said. She turned off, and he went straight, waving after her. "Good luck, stay out of trouble."

She texted the Pit Viper that she was on her way, and he gave her a corner to meet him on. When she saw him from a few blocks away, she felt her heart rate spike and wondered if she was going to faint. It was a little chilly, but he was there in jeans and a T-shirt—the sleeves of which, she noticed, were taut with the muscles of his arms. Ho boy.

"Let's go back to your place," she said the minute he was within earshot.

"Got it," he said, turning on his heel.

They rode the bus together in relative silence, much to Fiona's amusement—so much to say via text, but here they were, quietly smirking like dumb kids. Once in a while, an older person getting off the bus would make a point of ice-grilling him, and he usually nodded back to them. At first, she'd assumed he was just a local fixture like Emperor Norton in San Francisco, but after a while it dawned on Fiona that these bystanders and the DJ didn't know each other. They just saw something in him that people her father's age understood to be *bad news*.

He led her through his haunted neighborhood, up the dusty stairs, past the sonic graveyard. Once they were in the safety of his corner, he stopped, turned, faced her. After a pause, in which they both seemed to be presenting themselves to the other, she closed the distance between them.

This time, there was no hurry or outrage to make things dramatic and awkward; both moved at their own pace. She stepped into his arms, and they closed softly around her like the jaws of a Venus flytrap. Their lips met and deftly explored. He tasted like bubble tea. She kept her guard up, holding this one soft, tongue-less kiss long enough to let him know that this wasn't a precursor to anything, that this momentary pulse-speeding spark between them was enough. He, in turn, kept his hands crossed behind her back, and when they broke apart he looked at her with a smile of knowing gratitude.

"Feel that?" he asked.

"Yeah," she nodded.

"That's music," he said.

She pulled back and looked into those planetary eyes. "You really think you feel...some sort of power in me."

He laughed. "Well, not like *that*. You're not an X-Man. But I see in you the basic tools to do a lot of great things, Fiona. I see a lot of powerful songs that are going shamefully unwritten. I'd like to be here when they're set free."

Her logical mind told her it was flimsy. That he was a handsome dude from her past with a very intricate prop out of *The Evil Dead* who was playing her for a fool. But her gut believed it, or wanted to. Her gut told her to go for it.

"No marks," she said. "No hickeys, nothing like that. It implies ownership. That shit's gross."

He shrugged. "All right."

"No trying to pressure me into sex," she said.

"I would never," he said, neither casual nor offended.

"And no lying to me," she said. "If I ask you something, tell me the truth. And if I'm freaked out by it, or you do something that upsets me, I'm gone, and you can't come after me. Got it?"

"Got it," he said.

"Okay," she said. She kissed him again, softly, lightly. She pulled away from him, but reached out and put her hand in his, letting him know she wasn't backing off entirely. "Show me your book. I want in."

chapter
15

They spent the rest of the first Saturday lazing around the apartment, peering at each page of the book. He listed off the basics to her, his lips occasionally brushing her ear and making her shiver. Every so often, when he described something poetically enough, she'd turn and their lips would meet again, briefly. Then they'd turn back to the book as though nothing had happened.

There were three disciplines that the *Codex Canoris* covered: *musica universalis*, the Pit Viper's cosmic beats; *musica humana*, the internal music of the human body, usually expressed through singing and dancing ("SZA," he'd said, and then he'd nodded knowingly at her arched eyebrows); and *musica quae in quibusdam constituta est instrumentis*, the elusive music created when player and instrument came together perfectly.

The Pit Viper figured that if his music had no effect on her—or if it had a negative effect, like the headaches and nausea she'd felt in the past—then she was adept at one of the other two. Given Fiona's relationship with Betty, her discipline had to be the *instrumentis* (Fiona took a good five minutes trying to learn how to pronounce the full name, much to the Pit Viper's amusement, before she went with the shortened title).

Sure enough, while the cosmic atlases and the anatomical diagrams had no effect on her other than looking cool, the sheet music in the back of the old book felt like a live wire when she ran her fingertips across it...though maybe it was just the feeling of his skin on hers as he guided her hand to the page.

"You sure it's okay for me to touch this?" she said, fixated on the *Canoris*'s final pages. "If this book really is that old, won't the oil on my hands harm it?"

"Maybe it would harm a normal book," he said. "I think when something contains this much power, it's harder to harm it by conventional means. It has a life of its own, as it were."

"That's pretty scary," said Fiona.

"Oh, this book is definitely not to be messed with," he said and gave her a quick peck on the neck, making her whole body feel the way the *instrumenti* music did beneath her fingers.

"You're pretty daring for messing with it, then," she said.

"I enjoy things of a provocative nature," he said, and his breath crossed her ear. She pressed against him involuntarily, but then exhaled through her nose and loosed herself from his grip with an unconvincing laugh. Some part of her wanted to give in and jump on top of him—hey, a mysterious older musician who owned the floor of a building, it was what most Hamm housewives read paperbacks about while fanning themselves—but she was firm in her resolve. It was different than it had been with Horace, where she'd waited to be charmed to death. With the Pit Viper, she didn't want him to think she was weak. Her gut had always been her rocker radar, and to deny its instructions to hold off would, in Fiona's mind, betray the part of her that he seemed so smitten with.

As she got ready to go, he asked if she could come back next weekend. She told him she'd try but couldn't make any promises.

"Bring your guitar," he said. "Who knows, maybe you'll master the *instrumentis* immediately and become a sonic goddess overnight."

"You're giving me too much credit, man," she laughed, adding the last word to try and sound casual and not let on that she was burning up inside just looking at him. "Just because I've never been in a band doesn't mean suddenly my guitar is going to shoot lightning."

He smiled and shrugged. "True. Maybe I'm just pretty taken with you."

"That's fine, too," she said. She let her body sway as she walked out, relishing the sensation of his gaze on her.

At school that week, Fiona pissed everyone off at once — her friends, her parents, and her teachers. They all wanted to know why she was behaving like the cat who caught the canary, and she didn't feel like telling them. She'd never been much of a liar, but ended up doing a lot of shrugging and evading the truth, playing the Sullen Teenager card.

When Caroline asked her what the hell was going on with Calvin Hokes, she shrugged and repeated the nonsense she and Calvin had made up at the charity event. When Ms. Traubert asked her what she thought she was doing texting in class, she shrugged and said it was an emergency. When her father asked her how the band was going, she shrugged and didn't answer. She figured she was eighteen, which gave her the easy out of just being evasive and nonresponsive, because of hormones or mood swings or whatever child-psychology bullshit the internet was most in a huff over. The idea of using such a simple excuse would've made her sneer weeks ago, but now she didn't really care what it took to get them off her back, so long as they got the hell off. They all worried about how her life affected their own tiny self-centered universes, when she was living by a set of standards they couldn't comprehend, guided by a man from somewhere light-years away from Hamm. She felt her own potential, or at least whatever potential the Pit Viper saw in her, separating her from the masses.

It was especially strong at school, where everyone was still deep in the Pit Viper's thrall. She watched as Pit Viper mania grew in volume, causing the kind of gossip and peer pressure and clique mentality that she wasn't even interested in anymore. By now, even the freshmen were obsessed with the Pit Viper. Weber was making T-shirts in the basement of Powerdrive, and they were selling like crack. Rumors had reached a fevered pitch—the Pit Viper had learned to DJ from the Devil Himself at a crossroads; the Pit Viper had implants in his brain that allowed him to beat match perfectly; the Pit Viper was actually the illegitimate son of Diplo and Gwen Stefani, but had been abandoned as a child to avoid scandal. The closest anyone got to the truth was the rumor that the Pit Viper was actually Fiona's cousin Jake, who hadn't died but had run away and brought shame to her family, a story that would have once offended her but now just sounded silly.

For all their drama-mongering and fanaticism, only she knew the truth. Only she knew his back story and his secret... not to mention the feeling of his hands resting on her hips and his lips against her earlobe.

That Thursday, a familiar smell hit her nostrils, and she looked up from her locker to see Horace leaning next to her, wearing the forced calm of someone about to give a presentation in front of a classroom.

"Hey," he said.

Fiona felt annoyed, aware of the melodramatic one-on-one that was on its way. "What's up, Horace?"

"I was hoping we could talk," he said. "About how things ended when we last spoke, and what's going on right now."

Fiona knew Horace's request was totally reasonable—but it irritated her. Already, in his careful language, Fiona sensed the presumptions that were about to be made here—that she wasn't going to get to say her side of things until the end of a long confession, that *her* distance was going to be made equal to *his* insensitivity toward her, that she would be told that they were just going through a phase. Horace would learn nothing, and she'd either find herself bullied into stringing him along or get yelled at for saying the truth. And anyway, she had class. "Okay, can we make it quick? I'm heading to English."

Horace blinked a few times; he obviously hadn't expected that answer. "Actually, I think we have a lot to talk about. Any chance you can cut English, or maybe we can find time later—"

"Sorry, Horace, I'm really busy at the moment," she said. Her phone buzzed in her pocket, and she knew it was the Pit Viper responding to that clever-as-hell joke she'd just made about Turnstile, which only made this clumsy interaction feel more exhausting. "Anything else? If this is an emergency, you can call me after school."

He folded his arms and furrowed his brow. "Fiona, we have to talk about what's going on with us."

Her phone buzzed again. She considered going for the throat, being cruel, but she knew deep down that Horace didn't deserve it; after all, only a month or so ago she'd been overjoyed at the idea of hearing him say that he loved her. But she was over it, big time, and there was no coming back from that. It was as though Horace was a song she used to love but now found a little embarrassing—it wasn't that she *hated* him, only that she wasn't interested in retracing the past.

In the end, she went with honesty. "There is no 'us,' Horace. Not anymore."

Horace's face fell. "That can't be true."

"I've thought a lot about it, and I think it's best we see other people," she said, quietly and slowly. "The last time we spoke, it became clear to me that you aren't ready to be the kind of boyfriend I want—"

"Are you *kidding me?*" he cried, his eyes going pink and brimming with tears. "I screw up a couple of times, so you decide we're broken up without *telling me?*"

"You didn't think about me, Horace," she said in the same reserved tone. "When you planned to have a party where my cousin died, when you took those pills, how I felt never once entered your mind. How I feel needs to be a priority in your life. I excused it the first time, but I'm not going to excuse it again."

"What about Harry Suggs, huh?" he said, his nostrils flaring. "I excused *that.*"

"That was before we started dating," she said, a little sharper this time to let him know how shitty this line of inquiry was. "And if you'd told me then that it was some kind of debt to you that I'd have to pay off later by putting up with your insensitivity, I might have broken up with you right there."

She expected Horace to go all in and call her a slut—but

it was like he knew that was a losing battle. Instead, he just shook his head and opened and closed his mouth, over and over.

"Just like that," he said. "Just—" He snapped his fingers. "In an instant. It's all over."

"It wasn't an instant," she said. "It was a bunch of them. This is what I'm talking about, Horace. You don't want to believe what actually happened."

"I don't believe *this* is happening," he said, his voice finally cracking. "I can't believe it."

She sighed. This was already taking too long. She would be late for English, and she was dying to read the text messages waiting for her on her phone. She wanted to end this quickly, but without a mess. *Bloodlessly*, as the Pit Viper had put it.

She pulled his hoodie off the hook in her locker and held it out to him. He stared at it in horror, then took it from her, cradled it in his hands like a dead thing. After staring at it for a few seconds, his fists bunched it up in shaking handfuls, and he laughed without an ounce of humor.

"Whoever he is, I hope he's worth it," he said. Then he turned and walked away, the snake from the Pit Viper's album glaring at her from the back of his T-shirt.

chapter
16

The next Saturday, she and Calvin pulled the same routine — after the charity event, they went to go to "band practice," and Calvin split off so she could meet with the Pit Viper. Calvin's excuse actually turned out to be a perfect cover, because it allowed her to bring Betty with her. She'd also taken the time to do some homework and strengthen her alibi. Her band was named Bipartisan, though they'd considered Dracula Teeth and Nature In Analog. Two of the kids, the drummer and rhythm guitarist, were from the city, while the bassist, another girl, came from two towns over (she always thought of bassists as the two-towns-over band members, and anyway, her parents didn't seem to care so long as the fictional musician wasn't from Chicago or New York, where the "riffraff" came from). They were playing thrashier grunge-punk, though Fiona wanted to add more of a stylish influence, a little David Bowie and Dick Dale to get them out of the alternative niche. Their rhythm guitarist had an industrial piercing, which Fiona found gross but fascinating to observe. Calvin was in talks to get them a club show in the city, provided the venue would allow minors inside.

She'd made sure to pepper these details throughout conversations with her folks so that when Saturday rolled around, she was ready. "Ugh, our bassist is finally showing up," she'd said, rolling her eyes at a text message from the Pit Viper describing a dream he'd had about her. "I gotta go."

She tried walking to the Pit Viper's place on her own but quickly got lost on the outskirts of his labyrinth neighborhood and had to call him. This time, when she first caught sight of him, there was none of the giddiness or anxiety. She'd never felt this way about someone before—this at ease.

"Let me guess," she said as he strolled over to her, "your magic book makes it so that only you can lead people to your nefarious lair."

The Pit Viper laughed. "Or you grew up in a town with a population of less than fifteen thousand, and all the buildings in this neighborhood look the same to you."

"Watch your mouth," she said. "Us small-town folks are tougher than you think."

His grin grew sharp around the edges. "I guess you're your father's daughter."

Whoof. The comment left her dumbstruck. She blinked hard a few times, trying to make sense of it in her heart. In a split second, he had gone from the man she knew to the DJ he played onstage, a tough and bitter being who meant business. Suddenly, the ease was gone—he was still someone to be watched out for. They walked silently for a couple of blocks before she could find anything to say:

"Not cool."

He glanced at her and hunched his shoulders. "I'm sorry if that took you off guard. You have to remember, I'm not entirely over what happened." He touched the edge of his forehead, and as he brushed his hair aside, Fiona noticed the scar again. It looked small to her, but probably felt massive and ugly to him.

She nodded silently. He had every right to be angry. Her dad had beaten him half to death, and if *she* still resented him for it, how must the Pit Viper feel? Maybe it was the thought that he still considered her some small-town nobody. But there was something about the look in his eyes when he said it, a coldness that came over him that she recognized from when he'd bluntly mentioned the possibility of assaulting her. Even if there was a warm, compassionate human being at his core, he aspired to ruthlessness. She hoped it was only a defense mechanism, that the potent moments they shared together were him shaking off that armor.

Then they were back up at his place. This time, he was less cuddly, more focused on teaching her. He walked her around the equipment in his room and told her the stats for every speaker he owned, as well as the kinds of cables and batteries each item required and the history of that particular hardware, both through the ages and during his ownership. (When they reached an old, brass bell emblazoned with a chord symbol similar to that on the *Codex Canoris*, he said, "Got that in Turkey. Don't ask.")

She loved his maturity, how seriously he took her and his own life. It was refreshing, like cool bedsheets on a humid night. He was powder, marble, ice, a beam of clean light rather than the atmospheric shadows it left behind. His weren't the genres with their fashions and traditions, but the standout musicians, the acts that transcended their labels with their intelligence and vision. He was like his loft, a series of traits brought together and existing on their own in a wide-open space with nothing on which to brace themselves save his will.

Once they finished reviewing his setup, they sat down on his mattress, the book in his lap and Betty in hers. The Pit

Viper stared at Fiona as though for the first time, like she was the awkward tomboy from the teen comedy who had showed up to prom looking fine as hell.

"What?" she asked.

"You with a guitar," he said. "It all makes sense now. God, you look powerful."

"You're just turned on by a woman holding a musical instrument," she said.

"That's beside the point," he said with a grin that admitted she was right. She softened and chose to forget the comment about her dad. If anything it was just him being honest with her, which was what she'd asked for.

"But I'm serious," he continued. "The picture's complete. Now, we just need to make sure she—Betty, right?—we need to make sure Betty and you have the right kind of relationship."

"I'd marry her if the state would let me," said Fiona. "We're ready."

"We'll see." He slid the book in front of her, the chord on its cover staring at her like three black eyes. "Play for it."

"Play for the book? What should I play, 'Turn the Page'? 'The Book of Love'?"

"Just close your eyes and communicate with your instrument," he said. "With my discipline, I channeled sounds that are already out there into my master copy. The *instrumentis* is about the unity of player and instrument finding the notes that are already there."

"Ugh," she moaned, dropping her shoulders. "Can't I just summon my Patronus or something?"

"Be serious, Fiona," he said. "Concentrate. Speak to the book through Betty."

With a sigh, she closed her eyes and let herself drift. Darkness surrounded her, and as she breathed, she slowly lost herself in the void. She let her fingers idly run down

Betty's strings but never played them, just felt the grooved lines floating above the smooth black face of the guitar, her best friend, the thing she knew better than anything in the world…

She and Betty merged, creating music where there had been nothing a few seconds ago, causing a sonic big bang in the void through which she floated.

And as this new universe came into existence, Betty seemed to lift her head and stare into Fiona's heart.

Adrenaline drove through her like a railroad spike. She gasped and snapped her eyes open, feeling electrocuted. She clutched Betty to her chest like the guitar was a life preserver.

The Pit Viper stared down at the book with bulging eyes. He was half crouched, his hands planted on the floor to either side of the *Codex Canoris*.

The book was open to a page. On the page was a note.

It was a single note, a strange hybrid sixteenth. Its stem was bisected by a diagonal line to form a sort of cross shape, and its head was hollow and contained a narrow eye that reminded her of ancient Egypt.

"What was *that*?" panted Fiona, inching slowly away from the *Canoris* as her every nerve writhed beneath her skin.

"That's a *tonus cultus*," he said softly. "A 'worship note.' They're believed to be musical talismans of divine forces. They're also sometimes called *tonus culter*, which means 'blade note.'"

The latter definition definitely felt more like what Fiona had experienced—a slice down her psyche. But that wasn't what she was asking. "Why did I see it? Why did I hear it *in my fucking head*?"

"Because you and Betty found it," he said. "Together, you're stronger than the average musician."

Fiona stared at the note on the page. She hadn't just heard it, she'd felt it. She'd *known* it. Through Betty, she had witnessed an entirely different plane of music in a single instant. The eye of the note seemed to stare directly at her. *I see you.*

Her breath came out faster and faster. Her heart pounded a blastbeat in her chest. Her vision blurred. It was too much. She couldn't—it couldn't be—

"Breathe, Fiona." The Pit Viper was next to her, his hand planted firmly on her arm. His grip felt solid, and the look in his eyes was human, sympathetic to the shock she'd felt at having everything she knew shaken.

He knew.

Slowly, her shivering stopped. She breathed deeply, and inch by inch the world came back into focus.

"Thank you," she said.

"Peter," he said.

"What?"

"My name," he said. "My name is Peter. My mother named me after the saint."

Despite her shot nerves, she couldn't help but chortle. "It's not *Pete Viper*, is it?"

"No, it's Pete Covalch," he said. "It's Polish."

She started to laugh harder and harder, shaking with excitement.

"It's not funny," he said, blushing furiously, but then he started chuckling, too, and soon they both shook with laughter, the sounds intertwining in joyous harmony.

Fiona's breakthrough with the worship note shot the Pit Viper full of excitement. He bounced around the room with a pen and notepad, scribbling down everything from Betty's tuning to the position that Fiona had been sitting in when she'd hit the *tonus culter*.

Fiona laid back on his mattress and watched him take photos of the book with his phone and murmur about trying to recreate the moment in a controlled atmosphere.

He made a final scribble, tossed the notes on the bed next to her, and smiled at her. "We should go out," he said.

"Out?"

"Yeah," he said. "You just played music that hasn't been

experienced in close to a century. I think that deserves a little celebration."

"Where?" she said, both intrigued and nervous. Part of what she loved about being with him was how they were locked away from the world, feeding on each other's passion. She was worried he'd turn out to be like Horace, another guy who wanted to celebrate her minor triumph by getting trashed.

"Wherever you'd like," he said. "Record store? Vintage guitar store? Coffee, pastry, a view?"

Dear God, it was like he had a direct line into her subconscious. "All of those things," she said. Then, thinking twice, "As long as I'm home by eleven."

He laughed and extended a hand. "Well, come on, light's wasting." She took it and let him pull her to her feet, and then he didn't stop and yanked her into his arms. They stood for a silent moment, caught in each other's eyes, and then she nuzzled forward and kissed him. His kiss was as respectfully restrained as always, but this time, she pushed him further, opened her mouth, let her tongue brush against his. It was as though he understood, like once the boundary of *Home by eleven* was spoken, they would enjoy each other within it. She savored the nuance of him, something boys like Horace seemed desperately without.

"Are you bringing your guitar?" he asked as they got ready to go out (he had said nothing about Horace's hoodie being replaced with her old almost-too-small denim jacket).

"Oh, good call," she said, eyeing the case and imagining the hassle of carrying it everywhere with them. Her wrist would feel like wood in an hour. "Shit, she's a little heavy. Let me think…"

"It'd be cool if you walked around with her, like a samurai of old with a sword on his belt," he said. "Ready to draw her just in case the *instrumentis* strikes you. That said, you're welcome to leave her here."

"Is that okay?" she asked faux meekly, digging the domesticity of it. "It'll just be this once. And I won't start leaving a toothbrush and a change of underwear, promise."

"It's totally fine," he said, and, turning to go, added over his shoulder, "Toothbrush and underwear, too."

They pounded the pavement toward downtown, drinking in golden autumn afternoon light and cold air laced with vent steam. He strode at his usual steady pace, and for once Fiona didn't have to strain to keep up with him. She had been wrong—leaving the apartment didn't feel vulnerable; it felt liberating, like they were badass royalty with the whole city as their concrete playground. His icy air of mystery was completely gone, replaced by a jolt of geeky enthusiasm that made him loveably human. She was seeing a whole new Pit Viper—no, it was *Peter*, Peter Covalch, a strange and wonderful guy but a guy nonetheless, bright and alive no matter where some ancient book had led him.

The industrial maze gave way to funky storefronts and ethnic grocery stores. Peter waved her toward a fortune-teller storefront with a huge half-closed eye on the window, but rather than go up the stoop they trundled down the basement stair to a door marked only with a neon open sign. Peter pressed a bell; there was an ugly buzz, and they walked into an over-lit, cigarette-smelling room stuffed to the gills with physical music. Lining the walls were folding tables stacked with milk crates of vinyl records, not to mention cardboard boxes of cassettes and plastic bins overflowing with T-shirts and songbooks. From somewhere amongst the deluge of collector's items, The Smiths played out of crackly old speakers.

Fiona's mind boggled at the density of it; the place looked as though she'd have to suck in her stomach to fit down the narrow paths between the tables. Peter waved to the balding man at the counter in the back—the man glanced up and nodded but didn't wave back—and then motioned to the great musical mass. "The good news is, they have everything. The bad news is, it's totally unorganized. Just pick a box and start."

Forty minutes later, her fingers humming from flipping through vinyl and her shirt smelling of dust and rotten paper, Fiona had only made it through maybe a fifth of the crates. Though this record store felt more like an illegal gambling ring than the head shops she was used to shopping for vinyl in, its selection was superb, and she had narrowed her options down to a Record Store Day version of a Black Lips album, the new Mutoid Man, and Nick Cave and the Bad Seeds' *Murder Ballads*. She decided on Mutoid Man and, through some good-natured arm crossing and hand swatting, refused to let Peter pay for it, giving the disinterested old dude one of the ratty twenties her dad had foisted on her last weekend. She could've spent her whole life flipping through records, but she didn't want to cut their afternoon short. He didn't seem to mind; as they left the store, Fiona's vinyl tucked under her arm, he pointed ahead of them and said, "Home by eleven!" like it was a medieval battle cry. She laughed louder than she should have, delighted to see him being unabashedly silly, happy he wasn't ripping on her for being a teenager with a curfew.

The gear store he led them to was Buzzo Guitars, a vintage music shop she'd already been to on a family trip into the city. The fact that Peter wanted to show her somewhere she already knew about made her swell with pride. The inside was the usual hodgepodge of antique and new guitars, as well as the occasional fixer-upper (*Like Betty had been*, thought Fiona, and she accidentally said, "Aw!" out loud). They wandered the racks of old guitars, basses, and pedals, Fiona's eye poring over every one, wishing she could have them all but not sure what to do with half of them. Peter floated at her side and smiled when certain items caught her eye but never mansplained any of the hardware to her.

She stopped at the cases and found herself dreamily staring at a custom-made leather guitar case with backpack straps and an Ace of Spades inlay at the end of the neck, so that the card would float over the wearer like a thought bubble. Peter noticed her openmouthed gaze, leaned over the counter, looked at the price tag, and whistled.

"Don't even tell me," she said. "It's probably costs more than my guitar."

"It's definitely not cheap." He looked back at her with a puckish smile. "You know, if you want, I could—"

"No," she said, shaking her head violently. "No buying me elaborate presents."

"You could take Betty everywhere with something like that. Samurai of old, sword on the belt, agent of living music. Could be cool."

"Absolutely not," she said. It took all her willpower to turn him down, but she had to. She wouldn't let him shower her with gifts like some kept woman—at least, she thought with a Cheshire-Cat smile, not until she was sure that was what she wanted.

"Man, I can't buy you vinyl, I can't buy you overpriced guitar cases." He sighed in dramatized exhaustion. "What about baklava? Can I buy you a baklava and coffee?"

"You can buy me an entire tray of baklava," she said.

They sauntered another half mile, and when she saw the road-cone-orange lighthouse poking over the horizon of schmutzy brownstones, she prayed it was where they were going, which it was. The inside of Little Water Coffee was all aged blue-and-white linoleum, like a piece of Delft pottery and a failing diner had collided with one another. Everyone in line spoke to the too-tan woman with the pixie cut behind the counter in an Eastern European language that Fiona didn't recognize. When they got up front, the woman clasped Peter's face in her wrinkled hands and drew him close so that he could give her a peck on each cheek.

"My gorgeous boy," she said. "You beautiful man. I listened to your tape, it was awful, I hated it. What are you eating? Who is this?"

"Trill, this is Fiona," said Peter, motioning to Fiona.

"Do you like his music?" asked Trill, scowling at Fiona.

"Not really," Fiona said.

"She's too good for you," said Trill, looking at Peter like he was pitiful. "What do you want? No, don't tell me, apple fritters and cold brew."

"Baklava," said Peter.

"I'll give you a baklava and an apple fritter," said Trill. "Now that I've mentioned it, Fiona will not be able to stop thinking about it."

When she came back with their coffees and wax-paper-wrapped pastry, Peter said, "We're going upstairs."

Trill made a noise in her throat and waved as though to brush him aside, and Peter walked into the kitchen with Fiona hot on his heels. They meandered, Peter saying hi to every waitress, baker, and dishwasher before leading her toward a filthy curtain hanging over a doorway in the back of the kitchen.

Behind the curtain was a staircase so narrow that it appeared to have been built inside of the wall. Peter led Fiona up slowly for what felt like forever until he slapped open the door at the end.

They stood on the roof, staring at the miniature lighthouse which, up close, was larger than Fiona expected. Two younger guys in aprons smoking cigarettes started when they appeared, but then relaxed when they saw Peter. He shook their hands, laughed at a joke. When he said something and nodded toward Fiona, they both wagged their eyebrows at him and gracefully headed downstairs.

Fiona and Peter climbed up an iron ladder on one side of the lighthouse and plopped down in the main basket up top. It was both larger and smaller than Fiona imagined, the space cramped enough that their hips and shoulders collided but elevated enough that she felt a little dizzy, teetering over the circuit board of the city on all sides. Fiona felt high on it, the height, the closeness of him, the bright, cold city Saturday floating all around her.

He broke out the apple fritter, split it in a shower of glaze crumbs, and handed her half. She took a huge bite and washed it down with sharp cold brew.

"All I could think about after she mentioned it," he said, pointing to his remaining hunk of fritter.

"Yeah, dude," she said. There was a silence as they just took it all in, this perfect treat on a perfect day. Shook her head and took a deep breath, savoring it. "All right, I give up. If your goal was to charm the pants off me, this? This is the way to do it."

He shook his head. "Thanks, but this is a celebration. You did something impressive today, you and no one else. You *get* to have this. If everyone else out there"—he flung his hand out to the city, though Fiona could tell he meant a broader *out there*, the world, among the living—"could do what you do, be who you are, then they would get to appreciate this."

"But I didn't get here on my own," she said. "I didn't *earn* this. I'm only here because I'm with you. Besides, you can get an apple fritter anywhere."

"You're with me because you're not like everyone else," he said. "So you've earned me. I've earned you. We made it to each other. Finally."

Fiona wanted to laugh at his dramatic flair and tell him that he needed to get to know her better, but couldn't bring herself to do it. She knew she was easy prey, a teenage rocker with a mysterious older DJ from the heart of the city, but he just made her feel so damn rare and important. She leaned into him, and he wrapped his arms around her; she put her cheek on his chest, warm and firm under his shirt, and let herself hang above the world with him, surrounded by silence save for the steady rhythm of his heartbeat.

"Hey!" The voice called them out of their moment. They glanced over the edge of the lighthouse to see one of the smokers from earlier waving up to them. "You got people downstairs, man! Asking about you." Peter scowled, gave Fiona a kiss on the forehead, and leaped over the edge and onto the ladder, leaving Fiona to pick up the remains of their snack and follow slowly down.

Fiona got down the narrow stairs, past the filthy curtain, and through the kitchen before she could see Peter standing out in front of the counter, holding court with a crowd of excited onlookers.

Horace, Caroline, and Rita stood around Peter, staring up at him with rapt adoration.

Fiona stopped dead, felt her heels dig into the linoleum and her heart mis-beat in her chest.

Her plastic cup of cold brew fell from her hand and exploded on the floor. All their heads turned at once.

In an instant, she was in the kitchen with her back pressed hard against the tile wall next to the door. Her chest rose and fell as fear boomed through her. She felt caged, trapped by a place she didn't know in front of her and questions she didn't want to have to answer behind her.

"Ho boy." Trill stood by her, whisking something in a metal bowl. She stared at Fiona with vague disgust.

"Back door," whispered Fiona.

"To my right," said Trill.

She burst out of the door and power walked down a back alley. An overflowing dumpster oozed creeks of green water that made her nostrils burn. Through the haze of panic, she wondered what exactly she was running from. Was it the gossip that would no doubt follow if her friends found out? The weird way they might act, knowing that her distant behavior was centered around their new favorite musician? Horace? For whatever reason, it was imperative they not see her.

She didn't register the hunched figure at the mouth of the alley before she collided with him. There was a puff of weed smoke and a fit of coughing before they both fell into stunned silence.

"Oh, hey," said Keller, his look of worry transforming into confused delight. "What are you doing here? Hey, did you hear the Pit Viper's inside this bakery?"

Fiona's mouth opened and closed silently as she grasped for an excuse. Around the corner, she heard the faint dinging of a bell, and then Caroline's voice came soaring out into the air.

Fiona turned on her heel, trotted back into the alley, and crouched behind the dumpster, hoping it obscured their view. She felt Keller's eyes following her the whole way and seared with embarrassment as she tried to keep the top of her head from showing above the lid.

"I can't believe we saw him," said Rita. "Good eye, Horace."

"Yeah, even though Keller gave me fucking whiplash," added Horace, sounding sullen. "Think he liked the idea?"

"There is no way he's interested now, after me," said Caroline. "Holy crap, I am such a nerd. Next time, you just have to stop me from talking. Jam a sock in my mouth. It would be better for everyone. Doug?"

"Huh? What?" asked Keller.

"What's got you spooked, man?" asked Rita. "There a lewd flasher in the alley?"

"It's nothing," sputtered Keller. "Sorry. Just a little high."

"You didn't save me any, did you?" growled Horace. "Great, figures. Thanks, Keller, you jerk off."

"Okay, Mister Crankypants, let's go," said Rita.

Fiona heard the slam of car doors, and their voices cut out. There was a shuffling cough that could only be Keller's car starting. Once it rumbled off into the distance, she counted to one hundred and then stood up straight and walked down the alley with her head hung low.

Peter was waiting for her at the door to the coffee shop, mouth drawn and hands crammed in his pockets. Fiona's whole face burned with red-hot shame, and she couldn't even look at him as she passed and he turned to walk with her.

Outside of Central Station, she finally faced him. As she did, he took Fiona's shoulders in his hands and half crouched to look into her eyes. His expression had softened in a knowing, if sad, smile.

"All the worlds collided a little too quickly, I take it?" he asked.

"Something like that," she said. "I'm sorry. I shouldn't have freaked out. It's not like I'm embarrassed of you or anything."

"Sure," he said, but his tone said he knew better.

"No, seriously," she said. "My friends would actually have their minds blown by the idea. They'd be stoked."

"And maybe that's the problem," he said.

"Maybe," she admitted softly. "I just...I imagine how

things would change if word got out about…*us*." She waved a finger between them, sensing the pathetic understatement of the gesture. "And I'm not sure I can deal with that right now."

He nodded. "That's okay. We can take *us* a little easy."

"Well, I don't want *that*," she said. "Today was perfect. It was beyond perfect. And I want…I do want more."

He inhaled slowly. "Look, Fiona, you owe those people nothing. You're better than them and their silly little lives. It's why we got today, why you were able to speak to the book the way you did. So, if you want this to grow, if *you* want to grow, then you just need to be able to admit it." He let go of her shoulders and stood up, looking down at her more as a teacher than a companion or equal. "Take your time, but don't take too long. If you can't admit that you're destined for better things, I can't help you find them."

"I blew it, didn't I?" she said, resigned and deflated.

"Not at all," he said. "You're just not ready yet." He leaned forward and kissed her passionlessly on the lips. "I'll see you next Saturday. But you should get going. It's getting late."

As the train rumbled back out into the burbs, Fiona's foul mood stewed and stewed. She tried to listen to music, but every song sounded too loud and obnoxious, like the musicians were trying too hard; none of the singers got anywhere near the bleak, endless tunnel of unfathomable shame she felt. Earlier in the day, she'd sat next to him and created music that felt like a solar flare. They'd conquered the city like triumphant heroes and eaten flaky pastries on a lighthouse that sat above the world. But having her friends from home catch them together and know the reason behind her change in behavior would have made it all feel clumsy and naked. It was as though their presence was a gust of wind blowing away all the magic and mystery that Peter saw in her, revealing the small town in her heart. And it would make school a nightmare—Horace and Caroline wouldn't see the strangely beautiful afternoons alone with Peter, they'd just see zippers and bra snaps, the grossest scenes out of the worst anime.

Or worse, like Peter had said, they'd marvel at her. They'd be impressed. She'd be made to feel lucky, cool, the kind of shallow and thirsty stereotype that Tess Baron aspired to.

The train rolled into Hamm. Fiona got out feeling sour and resentful, wishing her small-town life would just disappear and leave her alone in the city with Peter. She told herself she was through with it, over, done. But twice, she heard a voice and looked quickly over her shoulder, frightened she might see someone who recognized her.

chapter
17

On Monday, the stone-gray sky cast a damp pall over Fiona's world. The light through her bedroom window was the same when she woke up at four, overwhelmed by dread and unable to sleep, and seven, when she finally crawled out of bed. It was one of those days that just wouldn't get any brighter.

When she finally left the house, a wind chillier than any this fall pierced her clothes, making her zip up her jacket and shiver as she got out her bike. Her eyes scanned the neighborhood, and she registered the first grinning pumpkins on lawns and shroud-wisped skeletons dangling from porches. She'd been too overwhelmed by her own problems to notice Halloween creeping up on Hamm, a time when people who would assault a young man indulged in a simple kind of scariness.

She was climbing onto her bike when Keller rolled up and honked for her. She considered blowing him off and riding away, but knew that was her being cowardly, not aloof. She dropped the bike, went to the car, and flopped into the passenger seat.

"So," said Keller after they'd rolled down her block a ways, "what's up?'

"Nothing much," said Fiona, casually. "What's up with you?"

"Nah, come on, Fiona, you know what I mean," he said, his voice sharp and hurt.

"Look, Keller, it's been a rough week, I don't really want to—"

"This needs dealing with *now*," he said decidedly. "First you freak out at Horace, then you start ignoring us, and now you're hiding from us when we magically spot the Pit Viper at some café. Three strikes. You owe us an answer."

Fiona chewed on her lips, trying to come up with the response Doug deserved. "It's tough, okay?" was the best she could do.

"Jesus, Fiona, help me here," he said. "Are you in trouble? Like, life-threatening trouble? Do you owe anyone money? Was hiding for our benefit?"

"Nothing like that," she said, wishing that her situation *was* that dire, that she had a real problem for him to help her solve.

"So, then, you're just being shitty for personal reasons," he said, and then glanced at her. "Because you have. Lately, it feels like you're too cool for us. Like you're better than being our friend. And I know Hamm kind of sucks, and we're not the coolest bunch in the world, but we're still your friends. We've always been."

"I know," she said, unexpectedly. Some part of her wanted to sneer, roll her eyes, say, *Who are you, Calvin fucking Hokes?* Instead, the same incongruous guilt from the day before washed over her, making her hunch into her seat. Maybe it was Keller that got to her; she could easily snap back at someone like Calvin when he stared or Horace when he behaved like a goon, but Doug was an all-around good dude, kind of doofy at his very worst. "I know. I've been unfair to everyone. There's just something…there's a lot going on in my life that doesn't concern you guys. And I guess I've been preoccupied by it lately."

"That's one way of putting it," Keller said. Fiona noticed that he was just circling blocks in her neighborhood—he wasn't taking them to school until they were ready. He gulped and then said in a shaky voice, "Is it what I think it is?"

Oh, Keller, you have no idea, she thought, thinking how silly his salacious ideas would look next to an ancient book containing the song stuck in God's head. But she didn't want to lie to him, and figured the more she tried to pivot around the truth, the more tangled the web would become.

"Yeah," she said. "Probably not all of it, but yeah. It's exactly what you think."

He silently nodded with an understanding look on his face, like he was well versed in the intimate workings of the human heart rather than a dude in a third-hand Chevy.

"And you don't want people to know because you're… embarrassed?" he asked.

"I just don't want people making assumptions until *I* know what's going on," she said, and then she decided to get some of it off her chest. Not specifics—she didn't want to accidentally fill any gaps in Doug's imagination—but the raw feelings she'd been living with for the last twenty-four hours. "For the first time in a long time, I feel like I'm doing something fresh and exciting, that makes me feel cool, and weird, and *different* every day. How rare is that, in Hamm? To wake up every day thinking everything feels new?"

He sighed. "You're not lying."

"But it's all raw as fuck," she said. "Like, sometimes it feels like I'm only living my dream if there's Hamm to come back to if things get tough. So the idea of having to dodge people's questions, or hear their assumptions spat back to me through the school grapevine…I'm not trying to do that right now. Right now, I want to let this happen in a controlled way, you know? Without Caroline wagging her eyebrows at me and Horace listening to a Sam Smith song on repeat."

Keller coughed out a laugh and nodded. "Okay, fair enough. Some of our crew can be super ignorant. But that doesn't mean they don't miss you or aren't worried about you. If you make them care, they'll care. Shutting them out will just make them readier to spread rumors and talk shit."

She nodded back. He was right—how were her friends supposed to know how she was feeling when it had been weeks since she'd said more than a few words at a time to them? Meanwhile, here was Doug with concern for her in his voice, telling her flat-out that she was missed. Sure, breaking up with Horace had been the right thing to do—she didn't regret that for a second—but the rest of her friends hadn't done anything wrong, and she hoped that she and Horace could at least be civil to each other.

And Rita. Rita had tried to talk to her about it. Fiona missed her so badly. If Rita was worried, then Fiona was doing something wrong.

"You're right," she said. "I'm sorry, Keller, I didn't mean to disappear. I've just been really preoccupied lately, and it's been making me act like a jackass."

"Happens to the best of us," he said and turned toward school. "Hey, this afternoon, maybe we all go out. You, me, Rita, Caroline, maybe Penny. Get a doughnut at Chance's or go see a movie or something, just get everyone in the same space together. Totally random. What do you say?"

After a moment, Fiona nodded slowly. The potential for awkwardness was high, but she could brave it. "Okay. Let's do it."

"Rad," said Doug.

"Thanks, Doug," she said, giving him a warm smile. Doug Keller, always a good dude. She hit the stereo, excited to hear what jam was waiting for her—Stiff Little Fingers? Wavves?

Instead, a track from Peter's album filled the car with its eerie pounding.

"Sorry," said Doug.

"It's fine," said Fiona, switching it off.

After school, she paced outside of Keller's car out in the parking lot, blasting Monster Truck on her headphones and simmering with nerves about seeing her friends. She'd managed to avoid her crew all day, telling herself over and over that she'd see them after school, and soon Doug's casual outing for a movie or whatever had become the focal point of her day. She'd catch a sliver of Penny Kim in a crowd, or hear Caroline's laugh down the hall, and think, *No, wait, after school you'll meet up, and you'll go for a ride, and you can be friendly to everyone, and if they accept you, your life in Hamm is all right and you can try and make Peter a part of it, gradually, eventually. After school, it'll all be made clear. Don't jump the gun, don't improvise.*

She turned to walk to the tail of Keller's car for the fortieth time, only to find Tess Baron in her path. The girl's extra-baggy sweater billowed around her in the harsh breeze, making her look larger than she actually was; Fiona vaguely remembered reading something about cobras doing the same thing with their hoods to frighten potential predators.

"Hey, Tess," said Fiona, pulling off her headphones. "Everything okay?"

Tess laughed in a pitying little way. Fiona thought it might have sounded biting in school, but the breeze carried it off, making Tess sound small and silly to Fiona.

"I know what you're doing," said Tess.

God*dammit.* She'd tried so hard to keep word from getting out. She mentally told herself to calm down—maybe Tess was just talking out her ass—but the knowing tone in the girl's voice turned Fiona's nerves up to eleven.

"Is that right?" said Fiona.

"Yup," chirped Tess. "I know people, and they tell me things. Your little Saturday hangouts with Calvin Hokes? Your breakup with Horace Palmada? I know *exactly* what you're up to, Fiona Jones."

Fiona clenched her teeth so hard she worried one of them might pop. She hadn't told anyone other than Keller. What was going on? Were Tess's friends in the city talking? That PM creep, maybe, or some other asshole Peter ran with? Either way, it was bad news. If her father and Edgar Hokes were already on the lookout, Fiona had to keep this as quiet as possible.

"Look, Tess, I've got no beef with you," she said, holding her hands up. "I don't know what this is you're trying to start with me, but I want no part of it. Whatever you think I'm doing wrong, I'll stop. Just, please, leave me alone."

"You need to back off," responded Tess, pointing a finger at Fiona. "This is mine, okay? I brought him to this stupid, sleepy little town. I want him. *He's* mine."

"Whatever helps you sleep at night," she said. "I don't care."

"You think I won't blow up your spot?" said Tess. Her eyes sparkled with sociopathic glee. "Your dad's always coming by to try and butter up my parents into joining the town council. What if, as a concerned neighbor, my father was forced to tell him that his daughter is spending her weekends with some guy, some *older* guy? Hmm? How do we think that would go over, Fiona—"

That. Was. *IT.*

In less than a second, Fiona had Tess's collar in her fist. She swung the girl's body around like it was nothing and slammed her back against the side of Keller's car, relishing Tess's cry of surprise.

Fiona's gut told her she should walk away, shake her head, and say, *Fine, whatever*, but the rage that welled up inside of her was palpable, so powerful she could taste it in the air around her.

This was exactly what she'd been trying to avoid, and she'd be damned if it happened like this...and anyway, truly, deeply, absolutely *fuck* Tess Baron. Fuck her stupid designer outfits and her perpetually dull eyes. Fuck her for thinking she could in any way tell Fiona what to do. Fuck her snobby tone when talking about the town council. The stunned look on Tess's face told Fiona that the girl had nothing on Peter, or on her. Tess was a pufferfish who'd tried to show off her spikes and was being rudely deflated. Good.

"Try it, Tess," deadpanned Fiona. "You think for a second he'd give me up for you? Why, I could stomp you right here, and he'd laugh about it when I told him later. You can play at being hardcore, but I'm the real deal. So, go ahead, push me. Spread a bunch of lies about me, get my dad involved. And"—she slammed the butt of her hand against the car's side inches from Tess's face, loving the sting on her palm and the shriek that erupted from Tess's gloss-covered lips—"see what happens, bitch. See. What. Fucking. Happens—"

"Whoa, whoa, whoa!" All at once, hands were on Fiona's shoulders, yanking her back. She finally let go of Tess's collar, and the girl ran off into the parking lot as fast as her trendy-ass chunky heels would allow.

Fiona shrugged off whoever pulled her away and whirled, only to face Rita, whose huge eyes were full of heartbreak and outrage. Behind her, Caroline, Keller, and Penny stood frozen in total shock.

"Jesus Christ, Fiona, are you out of your mind?" yelled Rita, throwing wide her hands. "You could've hurt her!"

"That was the idea!" snapped Fiona. "Did you hear the things she said? That human garbage pile needs someone to teach her what's what!"

"And that's *you*?" laughed Rita in disbelief. "*You're* going to beat the poser out of Tess in the parking lot? Jesus, dude, she's one of us, you can't just—"

"*US?*" Now it was Fiona's turn to throw out a laugh. "What group are we part of that includes *that* insufferable creature? How are you standing up for Tess fucking Baron, of all people?"

For a moment, Rita's face flashed insecurity, but then it hardened with resolve. "We've known Tess our whole lives. We grew up here together, we went to school together. Just because she sucks now doesn't mean we start beating on her when she acts the fool—"

"Rita, think about who Tess Baron is!" screamed Fiona. "That chick deserves a chewing out, a beating, and more! Think about who you're talking about!"

"Who are *you*, Fiona?" asked Rita. "Tell me *that*. I have no clue anymore."

Fiona felt the sting of Rita's comment, but it was quickly swallowed by complete resignation. She shook her head, a smile of brutal realization crossing her face. After all her worry and embarrassment, Peter had been right about them. All Fiona had done was fight back when some bipedal parasite had threatened her, but because she wasn't nice about it, or because she didn't play by the age-old rules of Hamm, Ohio, Rita considered her dangerous. Well, screw that. She couldn't be dragged down by people too stupid and afraid to see the world for what it was, especially when she had someone in her life who saw the hidden music behind everything. They were patient. They were careful. The Pit Viper told them to keep it secret. And to them, his word was law.

"Never mind," she said calmly, holding up her hands and turning around. "Don't worry about me, Rita. You have fun with all of this. Maybe I'll see you later."

"Yeah, hopefully you won't throw me against a car and take a swing at me like some schoolyard bully," called Rita.

"Hopefully!" Fiona called back over her shoulder, and began walking home alone.

chapter
18

"Tonight, we're going to tune," said Peter as they entered his room the next Saturday.

Fiona wasn't so stupid as to think he meant twirling knobs on guitars or drums. His conspiratorial tone suggested something different, something special. "What exactly are we tuning?"

"Ourselves," he said, like that was a given. His voice remained cool and level; he was obviously trying to hold tight the reins of his emotions after last time. "Basically, I'm going to tap into some planetary vibrations using the book and the master copy. The longer I open myself up to them, the more adept I am at their manipulation."

"Like getting calluses on your fingers," she said, displaying her playing hand.

"Exactly," he said. "Think of it as putting a callus on my soul. The goal is to eventually become so powerful that I don't need the master copy or the *Canoris* to wield the *universalis*. But that will take many, many tunings. If you try to hear too much of it at one time, you can go insane. From what I've heard, the last owner of the *Canoris* did that and ended up killing himself."

Fiona cocked an eyebrow. It had been cool at first, but she was beginning to wonder how much of Peter's belief in his musical powers was smoke and mirrors. Sure, she'd seen the worship note in her head and felt the book buzzing in her hands, but she knew that those had explanations, sleight of hand and hypnotic suggestion and all that psychic TV-show garbage. And even this "tuning" was probably just a lot of theater, like the séance she'd made her friends do one Halloween (she'd wanted to talk to Prince, but someone had manipulated the Ouija board to spell out "butt sex"). The more Peter believed in it, the more she was being sucked in, and the stupider she worried she would feel when she found out he was just a charismatic weirdo who'd robbed a library.

It was getting down to the wire with him, she realized. The last day she'd spent with him had had a soaring chorus with a shitty fade-out at the end—now, she wanted something real, something *she* could believe in. She'd been bold coming here this time, not even coming up with an excuse about band practice—she'd just ghosted and left the community center on her own. The interaction with Tess Baron had only strengthened her resolve. No more sneaking around. She had to be honest about how she felt, just as Lemmy intended.

Now, Peter needed to do his part. If Fiona was going to keep seeing him, she needed to know that Peter was for real.

"Are we doing it here or going somewhere?" she asked.

"The roof," he said. "Weather.com says moonrise is at seven fifty tonight, so we'll want to bring up all my equipment by seven thirty."

"How much do we need to haul upstairs?" she asked.

"Quite a bit," he said. "We'll start around three, I figure."

"You really think we'll need four hours to get everything up there?"

Peter nodded. "It'll take longer than you think. You'll thank me later."

He went about straightening things in his loft, and she stood standing, watching him. There was something else she needed to put to rest before she could continue.

"Hey, so you know Tess Baron, right?"

He nodded. "Yeah. She goes to your school. She threw the party I spun. She keeps trying to help set up other shows, too."

"You're not banging her, are you?"

He stopped and looked up at her, face painted with amused shock. "God, no. Why?"

"She stopped me at school to, like, lay claim to you," she said. "I guess she somehow found out I've been…seeing you."

"How'd you respond?"

"I told her that if she came at me again, I'd destroy her."

"Nice," he said, grinning. "As you should have. I figured it'd be something along those lines from you."

"But you're not…"

"No," he said firmly. "I don't do side projects. I'm all-in on you."

Fiona smiled back. His confidence in her always raised her spirits. Horace had wanted to be her white knight in shining armor, and Calvin Hokes figured he could be her superhero swooping in to lend her a hand, but Peter respected her enough to know she could handle herself. If anything, he enjoyed it.

The staircase to the roof was narrow and steep, and contained forty-seven steps. Fiona knew, because she counted them as she and Peter hauled speakers, PA wedges, and amplifiers up to the roof. She had imagined it would be like the time she and her dad had helped the Fiddlers move, making quips as they worked around corners and over blocky raised thresholds. Instead, the Pit Viper grabbed a bass cab and hauled it himself like it was nothing, and she was left to grunt through every item that her arms could handle.

By five thirty, her body creaked with exhaustion. Sweat poured from her pits and trickled down her spine. When he got stuck behind her on the way up the stairs as she huffed and puffed, she could feel the impatience radiate off him in waves. He obviously didn't like it when things were in his way, even literally.

An hour later, the vast majority of the Pit Viper's gear was on the broad warehouse roof. Microphones of different sizes and shapes sat perched in front of the amps and speakers like robot crows. The wires for everything eventually tangled into a lumpy, black braid that trailed down into the building.

The view made Fiona's heart sing. The city sprawled out before them like a wasteland at sunset. The taller buildings stood silent and still, reflecting the coppery clouds but not yet lit up by a thousand harsh, artificial lights. It felt right, Fiona thought, this momentary quiet as the sun slipped beneath the horizon. But soon it would be gone, and the noise of the city would bring out vampires and ghosts.

"We're done early," he said, stretching. Sweat had collected at his collar and under his arms, plastering his shirt to his sinewy body. She concentrated on the skyline and not his slick physique. "I'm impressed. Now we just have to wait for the moon."

"The moon needs to be up for a tuning?" Fiona asked.

"The moon is the key," he said. "It's basically a receiver that channels the frequencies of the other planets to us. All the sounds we're going to hear tonight are being transmitted to our equipment via Luna. It connects Earth's sonic frequency to that of space."

"That's some real Jerry Garcia shit right there," she said.

He smirked. "Yeah, guess so. Okay. An hour's practice, and then we meet back here for tuning."

"Do you have a spare practice amp I can use?" Fiona asked, hiking a thumb back at the tuning circle. "You made me bring all your other guitar amps up here."

He shrugged. "Practice on the roof."

Reluctantly she brought Betty upstairs. As she plugged in and turned on, there was still a thin sliver of the sun left, like a lake of fire on the horizon. She wondered how the guitar would react, playing properly out in the open for the first time.

But Fiona found no hesitation in Betty. The riffs came out of her in a flood, chugging and moaning into the open air as though the guitar had always wanted to be used outside of four simple walls. It was like Fiona and she were playing an epic prayer to the sunset over the city, digesting emotion in huge gulps rather than thin sips. Fiona squinted, feeling the raw energy of the music, the honest offering that came with playing in the open air with no one around to worry about. There was purity to it — no acoustics, no effect created by the size of a room or the material of the walls, just the notes that came to her the way they were, released through her guitar. Leaning back, wailing on Betty, she felt like the mystical being Peter kept promising her she was.

After forty minutes, she stopped playing, feeling strung out and dehydrated. For a moment, her fingers still humming from practice, she held her hand up to the air in the shape of a claw, cupping the last of the day. She could almost feel the weight of her music, the ways she might put it to use…

She dropped her invisible orb by her side. Ridiculous. What was she, ten?

She tried to start back up, but Betty felt spent for the night. The sun was gone, and Fiona watched the daylight die more and more with every second. The moon was on its way. It was Peter's time now.

When Peter finally returned to the roof, night had set in and the city sparkled with dots and waves of electric light, leaving the sky a bruised purple.

He didn't say a word, just walked to the center of the circle of amps with a laptop, the *Canoris*, and the master copy. He sat in a lotus position, like a meditating guru. Fiona sat facing him and watched as he plugged a cable into every port of his computer, each cord leading to a nearby central mixing board that in turn trailed dreadlocked wires to all the other devices surrounding them.

Peter carefully placed the record, still in its white sleeve, in front of him. He opened the book to a specific page, and after scanning it used a nearby distortion pedal as a paperweight to keep it open.

"Turn everything on," he commanded.

She stood, stung by his harsh instructions, and walked the circle, flicking switches and pressing buttons. Once every piece of equipment was awake and humming, she returned to the same position as before. She tried to speak, but he cut her off:

"We are going to try and distill a worship note that comes from the planetary tones of Venus and Saturn, with support from Jupiter," he said. He put in a pair of soft foam earplugs.

"We have an hour to get it, but we won't need that long.

I've tuned to this note before, but each alignment's different. Tonight's *tonus* will be stronger than my previous tunings."

"Should I be wearing a pair of those?" she asked.

He shook his head. "I want you to listen," he said. "You should know how this feels."

"Is it going to make me sick?" she asked.

"If only that," he said. "It will probably make you feel lots of different things, some of them painful."

She frowned. "But you want me to experience it," she said.

"Pain purifies," he said. "Like fire or boiling water. Cleansing your spirit of normality. You'll thank me when you're stronger."

The way he said it made her shudder. If he *was* crazy, if this was the thing that would trigger the madness he'd hidden from her thus far, then she knew she'd later recall this moment as the wake-up call she should've heeded. If she was going to leave, now was the time—

Before she could respond, he pressed a button on the mixing board, and from a handful of the amps and speakers came a deep note, so low that Fiona could feel it in her guts. It made her grimace. She wasn't sure soiling herself in front of him was her idea of displaying strength.

"What is that?" she yelled over the sound.

"The moon," he said. "The bedrock. Try not to talk." He cracked his knuckles and picked up his laptop. "Now, Saturn."

He pressed another button and a second note, this one harsh and crackly, like a scream compressed and distorted beyond recognition, spewed out of more speakers. Immediately, Fiona felt it enter her, carried on the back of that deep lunar rumble. With each second, she could sense Saturn's note burrowing into her body and mind, making her blood bubble like soda water.

He pressed another button, and a third note accompanied

the others, and then one more. By now there was no telling whether the notes were high or low, major or minor. The four sounds blurred together to become a steady wall of noise. The hair on her arms and neck stood on end and rippled like ocean waves. This was more than a simple sound, it was a new type of energy, music in its blinding and unadulterated form, shrieking out from somewhere beyond the clumsy use of human hands or constructed implements. It was like a drug, both enrapturing and poisoning her.

She squirmed. The sounds traveled along her nerve endings and made her feel nauseous, anxious, unable to move or look away. Warring sensations attacked her—an acidic burn of sound waves on her skin, a deep-set gastrointestinal rumble of the moon, but also a surging excitement that made her breathe fast and blink hard.

Amid it all, in the blue glow of his computer, sat Peter—no, Peter had vanished, and in his place was the Pit Viper, grinning like a lunatic as the noise engulfed them. He laid down his laptop and began twisting knobs and faders on the soundboard. Her teeth grinding and her mind reeling, Fiona watched as he picked up the master copy between them, discarding the white paper sleeve and cupping the record carefully between his two hands. He raised it aloft over his heads, and she watched as, surrounded by noise, the record vibrated, making it look less like a piece of wax and more like a flying saucer. Soon, it shook so hard that it was just a lightless blur in the air.

Without warning, he lowered the record and pressed a button on the laptop. The sounds all stopped at once.

As he put the master copy back in its sleeve, she thought she could see the etchings on it gleam bright and angry in the light coming off the city.

He looked back at her and asked, "How are you feeling?"

She tried to respond but couldn't. Slowly, carefully, she stood up and steadied her breathing, but even then, she had no words.

It was real, she knew. It was all brutally real, the book and the record and the musical power. Fiona wasn't sure of a lot of things in life, but she knew beyond any questioning that he had been telling the truth. He was no charlatan or hypnotist; he was a human being in control of powerful forces. Her gut screamed in simultaneous terror and joy.

He rose, and she saw his strength, saw the power running through every taut muscle and fluttering strand of hair. Her knees wobbled. He stepped forward and put his palm against her face. She looked up into his eyes, gleaming and bottomless, and found herself drawn into them. His thumb edged up over her cheek and ran slowly over her lower lip.

Her mind urged her to slow down and think about this. Her heart wept in amazement at him.

Her gut was all in.

She leaped onto him and kissed him fiercely, reveling in the crackle she felt where their skin touched. He pulled her close with grappling hands and solid arms. She dug her nails into his shirt and yanked, ripping it down the back. He bit her lower lip, and she bit back harder, relishing the taste of pennies where she broke skin. There was no moment but this, here, now, realer than anything she'd felt in months.

He hoisted her up, and she wrapped her legs around his waist. He carried her downstairs, and the cool shade of his lair closed around them both, enveloping them inside a duet that only they could hear.

chapter
19

She screamed as the moon lowered down to the earth. Its white surface gave way to a gaping mouth that screamed back. Betty was fusing to her hands in messy knots of scar tissue, her strings weaving into Fiona's flesh like sutures. A huge eye opened in the guitar's center and stared lovingly back at Fiona. The moon's crag-mouth hung open, and inside of it, she heard the sound of slithering coils. Something flicked its forked tongue at her and hissed.

Fiona sat up with a gasp, tangled in sweaty sheets.

Above her stretched the pressed tin of the warehouse ceiling. Around her, the room was lit powdery blue by the early morning coming in through the huge windows.

The night replayed in her brain, and she rubbed her face.

Peter lay on his stomach next to her, snoring softly. This close, Fiona could see the tattoo that took up his entire back, a diagram of the solar system. Each planet was surrounded by ancient-looking symbols and emitted concentric circles from it, like sound waves. They met between his shoulder blades, in a black triangle with a chord in white at its center.

The mathematical symmetry of it all was messily divided by ragged red welts left by her fingernails.

Fiona stood, mind reeling, and nearly tripped over one of his boots. Around them were strewn clothes, condom wrappers, and an empty bottle of wine they'd drank straight from the bottle. As she surveyed the scene, the rest of the evening came back in a blast of sense memory.

She shook her head. She couldn't believe it.

She'd been with him. She'd spent the night with him. It had been incredible, everything she'd been waiting for, but still, it hadn't been part of her plan, and...

Spent the night...

Panic lanced her. The unthinkable. The ultimate trouble. She found her jeans, dug through the pockets, recovered her phone. Twenty new text messages, twenty-two missed calls, all starting at eleven on the dot. Not just from her parents, but from Rita, Caroline, Filip Moss, and Calvin Hokes. She didn't listen to the voicemails, but what little of the texts she scanned told her what she needed to know—her parents were looking for her. People were worried.

In a daze, she found her clothes and bolted.

The air outside Peter's corner of the loft felt especially harsh and cold as she yanked on her jeans mid-stride. She was fully dressed as she hit the bottom stair and had her phone pressed to her ear by the time she was out the door.

Less than one ring in, it clicked on. "Hello?"

"Mom."

"Fiona, where the *hell* are you?"

"I'm sorry," she said. She did her best to cobble together a bullshit story with the pieces she had in place. "Band practice ran late last night, and then there was a party, and I didn't want to wake you up—"

"Cut the crap, Fiona," snapped her mom. "Calvin told us he

was covering for you. You're not playing guitar in any band."

"Shit."

"Excuse me?"

"Sorry, just…" She stopped dead and stared back into the blocky heap of warehouses. She'd left Betty on the roof last night. She'd been so absorbed with finally being with Peter that she'd entirely forgotten about Betty. It felt wrong, abandoning her guitar so soon after she'd felt such a powerful new connection between the two of them. And given how conflicted she was feeling, she'd need a good Betty session before the week was out.

She squinted into the urban collage. Would she even be able to find her way back to Peter's place on her own?

"Fiona!"

"Right, sorry! I'm on my way home!"

She ran, following signs and using the tall buildings downtown to guide her, finally swallowing her pride and asking for directions from a couple of sour-faced old men playing dominoes outside of a deli. Eventually, she found her way back to Central Station and bought a ticket. The whole time, she mentally apologized to Betty, and to Peter. It wasn't her fault, she swore. She would be back. Things had just happened too fast last night. She needed to sort this out.

She sat on the platform, waiting the hour until the next train to Hamm came rolling through. Her head in her hands, she reviewed the night in her mind, wrestling with the warring emotions that the memories stirred up.

So much of it scared her. The tuning, the way it had affected him, the way it made her feel—it was terrifying.

Suddenly, all of the aspects of Peter that she had considered cool and savvy felt inherently dark. He wasn't just strong of will, he was supernatural. Were Fiona's friends just sucked in by his well-made music, or were they under his command? She'd always appreciated the idea of his ancient music book, so long as it came with this huge grain of salt. Now that there was no question in her mind, she felt deeply upset by it.

But...

But she'd never felt this way before, about anyone. Fiona's respect for his talent and resolve had elevated to amazement. Last night, finally having sex with him, she hadn't felt brainwashed or tricked, she'd just wanted him, plain and simple. She hadn't felt horny, she'd felt *alive.* She wanted to call it love, but that only reminded her of the adorable warmth she'd felt for Horace, which came off as immature and hackneyed by comparison.

And on top of it all, as frightening as it was, she wanted to get better at his craft.

Sitting there waiting for the train, she realized she made music constantly—drumming her fingers, humming, foot-tapping out rhythms. Small music, maybe, but music nonetheless. It felt necessary to her, just like using Betty to unleash her emotions felt necessary on a larger scale. The past couple of times she'd gotten deeply angry, at Horace and Tess Baron, she'd felt raw power surging inside of her, pounding along to the beat of her heart. Music had always been her way of communicating with the universe, or at least understanding it. And now, just as she'd always felt the *right* of rock and roll, the organic beauty of guitars, drums, and vocals, she felt this.

Her phone buzzed. It was Peter, texting her.

PV: You left.

F: I know. I'm sorry. I'll be back, I promise.

No response. Her heart ached at his simple confusion. She wrote the longer text, explaining that she'd told no one about last night, that she needed to put her parents at ease. Still nothing.

The train rolled in, and she climbed aboard. As the readout in front listed the stops—Markus Boulevard, Wright, Locke, Warden, McFerrett, and Hamm—she closed her phone and did her best to clear her head. She couldn't get too caught up in his silence. There were more immediate concerns.

The house was quiet as she entered. Maybe the coast was clear. "I could kick your ass right now, I swear."

She winced—should have known better. Her mom was just doing that "silent but deadly" Mom routine. Resigned, she turned to the living room and found her mother on the couch. But while Fiona had expected her to be stiff and angry, Kim Jones just looked bedraggled and beside herself. There were dark circles under her eyes, and her hair stood out in all directions. She stared at the floor between them like it was a disappointing Christmas present.

"I'm sorry, Mom," said Fiona. "This was my bad, entirely. I should have texted you."

"You lied to me," said her mom feebly. "I was so excited to see your band. I kept thinking of asking to hear one of your songs. Have you burn me a CD. But I didn't want to pressure you."

"I know," said Fiona, leaning against the doorframe. She was trying to keep her cool, but her mother's tone of voice made her choke up. Getting screamed at would be far better than this level of disappointment.

"I called everyone last night," said her mom. "I woke up people in the city who I haven't talked to in years, asking if they'd seen you. I've emailed your picture everywhere."

"Look, Mom, I know I screwed this one up. I promise, the night just ran late, I had a beer or two, and my phone died."

She stepped into the living room, holding her arms out in front of her. "I'm okay. Everything's okay. It's like you say to Dad, I'm a big girl. I can handle myself. But this was my bad, totally, and I'm so sorry. It'll never happen again."

Her mother finally looked at her, and Fiona saw her eyes soften. She smiled. This wasn't irreparable. It might be okay.

The door opened and slammed, and they both turned to see Robert Jones stalking down the hallway. "Honey, I asked Bart and Darren if they could keep an eye—" He saw Fiona, and his face went violet with rage. "Well, well. Look who decided to show up."

"Dad, I'm *so* sorry," Fiona said quickly, hoping to cut off his anger. "I'm totally at fault—"

"You're a sorry excuse for a daughter is what you are!" bellowed her father. "Is this how we raised you to act, Fiona? Staying out all night, breaking your mother's heart, lying to my goddamn *face*?" Fiona reared back as her father closed in, spit flecking out of his mouth. "You tell us we don't need to worry about you, and then you just disappear! And when we ask your friends about your band, well, surprise, surprise, *it's not real*! Yeah, that's right, Calvin told us. No band, no shows, no practice space, all a big lie that you made that nice boy play along with, taking advantage of his feelings. You were just using that poor kid as a smokescreen while you were wandering off to meet some guy, huh?"

"Robert, please!" sobbed her mom.

"Kimmy, don't defend this girl!" he shouted. "Remember how upset you were last night? Fiona, I wish you'd been here. I wish you'd *seen* the kind of hysterics you were putting your mother through. Whatever fun you were having, whatever shit you were snorting and guys you were hooking up with, I hope they were worth giving your mother a panic attack!"

Fiona clenched her fists and put them to her temples,

trying to keep herself from freaking out. The sounds of her father yelling and her mother protesting were becoming noise in her head, and every second of it hurt worse than the last. Her body shook. Tears stung her eyes. She'd almost had it under control. It had almost been okay. And now he came here, accusing her of wanting to hurt her family.

"So who is it, huh?" shouted her father, shoving his face in hers. "Who's this cool friend of yours who you'd rather knock boots with than let your mother sleep at night knowing you're safe?"

That was it. Her dad wanted the truth? He could have it. What was he going to do, anyway?

"The Pit Viper," she snapped, turning to face him.

Fiona watched her father's rage fizzle out, leaving stark horror behind. "What…what did you say?"

"The Pit Viper," said Fiona. "I've been spending every Saturday with him for weeks. And I'm sleeping with him."

In the following silence, Fiona could hear her father's watch ticking and the fridge humming in the next room. Everything hung still, like the moment before a bass drop.

"Fiona, what have you done?" whispered her mother.

"Oh no," wheezed Robert Jones. "He's…oh no." He fell back into a chair, his mouth opening and closing again and again. Fiona's mother rushed over to him, grabbing his hand. Fiona observed him for a moment longer, righteous in her rage, and then walked up to her room.

The next day, she found herself on a social desert island. Her parents were gone when she came down for breakfast. She saw Caroline and Rita ahead of her as she biked to school, but when Caroline glanced over her shoulder and saw Fiona, her two friends exchanged a quick sentence and sped up. In chemistry, Horace sat at the other end of the room and refused to look at her. She eventually texted Peter saying, **This is a lot and I need time to think about it**, but still she got nothing.

But while Fiona didn't want to talk to any of them, having *no one* to talk to was killing her. If only she had remembered Betty. Betty would understand.

As she walked the halls of school, her father's shocked, horrified face kept running through her mind. He wasn't just angry about her sleeping with Peter, Fiona realized, he was genuinely scared. But why? He'd put the boots to that boy years ago like it was nothing. Why was he afraid of him now?

Filip Moss's comments outside the club came back to her and piqued her curiosity. She thought she'd been there for the entire story—*the whole sordid affair*, as Peter had called it— but dear God, she'd been nine at the time. Maybe there were other facts surrounding the deaths at the mill that Fiona hadn't heard about, evidence that made her father petrified. She needed to know more about what had happened when the Pit Viper had come to Hamm—

She stopped herself mid-thought, her sneakers skidding on the school hallway's linoleum floor. Not the Pit Viper, *Peter*. He had a name, like anyone else. He was a man, scratch that, *her* man, and even if he was strange and powerful and a little scary, she'd seen his eyes sparkle with joy and felt his hands seize her with desire. She couldn't get sucked into the madness of the crowds, casting him as the shadowy phantom in her town's past. He was Peter, and he was hers. If she was going to investigate what had happened at the old mill, it had to be for his sake, too.

After school, she went to the Hamm Library, a single-floor

building just off Main Street with a mural on the side featuring Dora and Pikachu reading Dr. Seuss together. Fiona hadn't been there in ages, but Mrs. Dirshowitz was still the librarian and still called her "Fionaroni" when she walked through the door. They hugged, and Mrs. Dirshowitzloudly remembered the day she'd spent helping Fiona finish her project on the Ivory Coast the night before it was due. It was exactly as Fiona had imagined it; she felt momentarily relieved that nothing ever changed in Hamm.

"I was wondering if you had old *Herald* archives here?" asked Fiona.

"Oh, of course!" said the busy older woman, motioning for Fiona to follow as she strode through the shelves. "A library this small, collecting newspapers is pretty much all we do. Well, that and loan our ten copies of *Fifty Shades of Grey* to unsatisfied Hamm housewives." She wagged her eyebrows at Fiona, who responded with an exaggerated grimace.

Through an Employees Only door near the back of the building and down a flight of stairs, Fiona discovered an endless basement lined with cobwebby shelves. Hundreds of dusty books and old boxes cluttered every rack, along with busted typewriters, ancient boxy computer monitors, and dinosaur-necked transparency projectors. Fiona couldn't help but blink in surprise—she'd had no idea the archives of the place were so vast. It reminded her of Peter's loft set to reading rather than music.

"If they're before 1945, they might be downstairs in the sub-basement," said Mrs. Dirshowitz as she pointed Fiona toward a wall of shelves labeled Herald Archives.

"They're after 1945," said Fiona, a little disappointed she wouldn't get to see the basement below this one, which no doubt housed a race of hyperintelligent rats and a mummy or two.

She'd expected microfilm that she could turn in a viewfinder, like in a detective movie, but no such luck in Hamm—the newspaper archives were actually old papers, stacked so thick and tightly that each cardboard box of them must have weighed a hundred pounds. They were also, Fiona soon found out, stored and labeled in no particular order, and she suffered through multiple back-twanging box retrievals and one big spider crawling across her hand before she found the right ones.

Jake had died mid-April, she remembered. The night she'd seen her father beat up the Pit Viper had been the second week of May. But when she found the papers for that May, she found nothing more than the usual fluff pieces and nationwide coverage. She read a police blotter from late April mentioning a noise complaint filed against the mill, and she read a piece on its permanent closure in the beginning of October that included one of the Goring family saying that the property held "too many bad memories." In between, the paper was a Frankensteined mess, torn apart and stitched together. Multiple articles were clipped out of the pages or blacked out with marker. There was no mention of Jake or Geraldine Brookham, no op-eds or letters to the editor from concerned townsfolk about the club rats invading their streets. No nothing.

Fiona harrumphed. It made no sense. This was Hamm, a place where Keller's brother driving drunk that one time was the stuff of legend. How could a town this small and insular not cover the biggest thing that had ever happened to it?

Back upstairs, she approached the front desk, where Mrs. Dirshowitz was checking out a stack of children's books for a dad and his son. When she saw Fiona, she grinned.

"Find everything you were looking for?" she asked.

"Not exactly," said Fiona. "Mrs. Dirshowitz, do you know

why there are no records of all those parties they used to have at the Goring Steel Mill?"

The bar-code scanner in Mrs. Dirshowitz's hand froze. Then she quickly went about checking out the books and handing them to the little boy across from her.

"I'm not sure what you mean, Fionaroni," she said in a tight voice.

"Remember, the Goring Steel Mill used to host these big raves?" she asked. "My cousin Jake, he passed away at one of them."

The librarian's eyes followed the dad and son as they walked out. "Uh-huh. Right."

"Well, he doesn't even have an obituary in the *Hamm Herald*, and I wanted to—"

The minute the door closed and they were alone, Mrs. Dirshowitz turned on her with robotic coldness, all emotion gone from her face. "Fiona, I don't know why you're asking me about such a morbid part of this town's history. I'm so sorry about your cousin, we all were, but you shouldn't dig up old stories you don't really understand. It doesn't help anyone."

"I…just wanted to find out what happened," said Fiona, taken aback by the kind woman's harsh tone. "Do you know something?"

"I know that your father is a good man," said Mrs. Dirshowitz, emphasizing the last two words. *Good. Man.* "And tonight, when you walk home and don't get mugged or harassed on the street, you should thank your lucky stars he was ready to do what he did for this town."

"Tell me everything you know about him."

Fillip Moss looked away from the glass counter filled with doughnuts and glanced over his shoulder at her. "Hey, Jones. What are you talking about?"

The word "Peter" sprang to her mouth, but she swallowed it. "The Pit Viper," said Fiona softly, hoping the other customers at Chance's Country Bakery wouldn't hear her.

Filip clicked his tongue. "Ah. Yeah, hold on. You want a doughnut?"

Once he'd gotten them coffees and himself a box of a dozen (a *dozen doughnuts, dear* God), Filip led Fiona to the picnic table farthest away from the local moms and other teenagers sitting outside in the crisp autumn morning. Fiona watched silently as he wolfed down two doughnuts in seconds. It didn't escape her that the last time she'd gone to Chance's had been with Horace, when they were in the throes of having just slept together and all was right in the world. Now, here she was watching a jock hesher pound frosted stomach cancer, wondering if her whole life was a lie.

Finally, after washing down his cheekfuls with a slug of coffee, Filip leaned forward and began speaking to Fiona in a conspiratorial whisper.

"So, some of my friends in middle school weren't from Hamm," he said. "Because of the outreach work my mom did, I got to know this crew of kids who went to school in McFerrett. They were super cool, but a lot of them were poor as shit, and they came from rough areas where there wasn't a town council. I didn't give a fuck; I thought it was awesome. They were hardcore, and good people, and taught me about stuff that didn't happen in Hamm. And they knew some of the guys who used to party at the old mill.

"Our parents just saw them as these invading hordes, but the Hamm club rats were these kids' siblings or their siblings' friends or whatever. Since a lot of them were poor, their older brothers and sisters were working the parties for extra cash—slinging pills and weed, sometimes selling sex or whatever." Her grimace must have broadcast a little louder than she had intended, because he pointed an irritated finger at her. "Yeah, not very pretty, I know, but these guys didn't grow up with families like ours, okay? They weren't doing charity trips on their Saturdays, they *were* the charity cases. All the stoner dudes from the city and the university wasting their parents' cash at the old mill on the weekends—that was their ticket out. Put together a big-enough wad and run away somewhere, start a life. It was good money, as far as bad money went."

He wolfed down another doughnut almost angrily. She made a point of keeping quiet, waiting until he was ready to talk again. Filip was spilling his guts, and it was taking something out of him.

"Anyway," he continued, calmed, "so I'm, what, nine? And the two kids, your cousin and that Geraldine Brookham chick, they OD. Our parents freak out. And I start overhearing my mom talking about how they're going to do something, put a stop to this. I'm too young to know what's up, I just know that there are dead kids and it's sad. So, then I hear her talking about someone called Pit Viper. I'm freaked out, because who the hell is called *Pit Viper*? Sounds like a bad guy.

"Then, the town clears up. My mom is all happy, and we start eating out on Main Street again. But then my mom does another community outreach thing in McFerrett, and she's there to talk about neighborhood watch or whatever, and there are all these people angry at my mom. They're saying she knows something about their kids just vanishing.

"So, I talk to this kid Jaime, who I was always really close with. I'm like, 'What happened?' and he's like, 'My brother's gone, the Pit Viper took him.' Now, Jaime's brother Keith was a bad dude, a real piece of shit honestly, so it wasn't like Jaime was too crushed about not getting beat up and called 'faggot' all the time. Besides, the kid's eight. But Jaime's mother is *pissed*. She keeps asking about that 'last party,' and my mom is doing a really bad job at sounding innocent. And I figured out that this Pit Viper guy had done something really bad, and maybe the Hamm town council had something to do with it.

"But that's not the end of it. Because Jaime's brother Keith? He was found *dead* a few months later. He and a bunch of the other people who disappeared. None of them were discovered nearby, of course, so there was nothing that could tie them to the old mill or Hamm or whatever. Ravers run away and OD all over the fucking place, right? But a bunch of those kids, not all of them but some of them, they died. The rest, I don't know. But as I got older, I got sort of curious about it. Where'd all the other kids go? Jaime was long gone, so I couldn't ask him, which sucks. Wish I knew where he got to. Anyway, it was obvious my mom didn't want to talk about it. So, I go online, do a late-night search fest. But it's like I told you: there's no public record of the old mill, even in the reports of local kids disappearing. The Pit Viper's nowhere to be found, which doesn't surprise me, but the old mill? Those parties were legendary, and it was where they found a deceased youth. But there's nothing. It's like the place never existed."

Filip devoured his fifth and sixth doughnuts and drained his coffee, like getting that big secret out into the open left a hole in his belly that he needed to fill. Fiona sat there with coffee cooling in her hand and mentally digested his story.

"Why haven't you told anyone this before?" she finally asked, feeling her stomach churn.

"Why do you think? Because it means my mom—" He sighed, shook his head, and rubbed his eyes. "Our families,

Jones…it means they were a part of this awful thing. When I finally asked my mom about it, she burst into tears and asked me to never tell anyone. Because they did it, Jones. I assume you know? Yeah, look at you, you know. They paid that dude, and he disappeared the club rats *somehow*. Anyway, my mom was racked with guilt. She figured they'd paid the guy to get rid of those kids, he'd done his job, it was over. It's all so shitty, you know? And now the Pit Viper's back, and everyone's so into him. And if they only knew…" He sat back and eyed Fiona, suddenly suspicious. "Why are *you* asking, anyway? What'd you find out?"

"I just remembered him from when we were kids," she said, deciding to keep her cards close to her chest for now. "After you mentioned there were no records of him online, I looked into him at the library and started to get creeped out. Figured I'd ask."

Fiona could see Filip's expression getting harder by the second. She had always assumed that his stonerdom had left him somewhat stupid, but his piercing gaze said otherwise. He didn't buy her bullshit story, and it made her anxious.

"That all?" he asked.

"Yeah," she said, uncomfortable under his eyes. "Look, I should go."

As she biked back to school, Fiona felt her skin crawl. It wasn't just Filip's campfire-story tone of voice, or the way he'd said that the club rats from the mill had shown up dead, or the way he'd seen right through her at the very end. It was something else he'd said, something that didn't fit right with what she knew for a fact.

She figured they'd paid the guy. He'd done his job. It was done.

Peter had never been paid. He'd said so at the winery sign. Fiona had always assumed it was a Hamm town council decision—send Robert, Edgar, and Darren to take care of things rather than give this creep their money. But if Harriet Moss thought he'd been paid, then her money had gone somewhere.

But where?

Fiona had a hunch. But it was the last thing she wanted to believe.

chapter 20

"Your father wants to talk to you after this."

Fiona glanced sidelong at her mother. Up until now, they'd driven to the city in total silence. Her dad had gone to the community center early, and Fiona was beginning to understand why. He probably didn't want to interact with her until they'd had their official fireside chat.

"I guess I'm in big trouble," was all she could think to say. Her mother exhaled slowly and loudly, and then said, "I don't know. He just wants to talk to you. You'll have to ask him."

"Ugh," said Fiona without meaning to. There was nothing more brutal than the passive-aggression, the loaded statements, the Big Talk looming in the distance. She'd had problems relating to her dad for years—nine years, to be exact—but her mother had never resorted to this in the past. "Look, Mom, I'm sorry for upsetting you the other night. But please, try and understand what I'm dealing with—"

"Let me tell you something, Fiona," said her mother, eyes glued to the road. "*You* don't understand a thing about what you're dealing with. You think it's easy raising a family in this world? Or trying to have a nice, simple life? Well, it's not. And honey, if you think for a second that you know what you're doing, or who your father is, then you're dead wrong."

Fiona felt anger stir the blood behind her face. Betty's absence that week had left her stranded; without a conduit for her emotions, they were just coming off her like ambient heat. "Do you know what he did? What Dad did to that boy?"

"I know *everything*," said her mom. "I know the stuff no one else knows. Anything you think would be a shocking revelation for me, I've known for years." Fiona sat back, wide-eyed. Her mom smiled cruelly and shook her head. "Fiona, I love you. You are everything in the world to me. But you really screwed up this time. Your problems are only just beginning."

Fiona stared out the window, feeling sullen and hollow. It was her first Saturday in a long time that wasn't full of joyful anticipation. She missed him so badly—his smell of sweat and wood, his muscular frame loping forward to meet her, the excitement in his eyes as he showed her a new page in the book. More than that, she missed being admired and revered. Everyone in her day-to-day slog through life in Hamm was treating her like a little girl caught with her hand in the cookie jar. She missed being seen as an artist, equal, and love interest. It had made her feel alive; now, she was a walking corpse.

They got to the community center and headed in silently. Caroline refused to look at Fiona as she put her apron on. Calvin waved to her, and it made her cringe; it was almost as if he was trying to be extra friendly to her now that her whole life was in shambles, perfectly poised to fill the void that he'd helped create by ratting her out. Only Filip Moss greeted her typically, but his expression was all too clear—he wanted to know what Fiona was hiding.

"How you holding up, Jones?" he asked, giving her a nudge with his elbow.

"I'm all right," she said casually, trying to laugh off her emotional strife, failing terribly. "Just got a lot on my mind."

"Yeah?" he asked, suddenly sounding less friendly, more intense. "Looks like something's eating you. Want to talk more?"

"I'm fine," she huffed and put some distance between them. She didn't want people seeing them, getting the wrong idea. And anyway, she absolutely did not want to talk about it.

When her father finally entered the room and stood up on a chair to address the gathered council, she was stunned. He looked terrible, in more ways than one. Sure, exhaustion hung on him visibly—dark rings around the eyes, hair slightly mussed, mouth half open with fatigue. But more than that, anger and suspicion lined his face. His eyes darted around the room as he spoke. For the first time ever, he genuinely seemed like he didn't want to be there.

"All right, guys, you know the drill," he said, his voice sounding haggard. "We're finishing our pledge pretty soon. Just keep up your spirits, be polite, and try not to spill anything hot. Don't want to send anyone to the burn ward." One or two people laughed half-heartedly, but most seemed to find the comment a little edgy, especially for Robert Jones. "Everyone ready? Good. Let's do this."

They got to work slower than usual. Fiona and Caroline were stationed together at hot liquids, handing out drinks along with packets of creamer and sugar. Fiona could see the hem of a green Pit Viper shirt poking out over the collar of her hoodie and heard her hum a melody to herself that Fiona recognized from the album.

For the first time in ages, Fiona wanted desperately to talk to her. When she'd started spending her weekends with Peter, Caroline was the easiest member of her crew to blow off. Her old friend was just too loud and self-important and *high school* to worry about offending. Now that she was feeling confused and alone, Fiona missed Caroline's boisterous attitude, the way it took all the bullshit out of the room.

"At least next Saturday will be the last one of these," mumbled Fiona.

Caroline tightened her mouth and stayed quiet.

"Any chance we can talk?" asked Fiona.

"I don't talk to strangers," said Caroline firmly.

Fiona sighed. So much for that. They shuffled around each other in silence for the rest of the morning.

The hours were painful, but as they neared the end of the charity breakfast, Fiona found herself trying to draw them out further so she wouldn't have to speak to her father. She wiped down tables she didn't need to and offered to help wash the trays, much to the surprise of the cleaning crew. Finally, she walked back into the dining room and discovered that she was one of only a handful of people left hanging around. Even the homeless guests were gone. There was no more hemming and hawing—she had to face the music that she didn't want to hear.

Robert Jones waited outside, staring at the sidewalk. In the naked light of day, there was nothing commanding or scary about her dad. He looked small and weak, dwarfed by the city around him; he kept his hands stuffed in his jacket pockets, and quick puffs of steam shot from his mouth. Every few seconds, he'd look up at the skyline and then say, "Hmm," and return his gaze to the concrete. Finally, Fiona swallowed hard, set her shoulders, and walked over to him.

"Hey," she said.

"Oh, hey," he responded, sounding like he wasn't expecting her, while his expression looked prepared, determined. "Let's talk. You hungry? I can never eat the food in there. Feels wrong when we're feeding people with real problems."

She was surprised by the offer and suddenly realized that she was ravenous. She'd felt sick with worry when she'd gotten up, so all she'd had was an apple before hopping in the car. "Yeah, actually. Want to head to Chance's or something?"

"No, let's stay here," he said. "As long as we're in the city. There's a deli around the corner with good knish. Have I ever given you a knish?"

"No. I've never had one."

"Oh, man. Come on."

He walked, and she flanked him, waiting for the icebreaker. She waited and waited, even as they entered a little bodega. The athletic twenty-something dude behind the counter lit up when he saw them enter and brushed down his stained apron with exaggerated debonairness.

"Robert, my man!" he cried. "Who's this? No way this is *the* Fiona."

"This is her," her dad said with a nervous laugh. "Fiona, this is Lon. Lon, Fiona."

"Fiona, it is the sincerest pleasure," said the guy, leaning over the counter and shaking her hand firmly. "I've heard so much about you. Your dad brags about you all the time. Says you're a killer guitarist. What do you play, funk? Rock? My brother used to date a rocker girl, but she was more goth. Wore tons of gunk on her face. You I'd peg as more of a New York hardcore chick. What're we having?"

Her dad got a mushroom knish, and she got plain. Lon heated up the knishes and handed them over the counter with a smile. Her dad tipped him an extra three bucks, about which he made a big show of thanking Robert Jones profusely. "I didn't know you had friends around here," she said as they walked out of the deli.

"He's not really my friend, just a nice guy," said Robert, shrugging. "And Lon's good people. I always tell him he

should move to Hamm after school, but he's not interested."
He cleared his throat and looked at his knish. "It's always
been about good people, you know?"

Her dad picked a stoop about a block down and carefully
lowered himself onto it. Fiona sat beside him, feeling more
confused than ever. She'd never pictured Robert Jones eating
lunch on a stoop or cracking wise with the deli guy. He was
supposed to be closed-minded, almost a redneck. It bothered
her to consider that he probably knew more about the city
than she did.

They munched on their knishes for a bit—hers was damn
good, but his smelled better, and she regretted not being
adventurous—until Fiona was too impatient to wait for him
any longer.

"I'm sorry about what I said the other night," she started.
"I was just upset."

Her dad didn't reply for a bit, but then went straight to
the point: "How much do you know?"

She sighed. *Here we go.* "I watched the meeting where
he made his presentation to the council," she said. "And I
followed you out to the winery sign and watched you and
Edgar and..." She went silent. It suddenly felt too horrible
to say.

She waited for his authoritative rage, but it never came.
When she finally glanced over at him, she nearly cried. Her
father looked so heartbroken. His eyes and mouth were both
downturned, and he chewed at his upper lip nervously.

Fiona had been villainizing him all week; hell, she'd been
doing it for nine years. It hadn't occurred to her until now
that his secrets were eating away at him inside like a cancer
of the soul.

"I'm sorry you had to see all that," he said.

"Me, too," she said, feeling a catch in her voice. Her

accusatory conviction began to falter. She wanted to hug him, but forced herself not to.

"That all?" he asked.

"I found out that everyone gave you the money to pay him off," she said. "But you didn't. Did you?"

Her father softly shook his head. He picked off a bit of his knish and tossed it to a nearby pigeon, chuckling humorlessly as the bird grabbed it and waddled away. Then he sat back against the stair behind them and ran a hand through his hair. "I need you to please, please put yourself in my shoes for a second, Fiona."

"Okay," she said, determined to be fair. "Shoot."

"Imagine you have a sister," he said calmly. "I know you always wanted one, so picture her, the sister you didn't get because we had our hands full with you. You and your sister grow up together, and she's always a little silly. While you spend your weekends working in the city, she spends them going out on Main Street in Hamm, safe and sound. She doesn't know anything about the real world. But you go along with it, because she's so sweet that, well, why not be silly? If she's that wonderful, she's allowed to be careless. Leave the hard work to us humps.

"So, your sister, she has a son, your nephew, who's just great but is even sillier and more careless than she is. And you watch this sweet boy grow up, and you're always a little worried because you've seen some things that have taught you that the world isn't nice to sweet people like him. And then he gets old enough to drive, and he starts getting mixed up with all sorts of bad people and bad behaviors…and then you get a call at three in the morning, from your sweet, silly sister, because her sweet, silly boy didn't come home. And when the police go out looking for him, they find him dead."

Fiona put a hand to her mouth to hold in the sobs.

The city around them seemed to hush a bit after her dad's last word, as though it was suddenly interested in his story. She wrapped the foil back around her remaining knish. The half she'd eaten now sat in her stomach like an anvil.

Her father closed his eyes, took a deep breath, and then opened them again, staring out at the sidewalk like he could see his checkered past chiseled in it.

"And all you want is to help her," he said. "You want to do anything, anything at all, to punish the people who did this, who...invaded your sweet, silly life with their big, ugly world. You forget the beautiful things, the good people and the fun nights, and all you see is you and *them*. So you pray for an answer. You pray for something, anything. And then one day, you're drunk and you're talking to a bartender in the city, and Satan himself sits down next to you."

She clenched her eyes and remembered Peter's words from nine years ago. *You made a deal with the devil, the time to pony up came, and you chumps didn't have a soul among the lot of you.*

"This...*fiend*, he's overheard your story, and he has all the answers," continued her father. "And you're a mess. So, you agree to his terms. And by the time you've signed your name in blood, you realize what he has in store. And it won't help. It'll leave more families without their sons and daughters. But it's too late. The deed is done. So, you figure you have two options: tell everyone who's counting on you, including your sweet little sister, that you only did greater harm...or hide it. You tell them that everything worked out, that you just handled it. You call in every favor you're owed, and you wipe all the evidence of this horrible truth from the lives of the people around you. And you tell your friends, and your community, you tell them all, *It's okay. What happened there was just a horrible mistake, but we took care of it. All is right in the world. Forget it ever happened.*"

As he finished, his voice cracked and a tear dropped from the corner of his eye, hitting the arm of his jacket with a *pat*.

Fiona did her best to hold down the gorge in her throat. She'd expected raised voices and denials and threats, but not this. Not her father quietly falling apart next to her. She'd always thought that the perfect exterior her dad presented the world was hiding the dark side she'd seen that night by the winery sign. Instead, it was the exact opposite—her loving, big-hearted father had been forced into ruthlessness to deal with the horrors beyond his front door.

"What did you do with the council's money?" she finally asked.

"Most of it we used to bribe people at the newspapers and police precinct," he said, wiping at his eyes. "We made sure that no one would ever be able to tie the disappearances to Hamm. Your aunt got a nice chunk of it, and the Brookhams got the same amount. Mostly to cover funeral costs and let your uncle Warren take some time off work to mourn."

"That all?"

Her father swallowed. "The rest...it was only eight thousand each," he said. "Edgar, Darren, and I split it. For their help...and their silence."

Fiona felt her guts churn and her temples pound. "You stole from the council," she said, trying to make sense of it. "The economy had just crashed, people were having a hard time surviving...and you stole from them."

"Do you think I used that money on beer and cigarettes?" he said. He glanced at her, saw the wisecrack had belly flopped, and continued. "That eight grand helped fund two Hamm council Halloween parades, two Main Street food festivals, and a junior high carnival. The people on the town council, they're good people, but they wouldn't give us that money to do those things, Fiona. Instead, they gave it to the devil to kidnap a bunch of kids. And I wasn't going to allow that monster the satisfaction. So, I used it to do the right thing instead. I made him go away, and I buried that horrible thing in our past. That's what you have to understand, Fiona, it's *always* been for the good of Hamm."

"What about Edgar and Darren?" she said. "What did they do with their money?"

Her dad shrugged. "I don't know. That wasn't my business."

"Dad," she said, trying to keep her breathing regular, "how could you?"

"Sweetheart—" He seemed to think better of being sentimental with her. "Fiona. Listen to me. This is never going to be something I'm proud of. But you need to know that the people in our town, I love them with all my heart, but they're weak. They've never needed to fight for anything before. So, when the people here, who know how to fight"—he waved his arm out at the city—"when they show up and do whatever they want, there needs to be someone to take charge. The last time I just let things slide, people came into Hamm who did us harm. So, I did what it took to get rid of them."

"By stealing from our friends," she said, feeling her eyes finally water up.

"If I told them what we actually did, they wouldn't trust me," he said. He was trying to stay calm, but more fat tears were pouring down his cheeks by the minute. "And there was no way he'd do it for free, out of kindness." He finally looked up at her with his bloodshot eyes, full of insecurity and fear. "You were telling the truth, weren't you? You're seeing him."

"He's been… We've become close," she said. "I met him the night you… At the winery sign. I gave him some food and water. He remembered me, and when he showed up at a party in Hamm last month, we began talking. He's teaching me things."

Robert Jones closed his eyes and groaned. "Teaching you what?"

"We've been studying music together," she said. Technically true.

"Fiona," he said, "I'm not going to pretend that you being… with boys is something wrong. You're young, it's natural, I get that. And I understand he seems interesting. Hell, he seemed interesting to me when I first met him. But that man…he's evil. He did something *evil* to those poor kids…"

The way he said "man" showed Fiona the kind of character he hoped to elicit in her mind: the Pit Viper as a mad genius, stubble on his chin, knife in his boot, craving his ill-begotten cash. But when she replaced her father's demonic ideal with Peter, her Peter, who believed in her talent and respected her freedom and seemed so in tune with everything around him, she couldn't make sense of her father's story. Maybe he'd made some mistakes, but Peter was no simple villain.

And anyway, neither was Robert Jones. He was right—the council only gave a damn about Hamm when their normal lives were violated. Maybe they'd needed a lie. Maybe her father had done the right thing.

Fiona felt her body hitch with sobs as tears ran hot down her face. The truth from her father had put things in perspective…but that had only made them worse. Her heart and mind felt like ill-fitting puzzle pieces, and her gut was nowhere in sight. She wished Peter was there to hold her, then immediately felt sick with regret at the instinct.

"I need to go," she sobbed, standing. "I need to think about this."

"Please, Fiona, wait," he said, dropping his knish and grabbing her arm. "Don't go to him. Please, I know I'm not a good man, but I can't lose you. I did this, all of this, for you and our family—"

She wrenched free from him and marched down the streets, weeping as she walked. The last time she looked back, her dad was watching her go, wearing the ashen and uncomprehending face of a man who'd been stabbed by his best friend. No one in the city around him seemed to notice his tears.

chapter
21

This time, she was determined to find his place herself. No phone calls, no shepherding. She was going to get to him if it killed her, carried on the chaos in her heart alone.

She kept rehearsing it in her mind. *Run away with me.* Four words that summed up the great rock-and-roll dream— leaving the old life behind, reinventing yourself on the road, holding on to nothing but each other. Forget college, and Hamm, and the simple future she had lying ahead of her. They'd go to California, because that was where musicians ran away to, the land of hot days in the practice studio and long nights on the stage. She knew the actual undertaking was probably more complicated than she could imagine—there were going to be cops they'd have to dodge and shitty motels they'd have to suffer through, maybe even a rat-infested squat or two—but it was about time she went for it. She wasn't long for Hamm, anyway. She'd known that for ages. And besides, she was quickly learning that what little of her small-town upbringing she thought she knew was all a miserable conspiracy in the name of normalcy.

But Peter made her feel different. An equal, someone who didn't hold her back but only pushed her to be better. Fiona would sell the farm for that.

She made it to the crossword puzzle of warehouses before she got lost. She would recognize specific structures—the placement of loading-dock doors, the way paint was peeling on block-long brick walls—and feel a sense of relief wash over her, only to discover that same design or appearance two blocks down. She would turn corners and find nothing but dead ends and alleys splitting off them. The few other wanderers she ran into were raggedy street people who eyed her angrily and hunched their shoulders.

For the longest time, she wondered if she was even in the right neighborhood, the right city, the right mind. Then, out of nowhere, Fiona turned a corner and saw a tag in silver paint: 'sounds.'

The letters seemed to lean in a direction, the final *S* dragging off like it was sprayed while the artist was being yanked away. She followed its lead and saw another 'sounds' on a door across the street, leaning toward a nearby intersection.

She followed the tags, finding them painted on different parts and heights of the buildings around her. Every new 'sounds' seemed to be written like an arrow, one part of the final letter stretching off, pointing her to the next scrawled word.

She didn't realize how close she was until she turned a corner and saw Peter a few yards away, standing outside of the door to his loft. The guy from the club, PM, was across from him, sucking down a cigarette and nodding along to the words Peter was saying that Fiona couldn't hear.

Something about the look on Peter's face stopped Fiona dead in her tracks and canceled the greeting she was about to call to him. There wasn't a trace of the guy she cared about there, but the cold, hard gaze of his alter ego. Her father's description came to her mind, and while Peter didn't exactly look like the devil himself, his unblinking eyes certainly suggested sinister intentions.

Peter nodded PM in her direction, and she had barely enough time to duck into a doorway before they came past her, so close that she caught a whiff of him that made her heart ache with memories of their past Saturdays, of the lighthouse and the book and the hours spent inches away from each other at all times.

"How long will he be there?" asked Peter in an icy voice.

"Forty minutes, no more," said PM.

"Hmm," said Peter. "Well, let's get there fast, then."

Once they were a block away from her, Fiona crept out of the doorway and followed them. She knew she should alert him to her presence, or even just go grab Betty and wait for him, but suddenly she was curious to see Peter when he didn't know she was around. His face, his tone of voice, it all suggested that he was on his way to some serious business. That, along with her father's confession, left her wondering what was going on, who he really was.

The farther they walked, the more decrepit and vile the buildings became around them. The clinical warehouses of Peter's neighborhood gave way to burned-out hovels and vacant lots full of rubble. Everything was strewn with fluttering trash and tie-dyed rotten yellow with water damage. A distant sloshing sound and a thick septic stink made Fiona think there was some sort of open sewer or murky canal nearby. Whatever the men were doing in this neighborhood, she knew it couldn't be good.

Finally, they reached a half-crumbled brownstone in the middle of a weed-choked lot. Though in total disrepair, the molding and ironwork around its stoop suggested that it had once been nice. A plaque set in the wall next to the stoop read, the Offices of Manute and, but the remainder was destroyed.

Peter and PM stalked up the stoop and into the doorless entryway. Once they were swallowed by shadow, Fiona snuck after them.

Inside, the building was disgusting and terrifying, full of rot and darkness. The floors were sticky beneath Fiona's feet, and a smell of piss and the wrong kinds of mushrooms hung in the air. She listened for Peter's footsteps, then realized they were gone, absorbed by the house. Slowly she crept down a hallway, toward a set of stairs.

Closer to the stairs, there was a door, and Fiona looked in to see if Peter had branched off there. The moment she poked her head in, the stench of stomach acid made her nostrils burn, and she reared back and coughed. Against one wall, barely visible in the light coming in from the half-smashed window, huddled a man and a woman, their eyes twinkling wide and hungry out of their emaciated faces. A third person was splayed out in the center of the floor, a puddle of liquid around their head. Fiona couldn't tell if it was a he or she.

"Oh God," she said, and then realized the horrible impropriety, and, worse, how publicly she had just declared that she didn't belong here. "Sorry," she mumbled and turned to leave, to flee this awful place.

From up the stairs, she heard Peter's voice.

Each step creaked and groaned under her feet, but none of them loudly enough to alert anyone, until she was at another hallway, not quite as repulsive. As she moved toward the doorway from which the conversation emanated, Fiona heard others along with Peter, mainly a deep, oily voice in an accent she couldn't quite place.

"And has it been as fulfilling as you'd hoped?" asked the voice, sounding a little tired, maybe even pissed off.

"So far," said Peter's. "But I'm not done yet. It's not enough to just have them love me. The final blow is necessary."

Despite her pounding heart and the sweat beading on her forehead, Fiona felt cold inside when she heard those words. She pressed herself flat against the wall adjacent to the doorway and peeked around the corner.

The room was dark, but the milky light slicing in-between the boards on its windows illuminated decaying murals on the walls, pictures of cypress trees and swans. Close to the door stood Peter and PM, their backs to her; Peter stood rigid, but PM hunched and shifted like a stray dog. Across from them were two figures; one was the towering acne-riddled guy Fiona had spotted at the club, wearing a pool-blue windbreaker. The central figure, meanwhile, was an older man in a pearl-colored suit with carefully combed black hair and wrinkles that seemed to flow together. He was short, but broad all over—broad shoulders, broad face, and a broad grin full of yellow teeth that he gritted intermittently, as though he ached somewhere. If Peter was a Pit Viper, she thought, then this guy was a poisonous toad.

"Oh, I'm well aware," said the squat man. "This isn't happening without a tribute. I don't need to remind you that you could be out working right now, bringing in real results, you know, instead of following this, eh, passion project. You're lucky that Hunter and Ericka are doing so well, otherwise this, this would be kaput. Bam, done, over."

"I just need a little more time," said Peter, voice firm but submissive. "Things are coming together. I promise you it'll be worth it."

The man cleared his throat with an ugly sound. "Yeah, well. Time I can give you. You ever find out the ratio? Just curious."

A pause, and Peter said, "I'd say about 57 percent of them will be female."

"Good," cooed the man. "Better than half, always good. Well, great, just, throw the party sooner rather than later, please?"

"Right now, the plan is Halloween," said Peter.

"Halloween's fine. I can wait that long."

"Thank you, Udo," said Peter. "I appreciate it. Really."

"Okay, okay," sighed the man, Udo apparently. "Anyway. Bill here—" He nodded to the huge figure at his side. "He said you had a special favor to ask of me. Have to admit, given how much I'm doing so far, the thought doesn't make me very excited. What's up?"

Peter's shoulders heaved as he took a deep breath in and out. "When this is over, I need passage for two."

"Two?" asked Udo. "What, are you keeping one of them for laughs?" A pause, deathly silent. "It's not a woman, is it?"

Fiona felt a chill stab through her. Her breath caught. Even without a view of his face, she could sense Peter easing up. "I think I've found someone," he said, almost pleading.

"Jesus, it *is*," said Udo, holding his palms up as if to Heaven. "Pete, kid, you're *killing me* here. What have I told you, a dozen times? Do I gotta remind you about *my* marriage?"

"She's different," said Peter.

Tell them how, thought Fiona. *Let them know.*

"Help me."

She barely had time to look toward the voice before ravenous fingers bit into the flesh of her arm.

The woman from downstairs clutched Fiona desperately. Her bloodshot eyes gleamed with glassy want; her papery lips quivered. This close, Fiona could smell her, sour dried pee and musty bad teeth. She reared back, but the woman pulled harder, and pressed her bony frame against Fiona's arm hard enough that she could feel every rib in the woman's chest.

"Please help me," gibbered the woman in a hoarse voice.

"I'll do whatever you want, anything. I don't need much. Just a little money, just some help. Please, anything you want, *just please help me—*"

Fiona wrenched against the woman's grip, but her hands refused to budge. She cried out and reared back a hand to strike her, and just like that the filthy woman gasped, went rigid, and bolted off into the shadows of the house.

Fiona barely had time to collect herself before a new hand closed around the back collar of her shirt and yanked her hard enough to give her whiplash.

She was swung in a wide arch and then let go; for a moment, she was airborne, and then she crashed hard on her side, scraping her hand on the rocky grit that peppered the floor.

Fiona scrambled to her hands and knees. She was crouched in the center of the meeting, with all eyes on her. PM's mouth hung open, his eyes vinyl-wide as they glanced between her, Peter, the older man, and back again. The big guy with the acne, the one who'd grabbed her, lumbered back over to her with a look of cool disgust and threw a shadow over her cowering form.

But worst of all was when she locked eyes with Peter. He glared down at her not with rage or embarrassment, but surprise and disappointment, as though he'd expected more from her. In his gaze, all her resolve and cleverness evaporated, and she wanted to crawl to him, to apologize and weep at his feet and beg him to take her back to his place.

But the tension in the room told her not to move. This was serious trouble here—not parent or school trouble, life trouble. Acting out of instinct was the wrong way to play this.

After a few seconds of silence, the old guy sighed heavily. "Well, obviously, this is a problem." He looked up at Peter, face twisted in annoyance. "Anyone you know?" Peter's eyes never left her. "Right. Bill, pick her up."

The pimpled giant started toward her, and Peter yelled, "Wait!"

"That's what I thought," groaned Udo, waving Bill back. "Jesus, Pete, this her? This your lady you're trying to book an exit trip for? Because you know this speaks poorly both of her character and your judgment. Please, I beg of you, say or do something that will make me less, eh, *alarmed* by what I'm seeing here."

"Fiona's cracking the third section of the book," said Peter. The old guy raised his eyebrow, and then, slowly, looked down at Fiona. She could barely see his eyes tucked into the wrinkled folds of his face, but they sparkled out at her eventually, hard and black.

"Is that right?" he asked her.

"Yes," she said in a soft, faltering voice. She tried to stand, but Bill leaned in and grabbed her by the shoulder to shove her back down. Udo held up a hand, and the huge man let go of Fiona and stepped back, letting her rise to her feet.

The old man regarded her for a moment then extended his hand. "Udo Platt. A pleasure."

"Fiona Jones," she said, taking the dry hand in hers and shaking it.

"Pretty name," he said. "Pretty name for a pretty girl. So, you're working with the sheet music, huh? That's something. That's *new*. What do you play, flute? Lyre?"

"Electric guitar."

The man laughed in his throat and shook his head. "That's for ugly British guys, cupcake. You sure you don't want to try another book? Got plenty better suited for women. Maybe *Le Livre de la Vermine*, or a Warden's handbook?"

"You should hear me play," she said, trying to sound tough against the overwhelming terror that she'd never leave this room alive, that Peter wouldn't, either. "Well, I can't wait," he said, folding his hands over his paunch. "And you're from this town our mutual friend's all hung up on, this little suburb, with the mill and the whatnot? I'm surprised you're kosher with what Pete's got planned for all of them. You one of those kids who hates her parents?"

What? Fiona's mind raced for a snappy answer but came up with nothing. She took a quick look at Peter, who stared at the floor and clenched his fists at his sides.

"Oh, she doesn't know?" said Udo with a smile. "Wonderful. Rich. Listen, Pete, why don't you have a little talk with your lady friend and get back to me on how many people you want on your reservation. Meantime, be careful. And you, young lady, good luck with your, ah, music lessons." He smiled and then flicked his fingers at them. "That's all. Beat it."

chapter 22

The air outside still stank of refuse and sewage, but Fiona gulped it down as they burst out of the door and onto the street. Peter marched purposefully but silently next to her; he didn't need to say anything, given the rage coming off him in waves. PM, meanwhile, wasn't so reserved.

"Are you fucking kidding me, dude?" He swooped in front of Peter and blocked his path. "What are we doing, Viper? You do realize what just happened in there, right? That we almost *died*, that, that Udo and Bill Blemish nearly murdered us and buried us in the basement of this fucking house, *right*? All because the cooze who I've been fucking *warning you about* for fucking *weeks on end* decided to *follow us —*"

"Watch your mouth, Perry," said Peter. "And get out of my way."

"For *this*?" laughed Perry, jabbing a finger at Fiona. "Over some small-town chick who you had a precious moment with? Christ, *I'll* give you an apple if it'll make you listen to me over common fucking sense! She followed you! For all we know, she's a cop!"

"That's not true!" choked Fiona, shaking with fear. "Peter, I would never—"

"Shut the fuck up, whore!" PM laughed. "Like we'll believe a thing you—"

His snarky voice cut off in a squawk as Peter seized him by the throat. Fiona felt her anger and annoyance blown away by a cold inner wind as she watched Peter draw the scared man in close and stare him down with blank, dead eyes. Maybe it was only emotional suggestion, but she swore she felt a ripple in the air like those she'd sensed during the tuning, as if Peter had given off a small wave of sound without monitor or book to aid him.

"I told you to watch your language," he said. PM tried to twist from his grip, but Peter gave him a sharp throttle, and the man put up his hands in surrender. "Don't call her anything like that again. Understand? You just do your job and be ready on the thirty-first." Then he let go, and PM went storming off down the street, shaking his head and grumbling as he went.

She and Peter walked back to his place in silence, both obviously reviewing in their minds what had happened and waiting until they were alone to say what they really wanted to say. As the buildings returned from squalor to simple geometry, as he threw open the door to his place with a *bang*, as they climbed the stairs two at a time and marched down the aisle of lost sounds, they remained silent.

Once in his corner, he walked over to Betty's case and gave it a hard shove with the heel of his sneaker. It slid across the floor with a leathery hiss.

"Take it and get out," he said.

"I'm sorry I followed you," she began, trying to remain calm.

"I bet you are," he laughed, rolling his head back and

looking up at the ceiling. The words stabbed her between the ribs. "I bet you're just racked with remorse."

"But it sounds like I had *good reason* to!" she said, her voice cracking. "You're arranging passage for me? With *that* guy, who acted like all this power you've got and the potential you see in me is, what, some kind of tool, or weapon?"

"You don't even know what you're talking about," he said. "Udo gave me the *Canoris*. He funds my experiments and training—this, all this." He waved his arm across the room. "All the luxuries you've enjoyed these past couple of weeks—"

"All I enjoyed was *you*," she cried, and now she couldn't help it. The fear she'd sensed in that shadowy house, the story her dad had laid on her, the loneliness she'd felt all week without him, it broke through the dam. Tears rushed down her cheeks, and she wailed at him. "None of this matters to me at all without you!"

"Then why'd you leave, Fiona?" he snapped. "We tune, we *finally* sleep together, and then you leave! What was I supposed to think?"

"That I was scared!" she sobbed. "That I needed to figure out the rest of my life! My mom was freaking out when I spent the night here, calling the police!" She swallowed hard and forced herself to bare it all. "You keep telling me I'm better than the people I grew up around, but...but in a lot of ways, I *am* those people. I *am* a small-town girl. So this, the book, your power, *you*, it's new! It's scary! So I ran home, yeah, because I was *freaking out*. If you care about me, you need to care about *that*. You can't just expect me to drop everything and everyone I know in an instant."

He paused as she wept and then said, "What if you could?"

"What?" she asked. When she looked up and wiped her eyes, he was staring at her, thinking, planning.

"What if it could all be different in one night?" he said.

"What if you could leave everything behind, and it could just be us?"

"What are you talking about?" she said.

He went to his desk and retrieved a piece of paper that he thrust into her hands.

It was a flyer. At the top was a black shadow, out of which slithered the silhouette of a snake, its forked tongue flickering. The reptile made the *I* in the second word scrawled in large letters beneath:

PIT VIPER
HALLOWEEN
THE OLD MILL
GET THERE BEFORE 9PM
DON'T TALK ABOUT IT
DON'T EMAIL ABOUT IT
JUST BE THERE
SCHONERPLATZ SCHONERTAG

Her hands shook as she looked between him and the flyer and back again. "This…this is what you were talking about with Udo," she said.

"It is," he said.

"What…" Slowly, it came together in her head, the melody and the rhythm of his meaning finally matching up. "You're going to take them. You're going to take them like you took the club rats."

"It's what I came here for," said Peter softly. "It's what I'm owed."

"And…do what?" she asked, remembering Filip Moss's story, the way he'd told her that Jaime's brother was *found dead*. "Are you going to kill them?"

"No," he said. "I told you, that's not what I do. I'm wiping them clean, that's all. Taking their minds, their wills."

"And then you'll just, what, give them to that slimy cretin in there?" she said. "Do they end up like that woman who grabbed me? Violated and addicted and alone?"

He screwed up his face, and she knew right then that she'd hit it on the mark. Still, he fought not to crush her entirely.

"It's none of my concern what happens to them after that. What matters is what happens to us."

"You *can't*," she repeated. "Look, I'm so, *so* sorry for what my father and those men did to you. You know I am. But these kids, your fans, they're good people. You can't just brainwash them and sell them off—"

"*Good people?*" he said, disgust in his voice. "Do you even hear what you're saying? Those people stiffed me, and beat me, and left me for dead. You're the only one who cared about me, the only one who has any strength among them, but when the going gets tough you're the same as them. You retreat to this sheepish sentimentality, to Hamm and your mommy and daddy and weak-minded friends who are all too ready to jump onto the next fad or trend and then pay someone to kill it if it gets out of hand. You're better than them, you *know* you're better than them, but you treat them like they *should* be your equals. Why? Why humor that weakness?"

"They're just scared," she squeaked out, remembering her father's face. "Like me."

"Scared," he said, like the word tasted bad. "Scared enough to call me in to do their dirty work and scared enough to have me assaulted afterward." For a moment, his veneer of strength faltered, and he was no one but Peter, her Peter. "I was scared that night, Fiona. I walked for *miles*, wondering if I would ever have the strength to overcome what your dad did to me. And all I had to hold on to was an apple, some water, and the thought that there was someone different out there, who wasn't scared of me. By the time I got to a phone, I was stronger that I'd ever been, stronger than any tuning could make me. And I told myself I'd come back and show these people what their weakness gets them."

Fiona heard the scrape in his voice, felt the shiver in his grip. As tough as he was trying to be, he was breaking down.

She could see the human being inside him through the cracks in his demeanor. Suddenly, all she wanted was to not let the world ruin that person the way it had ruined everyone else in her life.

"Let's leave," she said, advancing toward him. "Right now. Let's just go away."

He blinked, stunned, and then shook his head furiously. "You fled from me twice, Fiona. Last time was too much for me. I can't trust you now."

"Please," she said, taking his hands in hers. "I promise, I'm not scared anymore. Tell Udo it didn't work out, and we leave. You, me, and a couple of bags. We'll leave all of this." She felt herself shaking now, too, and launched herself desperately into the dream, hoping it would work. "California. We'll go to L.A., and we'll get a shitty apartment together, and it'll just be us and our music. No small towns or gross benefactors, just our potential, together. No revenge. Let's just leave."

Peter's shoulders lowered slowly. His lips quivered, his eyes shone. His hands tightened on her, and he began drawing her close to him—

"I knew it!"

Both their heads snapped up, and they leaped out of each other's embrace.

A few feet away, Edgar Hokes grinned malevolently, a tire iron clutched in his hand.

chapter
23

"Mr. Hokes," said Fiona, reaching out a hand, "put that down."

"I knew it," repeated Edgar Hokes, pointing the tire iron at Peter. "I knew you'd be back, you little shit."

Peter looked from Edgar to Fiona, face twisted in outrage. "Is this why you followed me?" he whispered. "Is this your big plan all along? Finish what your father started?"

"I swear, I have no idea how he got here—"

Peter stormed away from her, heading to his desk. She scrambled after him.

"Please, Peter, you've got to believe me! I had nothing to do with this!"

"Get over here, buddy!" shouted Edgar Hokes, his face reddening as he stormed toward them. "You think we were joking when we told you what would happen if you came back to my town? This is long overdue."

Fiona turned and ran to Edgar, hoping to keep herself between the two men before things went entirely ass-up. "Mr. Hokes, stop it, okay? You need to put that tire iron down and just listen—"

Edgar grabbed a handful of her hair, and she cried out as hot needles stabbed into her scalp. He wrenched her head back hard enough that her knees buckled beneath her, and she hung from his grip. Through the pain, she recognized that she'd always known Edgar had this in him, but seeing it—feeling it tearing her hair out at the roots—was horrifying. What was about to happen?

"You just wait, skank," spat Edgar, staring down at her with a look of triumph on his flat face. "Your father believed you, my Calvin believed you, but you didn't fool me for a goddamned *second*. I knew you were trouble on two legs. When I'm done with your boyfriend, I'm going to teach you some manners and make sure your father knows exactly what kind of daughter he rais—"

Sound hit them both like an uppercut.

Edgar let go of Fiona with a shout, and they both slapped their hands to their ears. The tire iron tumbled to the floor, but Fiona couldn't hear its clatter over the noise. Music, tangible in its volume, throttled the room. Every speaker in the loft unleashed a flood of sonic power.

Peter stood at his turntable, watching the master copy spin. Though the whole room shook in Fiona's vision, he stayed perfectly still.

For Fiona, covering her ears helped, though she could still feel the vibrations deep in her marrow. But Edgar wasn't used to Peter's music and wasn't so lucky—he stumbled to his knees, his eyes and teeth clenched tight. Foam dotted his lips, and the veins in his temples swelled until they looked like fingers under his skin. Finally, he lurched forward, his hands falling away to reveal trickles of red coming out of each ear.

All at once, the music stopped. Peter returned his record to its sleeve and walked calmly over to them. In him, Fiona saw no signs of the person who'd held her and kissed her. The cracks in his persona were sealed, and the brightness in his eyes wasn't the possibility of tears, only hardened mania.

Peter was gone.

The Pit Viper squatted down in front of Edgar Hokes and peered at him as one would at an insect in a glass case.

"You know," he said in a soft voice, "even though three men beat me that night, I always remembered you as the mean one." Then he stood up straight and walked over to Fiona. After silently observing her, he exhaled slowly and carefully. "I'd tell you to leave, but I know I don't have to," he said. "It's what you do." And then he turned his back on her.

She lifted Edgar Hokes the same way she'd lifted Horace that night in the city, with one arm over her shoulders. But the older man weighed at least a Horace and a half, and by the time she'd lugged him down the stairs and piled him into his car, her collar was damp with sweat.

Fiona drove the Hokes family SUV carefully, riding the brake. She had her license and wasn't terrible behind the wheel—she'd grown up in a small town, driving lessons had been a social necessity, even if she spent every cent she ever earned on a guitar instead of a car—but she found driving while sobbing difficult, and the last thing she needed was for the cops to pull over an ordinary speeder and discover a weeping unlicensed teenager with a bleeding, incoherent man in the passenger seat. The highway was terrifying, but Edgar's GPS saved her life and got her back to Hamm in one piece. The entire drive, Hokes just moaned and rolled his head back and forth in the seat next to her. Once again, she was reminded of Horace tripping his face off, mumbling his stoned visions into her ear on the train.

Obviously, Peter had grown stronger since then. Horace had only had his mind blown by the power the DJ had wielded, and he'd been under chemical suggestion. Edgar Hokes might have had his eardrums ruptured.

By the time she finally reached the Hokeses' house, Edgar's hair had turned white. She gagged and reared back, repulsed by the sight of it. She left the car in the driveway, rang the doorbell, and ran through the backyards of town.

A few yards away from her family's house, the weight of it all slammed into her, and she put her hands on her knees, caught her breath, and wept.

She'd lost him. She knew that. For a moment, they had been unstoppable, beautiful and mysterious and actually learning to love someone like each other—and just like that, her father was right, and everything else was dead. Peter, the person she'd come to know and believe in, was gone, leaving only the snake from his album cover behind.

Even if he didn't feel betrayed by her, what she'd overheard in that hovel in the city meant she couldn't trust him. Fiona would get a way out, but Udo demanded a tribute. More than half female to male, always good. Kidnapping her friends and avenging himself on the people she loved had always been Peter's plan. She was just an unexpected bonus, and now he considered her nothing more than another busted amp in his graveyard, an emotional conduit that proved it couldn't follow through on what he asked of it.

That wasn't the Peter she'd known. Or worse, it was, and she'd overlooked it because of how he'd made her feel. In reality, it didn't matter anymore. She'd had the crushing truth shown to her in no uncertain terms. If she ignored it, she was looking the other way willingly. If she accepted it, the world broke her heart yet again.

Once she got back to her silent, miserable house, she sat on her bed and wondered what she was going to do. Maybe her classmates had seemed pathetic and weak to her, just like Peter had said they were, but they didn't deserve this. It wasn't their fault that the Hamm town council had called in some mercenary to deal with their problems, or that her father and two other men had robbed all of Hamm to keep the money out of his hands. They didn't even realize they were being affected by his music; for all they knew, they'd just found an incredible new album, a modern classic. Peter's vengeance was going on over their heads.

Originally, the idea of being elevated above her classmates had made Fiona feel special, but now that she saw what was at stake, she just wanted to be one of them again. She wanted to keep the people around her from getting hurt.

And Peter...

She hugged herself tightly and shook her head to no one in particular. She wasn't sure how she would deal with him, but he had to be stopped. If the look in his eyes when Edgar Hokes appeared was to be believed, he was too powerful and too angry to be left alone with the hopes that he'd go back on his plan.

She needed to do something. But what? Who could she turn to? Who would believe her insane story, or understand her without judging her?

There were two rings, and then a belch of double bass drums and guttural screams filled the line. It quieted quickly, and a voice said, "Hello?"

"Filip, it's Fiona," she said.

"Finally," said Filip. "What up, Jones, what'd you find out?"

"We need to stop him," she said.

chapter
24

The crowds filing into Hamm High looked readier for St. Patrick's Day than Halloween. But it wasn't Irish green, Dropkick Murphys green, being rocked on every shirt and messenger bag. It was its own shade, a neon green that had swallowed the color palette of the school whole. Pit Viper green.

Fiona sneered from the cab of Filip Moss's truck. Normally, Halloween was one of her favorite holidays, a chance to listen to a lot of Rob Zombie, hand out candy to tiny Avengers, and go to a party wearing Alice Cooper face paint. This year, though, it felt wrong, and she knew why. All the cutout ghosts and pumpkins in the world couldn't wipe away Peter's stranglehold on Hamm's teens. His presence was like a shadow stretched across her town, dark and long and impossible to get a firm grip on before it slithered away and you were left frightened as to where it might turn up next.

The secrecy that the party flyer commanded had been taken as law—Fiona would only catch muddled snippets of conversation or find shreds of torn-up flyer on the stairwell floor. The green shirts everyone was rocking were only revealed or put on at school, probably to keep parents from knowing about the plans that were in the works for Saturday. Fiona couldn't pin down any gossip, especially with how she'd been acting lately. She only knew it was happening. They were talking about him, the Pit Viper, her Peter—

"Jones! Hey, earth to Fiona!"

She flinched as Filip snapped his fingers at her like she was some dog. Before she'd become his coconspirator, Fiona had always enjoyed Filip's company, succinct and edgy metalhead that he was. But like the few other metalheads she'd known, he was proving brusque and unforgiving in his driven state, especially with such a heroic purpose behind him.

"Sorry," she grumbled. "I just disappeared into my own head for a second."

"Stay with me here," he said. "No losing focus. If this guy is as much of a, you know, *whatever* he is, then we can't let our guard down for an instant. He's got us both at a disadvantage."

She'd told Filip what he'd needed to know, which was most of it. She had admitted to meeting up with the Pit Viper privately and watching him use the *Codex Canoris*. At first, Filip had been incredulous about a book full of sonic ritual craft, but he'd warmed up to the idea when Fiona had described how Peter was using it to brainwash the teenagers of Hamm (and besides, heavy-metal dudes love a good ancient book of black magic). It was then that Filip admitted he was compromised—that he'd found himself downloading the Pit Viper's music without meaning to and blasting the album in his truck for days before realizing what it was. He'd just figured he was getting swept up in a fad the way you sometimes did, but the more he'd thought about it, the more he'd known that there was foul play afoot. "It's like every time I listen to the music, it makes more sense to me," he'd told her, sneering as he deleted the album from his phone.

The hardest part had been admitting that she'd slept with Peter. Not because of any concept of slut-shame—Fiona was secure in her hungers and wasn't going to let some dude like Filip Moss make her feel bad about them—but because she felt like she was betraying Peter by telling anyone. Even if it had been a moment of careless passion, it had been *their* moment, and turning it into a story point that she blurted out to Filip made it feel sordid and cheap. Filip had in turn been decent about it, simply shrugging and mumbling that everyone made mistakes—"Between us, I once smashed Tess Baron." Still, Fiona felt torn up inside by putting such a meaningful secret out in the open.

"I'm thinking our best option is to cut power to the old mill," said Filip. "There are still electrical wires running to the property for the motion sensor lights, to keep trespassers away. No electricity, no party."

"All right," she said. "Do you want to go after school today, or do we cut?"

"Neither will work," he said, shaking his head. "Ravers are all amateur electricians. If they're given enough time, they can rewire any structure. We need to cut the power right before the party, so that they can't get things up and running at the last minute. That's when we call in the council. Our folks and the police get there while everyone's waiting for the party to pop off, and the whole thing gets shut down. Hopefully, people get arrested. Hell, hopefully every kid at Hamm High ends up in a cell, safe and secure. What matters is, this party doesn't happen. I don't care how powerful a hypnotist this guy is, I bet he can't mind-control a bunch of cops with guns raised."

Fiona sighed. "I still don't like involving the town council. My father got us into this mess…"

Fillip looked like he was about to snap at her, but at the

last minute he stopped himself and did his best to be calm. "I know. I feel you. They definitely fucked us here. But it might be for the best, you know. If we're paying for our parents' sins, then maybe they need to lend us a hand."

Fiona nodded. Deep down she knew that Filip was the one thinking straight; she was clouded by emotion. It was so often the opposite, her gut showing her the right way and making her sure what she was doing was right. But she hadn't been sure of anything for a while now. Normally, Betty left her emotionally focused, mentally lean. But Fiona had been so terrified by watching Peter drop Edgar Hokes that she hadn't grabbed her guitar on the way out. Now, Betty was with Peter.

"So how do we keep them from stopping us?" she asked.

"We throw them off guard," he said, "by distracting the Pit Viper, stopping the show in its tracks. They're all working for him, and if he's telling them to stand down or hold off, that buys me precious minutes to make sure our folks get there before they realize what's happening."

"Buys you?" asked Fiona. "Where am I during all of this?" Filip nodded, as though he'd been expecting this. "So, bear with me: you're the one distracting the Pit Viper."

Fiona sneered. She knew what *that* meant, and it felt cheap and horrible. "Awesome. I come to you with this, and you make me the bait."

"Jones, you *can't* make this about you," said Filip. "If this guy wanted to date *me*, I'd be out there in his lap calling him *daddy*. But no, I'll be the guy on my hands and knees in the bushes cutting wires and trying not to get murdered by a bunch of club-kid junkies." He must have read the look on Fiona's face, because he raised his palms defensively. "Look, just be at the mill when he arrives. Stop him and ask if you can talk to him. Get him distracted enough that he'll hold off the party for a few minutes. You don't gotta blow the guy."

She winced at his crassness. "What if he doesn't buy it?"

"He doesn't have to buy it; he has to give me time," said Filip. "Don't get me wrong, Fiona, whatever you want to say or do after we've shut down this party is your choice. What matters is, we keep these guys from taking our friends and neighbors."

Fiona stared out at the crowds in front of the school, huddling and laughing and talking about the Pit Viper, and she wondered how worth saving they really were.

"I have to go to class," she said, cracking the door and hopping out of the truck. "I'll be in touch, though."

"Stay in touch!" called Filip after her. "Don't disappear on me, Jones! I can't do this without you!"

She trudged off into school, her head down. She passed Caroline and Horace in the halls, both of whom shot her dirty looks as though they knew about her role in Filip's plans. Clutched in Caroline's hand was a half-crumpled flyer; Fiona could just make out the head of the snake on it.

She grimaced. A distraction for Peter. What was she supposed to do, show up in tight black leather like Sandy at the end of *Grease*? Bring an apple and a bottle of water, really yank on those heartstrings? Could she pull off the "Run away with me" routine again after he'd already decided she wasn't worth his time? Or would she just have to stand in his way and weep and beg for forgiveness until he either took her in his arms or shoved her to the side?

Thinking about it chapped the edges of her brain. She missed her guitar; without Betty, Fiona felt overwhelmed and uncomfortable, constipated with emotions that needed to be wrung out through rock and roll. It dawned on her that she hadn't listened to music in days, and she carefully reached for her headphones, fantasizing about some Volbeat or Wolfmother or Dead Kennedys to calm her down. That's what she needed—a little music, a little personal enjoyment. Then, she could keep worrying about the impending doom coming to her hometown.

She pushed the headphone to her ear and reached for the right, her eyes softly closing in preparation for a soaring riff—

"Yo."

Her heart shrieked in disappointment as she yanked the headphones off and turned on the person talking to her. Vince, or Swordfish, or whatever the hell he wanted to be called, was at her one side, so close that their elbows brushed. He had a stern look on his face, like he was about to deliver some lousy news to her.

"What's up?" she said, hoping her voice conveyed her irritation. She had class to go to and music to listen to. She didn't have time to explain how she knew the Pit Viper—

"Don't do anything to fuck this up," said Vince.

"What?" she asked, trying to move away.

He lurched forward, blocking her path abruptly. Fiona stepped back, shaken by his proximity. This close, she could see his solid shoulders and huge hands; she'd forgotten that he'd been the bouncer at Tess's party, but now it was the only role in which she could picture him.

His head lowered, inches from hers, and he gave her an intense, pointed look.

"Don't do anything to fuck this party up," he said, quietly but tersely. He waved a folded piece of white paper under her nose. "You got me? You stay out of this. It doesn't concern you."

"Excuse me?" she said.

"I hear lots of things, Fiona Jones," he said. "I hear about stories from people like Tess Baron and Caroline Fiddler. Stories about you and a person of interest, a certain DJ who's going to be coming to Hamm this weekend. And neither you nor I need said person being discovered by our parents, or anyone's plans messed with. Very bad things could happen to people if anyone's alerted to secret happenings going on in Hamm. Got it? Understand? So just back off, keep your mouth shut. Everything's fine. Okay?"

She stood fixed to the spot, shock running through her in waves of prickling cold. Vince kept his eyes on hers a moment longer, just to emphasize the gravity of his words, before he turned and walked calmly away.

For teenagers in a small town like Hamm, Mischief Night was an important ritual. The night before Halloween was all about unleashing your demons and getting a year's worth of prank-based revenge on whatever teacher or counselor (or, occasionally, town council member) had made the previous ten months a living hell. It was even somewhat encouraged by the residents of Hamm, locals who made a big show of hiding in the bushes with hoses or hanging signs reading *throw an egg—I dare you.* Make no mistake, if you got caught TP-ing a house or igniting a bag of dog crap on a front porch, you got hauled back to your parents' place and made into a spectacle in front of your poor mother. Worse kids, the spray-painters and rock throwers, were even known to spend an evening in the drunk tank at the police station. But they usually came out of it with nothing more than their name in the newspaper and an elevated sense of their own badassery. No charges were ever pressed—to do so would feel like humorless overkill. Teenagers, right?

The general consensus was that Mischief Night took the heat off Halloween, when little kids were out with their parents and prominent locals were throwing parties. Hamm was the kind of town made for trick-or-treating and outdoor decoration displays. The fewer pranks pulled on Halloween proper, the fewer complaints were received by local police from residents furious that their children felt terrorized and their costumes were ruined. The town's teens, in turn, played along and planned their illegal fun for the thirtieth and their costume parties and slasher-movie marathons for the thirty-first.

But as Fiona left school that Friday, she heard no chortled plans for sophomoric revenge. No one called out that they'd see each other later (wink, wink) or that tonight was going to be killer. Even since her recent self-imposed social exile, she'd still been able to pick up on a rumor or two (plenty of them being about her, of course). Gossip wasn't hard to intercept at Hamm High—no one was graceful enough to truly keep anything secret, and none of the secrets being whispered were that scandalous.

But this Friday, the escaping crowds were almost eerily quiet. Everyone from her class left school with a sense of duty in their eyes. The most she overheard was the occasional soft-spoken, "Saturday." Not even Halloween—*Saturday*.

Everyone was being extra careful, she realized. No one wanted to be the person who blabbed too loudly about the old mill and got overheard by a nosy parent or teacher.

Especially not Fiona.

The next morning, Fiona checked her email and phone frantically, and only afterward admitted to herself that she'd been hoping for a message from Peter. Her mind had been circling this day in an ever-tightening orbit, and now that she was at ground zero, she almost hoped that it would all turn out fine. In her fantasy, the email waiting for her explained that he'd canceled the party, booked them a flight, made arrangements to house them in a monastery somewhere where the monks had set up a practice room for them in the basement.

In the fantasy, Peter apologized. He said he'd made a mistake, and that all that mattered now was their future together. He told her that he loved her.

But there was nothing. Fiona hated herself for feeling disappointed.

Her mom and dad had left for that Saturday's town council function—preparing for the children's parade downtown—without her. She stared at her mother's note, telling her to get some rest and requesting her presence later on that night. She could read between the lines: the less Robert Jones had to see his daughter right now, the better. Since their conversation in the city, he'd treated her like she was invisible. Tonight, though, they finally wanted to have another talk, all three of them. This one would most likely be less of a sympathetic confession and more of a hard position on her recent behavior. Too bad she'd be out at the mill, trying to save the town.

She shuddered at the thought of what was ahead of her. Filip's idea of a diversion sounded fine in practice, but with Peter actually standing in front of her, staring her down, it would be more difficult. She wasn't sure she could lie to him, much less do so convincingly. If she was going to throw herself at him, it would have to be for real.

If he said yes, she'd do it. Even after finding out what he had intended for Hamm, she'd still run away with him. She'd give it one more chance. Maybe she could make the guy she knew, the brilliant and hilarious dynamo who lived for music, the guy he was all the time. Maybe, with enough nourishment, his noble side would come out on top.

A normal Saturday felt like bullshit given the circumstances, but she tried her best. She made breakfast but felt sick after three bites of a bagel. She flipped on the TV, but the loudmouthed real housewives she found there just made her feel annoyed and anxious. She thought about going for a walk, but the idea of strolling among kids dressed as monsters made her feel out of place and pessimistic. And anyway, where could she go? With only her bike at her disposal, it meant pretty much one place outside of Hamm—the city, which she kept picturing as a maze of gray blocks with huge albino snakes slithering among them.

She sat in her room and blasted music, hoping it could reboot her sanity the way it had done so often in the past. She tried the chiller stuff: the Pixies, Jefferson Airplane, The Hurray For The Riff Raff, Hawkwind. None of it worked. Peter occupied every love song's melody, loomed behind every bridge and chorus. She could feel his power aimed hungrily at Hamm and imagined him bent over his turntable in that shadowy tomb of a warehouse, his fingertips skimming the pages of his ancient book, his lips mumbling arcane passages. Sound bars leaped on laptops and tape players until the darkness glowed a flickering blue that made his eyes look like twin galaxies…

Her phone buzzed in her pocket. She looked to it excitedly, only to discover Filip calling her.

"What now?" she said.

"Real nice," said Filip on the other end, a symphony of hammer strikes and yelling in the background. "Why aren't you downtown? I wanted to go over final plans with you."

"My parents didn't wake me up in time," she said.

"Okay, so come by now."

Fiona prickled with anger. First he was casting her as bait, now he was ordering her around? If not for her, there wouldn't even be a plan. "I'll be there, Filip. Calm down."

"You'll be there? You'll be where, when?"

"I'll be at the mill right before the party—"

"The Goring Steel Mill covers almost two acres of land," said Filip. "There are six entrances. Which one are we meeting at, Jones?"

"Jesus, Filip, then I'll meet you at your place beforehand!" she snapped. "Calm the fuck down!"

There was silence on the other end, and then Filip calmly said, "Don't be getting cold feet on me, Jones. This is serious."

"You think I don't know that?" she snapped. "Someone threatened me at school this week! I'm scared I'm going to get beaten to death!"

"Who?" asked Filip.

"A kid named Vince, who Horace calls Swordfish," said Fiona.

"No idea who that is," said Filip. "But keep an eye out. If you see him lurking around, let me know. This is good. We're finding out who he has on his side."

"Yeah, that's great, Filip," she said. "If he comes crashing through my window and smashes my skull in with a crowbar, I'll text you."

"Did you think this was going to be easy, Jones?" he said. "Of course we're getting threatened. Of course people want to hurt us before we stop this. This isn't a Nancy Drew mystery, dude, this is crime. Nasty characters are involved. People might get hurt tonight. We have to be ready for that."

"How comforting. Awesome bedside manner, Filip."

"Don't get soft on me. Call me if you need me. Otherwise, my place, seven." Then he hung up. Fiona stormed to her room, shaking her head. She'd been up for just over an hour and already she wished she had never gotten out of bed.

The doorbell rang, yanking her out of sleep.

She sat up and wiped crumbs from her eyes. Outside her window, the sky was fading from afternoon to evening and the occasional pod of costumed kids shepherded by a single parent trundled slowly down the street. The parade would be over. Her mom and dad would be home soon.

She'd slept for longer than she'd expected to. It was like her heart was working overtime, and it had wiped her out. She'd lost the day, she realized—lost any chance she had of backing out of Filip's plans, or even giving up and offering herself to Peter one last time in exchange for her classmates. By now, Horace and Caroline were probably filling their backpacks with glow sticks and Gatorade. By now, Peter's crew was loading the back of a car, and he was staring past the city skyline and out to Hamm, where his revenge was finally waiting for him.

A bowl of candy was sitting in the foyer by the front door (thanks, Mom), but she found herself holding it out to a FedEx delivery guy, heavyset with nerdy glasses.

"Are you Fiona?" he asked. When she nodded blankly, he handed her a tablet and said, "Sign with your finger." Then he handed her a large but light box, took a bite-size Mr. Goodbar, wished her a happy Halloween, and went back to his truck.

She took the box back up to her room, stunned and a little worried by its arrival. There was no return address, and the label was home printed. For a second, she imagined a bomb delivered by one of Peter's cohorts, that PM creep or someone else, but the package's size and relatively manageable weight didn't suggest that. She shook it and heard the contents inside flop around amid the rustle of tissue paper.

Fiona used a key to cut the tape on the box and carefully opened it.

From a bed of orange paper and black leather, the Ace of Spades stared up at her. Carefully, her throat swelling and her eyes stinging, Fiona pulled out the custom guitar case, the one she'd lusted after on their perfect day.

A note tumbled from its folds. She bent down, picked it up, and opened it. Inside, in Peter's scrawl, it said, *Samurai of old.*

Fiona let out a choked sob. It was a peace offering, an extended hand. He wanted her to know that after everything that had happened, he still wanted Fiona by his side. If she wanted to, she could go to him, put Betty in this case, and then she and Peter could join hands and walk out of this town and into—

She froze. Her romantic fantasy hit a brick wall with a sickening thud.

Betty.

The longer that fact rolled over in her head, the heavier it felt.

She opened her hands, and the leather guitar case fell to the floor.

He had Betty at his place. It was in Peter's possession.

Fiona's brow furrowed. Her hands clenched; her fingernails bit into her palms so hard that they oozed blood. Fiona felt one layer of armor after another clap down over her heart, until it was a red-hot mass of riveted steel and spiked chains.

Fuck her classmates. Fuck Filip, fuck her dad, and fuck Hamm. Fuck this guitar case. Fuck all the noble, superheroic aspirations that she was supposed to be doing this for, and fuck what might have been. Peter had Betty, her best friend, the tool with which Fiona had carved her personality out of stone. In a dusty loft in some dank industrial warehouse, Betty was sitting there wondering what the hell had happened to the awesome sister who'd once wielded her. Wondering when Fiona had become just another chick feeling torn up about a shitty guy. Betty was disappointed; no, Betty was *pissed*. Fiona had resurrected her from her pawnshop limbo only to abandon her in the home of a hot DJ who would probably just add Betty's hollow carcass to his collection of utterly destroyed gear. And she hadn't even gotten to be in a band yet.

Was that all there was? Did all those nights of cathartic venting and untamed riffs mean nothing to Fiona? Because it sure seemed like it with Fiona here, messed up over a boy while clutching the expensive gift he'd bought her, pining to be his sweetheart instead of just hunkering down, gritting her teeth, and getting her fucking guitar back.

Fiona realized she was standing again. A glance in the mirror showed cords rising out of her neck. She felt crazy, unhinged, unstable, but then again, given the stakes, she was prepared to lose her mind. This was her gut speaking, and her gut wanted Betty back, *now*. Now was not the time to brood alone in her room like some emo shmuck who wrote sad songs about the girls he'd cheated on. Now was the time to rock and roll.

She opened her desk drawer and produced her girl-gang emergency kit—a pink-handled switchblade and a can of mace she'd bought with Caroline and Rita on a city trip last year. Even the small knife and purse-size pepper spray felt like too much—she'd made it this far in her life without stabbing anyone, and she wanted to keep it that way—but if there was ever a time to break out the heavy artillery, it was now. Who knew what they'd be up against?

The doorbell rang. She ignored it, caught up in her fury. A second ring, and Fiona groaned and headed to the stairs. One set of trick-or-treaters, and then she was done.

She snatched up the candy bowl a second time and yanked open the door. The boy in the Halloween mask outside was surprisingly tall. She started to say so, but then he tackled her.

Bite-size candy scattered across the floor. Fiona cried out in panic and struggled, but her attacker's muscles were wiry and hard, and he kicked the door closed before any passing neighbors could see them. One of his arms wrapped around her waist, pinning her own arms to her sides and stopping her from reaching the knife and mace in her pocket. The other slapped a damp rag over her mouth. She realized what was happening and began screaming in the same instant, but every shriek brought burning chemical air into her lungs.

"Hush," said a familiar voice in her ear.

The room around her blurred, blended together, and sank out of view.

Light, first. Then noise, rhythmic, insistent.

She sat up, shaking her head, a blast of dizziness and nausea overcoming her the minute she tried to think. What had...where did...

The sound again, less muffled—a knocking at her door.

"Fiona!" yelled her mom through a pillow. "Your father and I would like to have a word with you, now."

Fiona shook her head. What had happened—

She recoiled as it came back to her—the man in the mask, the chemical rag. She patted herself down and realized she was fully clothed, nothing bruised or broken, in her bed, wearing her shoes. A scan around her room showed nothing noticeably missing or destroyed. She wondered if it had been a nightmare, but her pounding head and the sting in her nostrils suggested she'd inhaled something poisonous. She was glad she hadn't been assaulted, but the nonsense of it baffled her.

Why did the intruder just knock her out and leave here there? It felt like...a waste of time.

Her eyes flew to the window—darkness, night. She pulled out her phone—8:42 p.m.

Filip was alone. If he'd come by looking for her, she hadn't heard him. Someone was trying to keep her from getting to the mill.

8:42. The flyer had said nine. She could still make it.

Fiona burst out of her bedroom, nearly trampling her poor mother along the way. Her father came out of their living room, and their eyes briefly met, hers no doubt wide with panic and terror. Then she was out the door, on her bike, and pedaling as hard as her legs would allow.

Maybe Filip had cut the power. Maybe no one had shown up.

It wasn't too late. There was time.

chapter
25

The Goring Steel Mill loomed on the edge of town like a set piece out of *Castlevania*, huge and sprawling and somehow blacker than the night sky against which it stood. The three fences that circled it were topped with spirals of barbed wire and thin wisps of ensnared plastic bags that fluttered in the breeze like captured ghosts. The main building was surrounded by a network of small sheds, pipes, generators, and any number of garbage piles that had collected there since the business had closed in the 1980s and people had just begun using the spot as a dump.

As she sped down the country road that led to the mill, Fiona thought it looked like some kind of shadowy giant, like Death Himself was loitering just outside of Hamm, silent and patient.

Dread crept into her belly. Silent. Patient.

Something was wrong.

There was nothing unusual about the place — no pounding bass, no blinking lights, not even the drunken laugh of a partier hanging out nearby. She'd planned on ditching her bike at the first fences on the edge of the property, but suddenly she wasn't sure if she needed to. The gates all hung open, their chains cut…but no one guarded them. No one waited inside of them.

Fiona rode into the shadowy center of the grounds, her eyes scanning the industrial scenery and finding nothing, just deeper and deeper shadows. There were no decorations or graffiti, no lone shoe or half-crushed beer can that would indicate people had just been there. There wasn't even the electric hum of a generator. The only sounds she could hear were her own heavy breathing and the scurry of some animal in the bushes nearby.

For a moment, she wondered if she'd screwed something up. Was it the right night? Had the person who'd knocked her out warned Peter about her plans? Had Filip succeeded, forcing them to cancel the party? She tried calling him again, but it went directly to voicemail. But even if he had, her phone said it was only 9:20. Would the whole celebration apparatus have left so quickly?

If anyone had been here, they were gone.

Something was terribly wrong.

"Hello?" she said tentatively, her voice tiny in the huge darkness.

A figure stepped out of the shadows, and she spun, brandishing her mace.

"Fiona, right?" said the voice. "Rita's friend?"

Fiona exhaled, feeling like her heart might explode. Dave Hettenberg, the lacrosse player who Rita had hooked up with at Tess Baron's party, smiled awkwardly at her with his big lantern-jawed face. His bad cardboard-box robot costume and cell phone flashlight only added to his gumpiness.

"Are you working this thing?" he asked, trotting over to her the best he could. "I thought Tess said you weren't coming."

Fiona nodded slowly, trying her best to play along. Dave seemed to have a better grasp of what was happening than she did, so he might be able to clue her in. "Just...seeing where everyone else is."

"Yeah, totally," he said. "I was scared that, like, 'cause I was late, there'd be no one left to send me— Oh, shit, I'm sorry." He pulled the party flyer out of his pocket and presented it to Fiona proudly. *"Show-ner-plots show-ner-tag."*

"Sorry?" said Fiona.

Dave lowered the flyer, looking nervous. "Isn't that the password? Rita told me that I needed to present it at the map point, or I couldn't find the venue. Where are we going from here, anyway?"

"Map point," said Fiona.

Map points are for warehouse gigs, Vince had said. *Where you don't want the cops showing up.*

She put a hand to her forehead, feeling clammy and shaken as she put two and two together. Of course he hadn't spun at the old mill. It was too predictable. He was cleverer than that. He knew it wasn't safe here, given his history with the town. So, he'd put the mill on the flyer, but he'd made it a stop along the way.

He had planned it out ahead of time. Of course he had.

"Sorry, is that not the right password?" asked Dave, suddenly looking deeply nervous. "It did seem weird that it was in German."

"German," she repeated.

"Yeah," he said. "I looked it up, because it's spelled so funny. It is *Schonerplatz Schonertag*, right? Beautiful place, beautiful day?"

The reality crashed down on her like a thunderclap.

"Oh God," she said. She picked up her bike and began frantically riding back toward the front entrance to the mill, leaving Dave Hettenberg yelling after her in confusion.

Just past the fence, light grew in the distance and then flared in the night, stabbing at her eyes. Gravel sprayed as a car careened toward her. She skidded her bike to a halt just as the vehicle pulled up in front of her.

"Fiona!" yelled her father as he yanked open the car door. He scrambled out into the headlights and seized her by the shoulders. "What the hell is going on here?"

"Did you hear from Filip?" she panted.

"Hear what?" asked her dad, his face a total blank.

Filip never called them. He'd never gotten a chance. It was wrong, all wrong. "Dad," she said, "we need to leave, now."

"What are you doing?" he yelped, his eyes shiny with tears. "You scare the shit out of your mother, you rush out of the house without a word, and now I follow you here, of all places—"

"He's back, Dad," she said. "You were right. He's taking them. He's taking all the kids."

Robert Jones's face dropped from stricken to slack. "Where?" he said. "Here? Is he inside?"

"The winery," she said. "He's at the Hamm Winery."

Something about the Hamm Winery's abandonment made it creepier than the mill. The mill felt like something out of a doom metal track, dystopian and covered with decades of dust, but the winery was too precious and off the beaten path to fall to the same level of ruin, and so the grounds off of State Road 217 had remained relatively untouched. The cottage where visitors used to sip that year's newest vintages and eat locally sourced meals was boarded up, and the barn where they'd kept the fermenters now sported some small-time graffiti and empty bottles left by local kids, but overall the place was preserved like a frog in a laboratory jar. It felt eerie, as though the residents had disappeared in an instant; if the mill looked like somewhere five years after the apocalypse, then the winery looked like the world had ended five seconds ago.

It was 9:51 when they arrived. Fiona bolted from the passenger-side door before the car had even stopped, while Robert Jones stayed back at the car calling the last remaining council members. She ran across the grassy grounds; the rolling hills that were supposed to feel pleasant were now just a pain in the ass to get over.

The cottage was dark and silent, but there was a light on in the barn.

Fiona skidded to a halt inside the open barn doors.

No one. Not a soul.

She walked across the wooden floor of the huge empty space lit by a single bare bulb dangling from the ceiling. Her eyes darted around the room, desperately trying to find evidence of the party, a burned-out glow stick or a scrap of neon confetti, but there was nothing. The barn smelled of old wood and cut grass, not cigarettes and sweat and booze.

But she could sense energy in the absence here, like the party's ghost was haunting the space. She was missing something.

There, on the floor.

In the dust at her feet were footprints. More importantly, shoe prints—the patterned soles of a thousand sneakers making their way across the dirty ground. Chuck Taylors, Timberlands, Vans, Nikes, Doc Martens, Adidas, even a John Varvatos dress shoe or two, swirling and overlapping in the dirt at her feet like instructions for some sort of bizarre waltz.

Dancing. The feet had been dancing. Slowly, she followed their rhythm, trying to understand where they'd gone.

She heard another car roll up outside, then another, then a fourth, but she was too engrossed by the shifting footprints in the dust to notice. The fine print of the party began to show up in her vision—a sticky patch from some spilled drink, a single colored bead. Finally, at the backmost part of the room, she came upon a square patch in the dust with only a single pair of shoeprints leading to and from it. Expensive high-end kicks, their movements limited to a tight margin.

Peter.

"Oh my God," said Harriet Moss behind her. People rushed into the barn, their frantic footfalls ringing through the huge space like the applause of skeletons.

The entire Hamm town council stared at Fiona Jones. She eyed them back in pity. These adults, who had for so long protected their town, who Fiona had admired since she was a little girl, now looked bedraggled and weak against the gaping maw of the empty building. Her father stood at the middle of the crowd, his hand on his forehead, staring at the dusty sneaker prints at his feet.

"Where are they?" asked Nathan Liddel in his high, whining voice.

"Caroline?" called Darren Fiddler, his voice extra small in the empty room. "Caroline, are you in here?"

"They're gone," whispered Robert Jones.

"Gone where?" snapped William Chatsworth, his barber's mustache seeming to twitch. "Where did they go? Bob? What happened?"

Christine Nye was on her cell phone. "I'm calling the police."

"Christine, wait," said Robert, just loudly enough that she could hear. "Just, wait a minute." Christine lowered her phone instinctively at Robert Jones's command, but her face wanted to know why.

"Why would he take them away from us?" said Harriet Moss. "We paid him. Why did he do this to us?"

"Who?" asked Bill Chatsworth, still flabbergasted. "Where are they?" shouted Janelle Hokes, barging in and heading straight for Fiona. "Where'd he take them, Fiona? Tell us now!"

"Now, hold on, Janelle," said Robert Jones. Fiona opened her mouth to speak, but before she could say anything, Janelle's meaty hands clamped on her shoulders, pulling Fiona close to her sweat-shiny face; Fiona smelled white wine and gasoline.

Janelle's fingers dug into Fiona's flesh like steel claws. "Talk!" she bellowed, giving Fiona a hard shake that made her head whip back. The angrier Janelle got, the more the crowd focused their collective fear on Fiona. Slowly, the town council closed in, their shock transforming into rage. "Where'd he take my boys? What did he do to my Edgar?"

"Let me go, Janelle," Fiona yelped.

The hands tightened, and Fiona squeaked with pain. By now, she was trapped in a circle of adults peering down at her, hungry for answers.

"My husband comes home with his inner ear destroyed, puking for days, can barely stand up, and then this happens, and you don't think I see the pattern?" shrieked Janelle. "You don't think I know what's up, you bitch? *What happened?*"

"Janelle."

"You tell us, Fiona, you tell us now or so help me—"

A click, metallic and recognizable, overtook the noise in the barn. The town council's rage dissipated, and they stepped back defensively.

"Janelle, take your hands off my daughter," said Robert Jones firmly.

Janelle Hokes released Fiona and took a step back. Fiona's dad stood with his arm extended, a snub-nosed revolver in his grip. She watched the dumbfounded townsfolk creep back slowly, giving him plenty of room.

"Jesus, Robert," whined Darren Fiddler, "drop the gun."

"Anyone who touches my daughter gets shot," responded Robert Jones. His voice never wavered, though the gun in his hand shivered. The barrel followed Janelle Hokes until she was a good twenty feet away from Fiona.

"Robert, what's going on?" asked Christine Nye, her phone now at her side.

"He came back," said Janelle, relishing the chance to reveal the town's hideous secret. "The Pit Viper, that damn DJ we hired. He took our children, Christine. He lured them here and took them all—"

"But *why*?" cried Harriet Moss. "We did everything he told us to! We gave him all that money! Why would he do this?"

Silence. Both Fiona's father and Janelle Hokes stood perfectly still. Only Darren Fiddler shook his head, kneaded his hands, and swore.

"Church basement," said Robert Jones softly. "We meet there in thirty minutes. Nathan, Joan, you stay here and call the cops fifteen minutes after we leave. Tell them there was a concert here, and our kids are all missing. Tell them you have no idea who took them or why. They need to just use what evidence they have here.

"Fiona," he continued, "get in the car. You've got some questions to answer."

She nodded and slowly walked to her father, doing her best to avoid the line of fire.

. . .

Ironically, they stashed her in the old kids' room, the one with the Golden Books that she'd escaped the night she'd first seen Peter. Now, her father had told her to stay put or else, and one or two other council members had given her hard stares that were meant to be threatening.

Being alone with her thoughts drove Fiona insane. The failure to stop Peter was on her—her indecision, her emotional hangover from the high of being his. If she'd discussed the game plan with Filip earlier that day, they might have had a chance. She could've figured out that the mill was only a ruse, but she was too tangled up in her own emotional melodrama to focus. Peter had done what he'd said he was going to do, as much as she'd prayed he wouldn't. Now it was all a mess—her friends and classmates kidnapped, Filip possibly hurt or worse, Peter completely consumed by his revenge. Janelle Hokes had every right to be bloodthirsty.

Hard as she tried, she couldn't make out what anyone was saying down the hall, but there were shouts and screams and sobs. The sound of a piece of furniture being knocked over or tossed rang out at one point, so she guessed her father had explained what had actually happened to the money they'd gathered for Peter, and the rest of the council members weren't pleased.

As she sat on the floor of the moldy room, her back against a wall with a smiling rhino painted on it, Fiona wondered about her classmates. Was there anyone left besides her and Dave Hettenberg, who was probably at home thinking he'd missed the Halloween party to end all Halloween parties (which, technically, it had been)? The only other person she could think of was Filip, but he was nowhere to be found, meaning that Peter might have gotten him.

She kicked herself for letting Filip go it alone. Whoever had chloroformed her had been aware that she might ruin

Peter's master plan, which meant it was well underway now. All signs pointed to Vince, aka Swordfish, with his threats of violence and his broad frame that would be perfect for tackling her. But that hadn't been his voice whispering in her ear, though it had been familiar. Was there someone else involved? How much did she still not know?

What she did know was it couldn't be over. Not yet. Peter was out there somewhere. He'd have to do something like what he did to Edgar Hokes on a large scale to wipe their minds so thoroughly, which would take time, patience, discipline. And then, he'd give them to Udo, who would use them for... what? Human slavery? Prostitution, running drugs, manual labor? What would a man like that do with a whole crew of brainwashed teenagers? Nothing good, certainly, given how many of the mill rats had been found dead.

The hideousness of that thought relit the fire under her ass, and she stood, steeling herself. Her friends were gone, but they hadn't just disappeared. He hadn't sucked them into another dimension or trapped them inside a gem. Peter had said it himself: he wasn't a wizard, and this wasn't a fairy tale. His power—whatever it was—was practical. Her friends were still around somewhere, even if they were under his control.

She could get to them. She could get to Betty. She could fix everything.

Or she could die trying.

But not with the council's help. They were part of the problem. The adults would go blundering into the situation with blinders on and would find nothing but an empty loft apartment full of broken sound equipment. And even worse, they might get all her friends killed in the process. They didn't know what they were up against. It was on her to save her classmates, but she had to escape the council first.

She got on her hands and knees and looked under the

door, the carpet scraggly and crumby on her cheek. No feet outside the door, just a smell that didn't belong here—cigarette smoke.

Hope hit her in an overwhelming wave. A chance, slim and unexpected but very, very real. Of course that's who the council had assigned to guard her. She was locked up here, but breaking a chain was as easy as finding a weak link. And she'd known who that was for years.

Darren Fiddler stood by the water fountain outside the door to the main church basement auditorium, ashing into the drain. As Fiona crept toward him, she considered who Caroline was versus her father. Caroline's domineering behavior came mostly from her mother, Grace, a clinical hard- ass who had no problem causing a scene at a restaurant or storming the principal's office if it meant getting her way. Darren, on the other hand, was calm, contemplative, easily worried but perpetually helpless. His presence on the town council had always felt like a gift bestowed by Fiona's dad, who recognized the gentle good in Darren. But now that they were conducting serious business, Darren had been left outside to watch the door like a servant, ready to summon Fiona whenever the grown-ups told him to.

"Mr. Fiddler."

Darren spun around, dropping his cigarette. He gaped at her like a child caught stealing seconds on dessert.

"Get back in there, Fiona," he tried to command. "We need to talk to you."

"Listen, Mr. Fiddler," she said, calmly and quietly, worried he'd get so loud that the others would hear them. "I know where he took everyone. I know where he took Caroline. I can get her back, but you need to let me go."

"They've got to— We want to speak…" he gibbered. "No one—we don't know what's going on. What happened, Fiona?

What happened to my daughter? I just want this over with."
His eyes teared up. "I never meant for things to get so bad
that night. We were just doing our jobs—"

"Mr. Fiddler, please," she said urgently. "I need to leave
right now. If you keep me here any longer and waste time
questioning me, you're going to lose them. Caroline's going
to wind up dead." Darren flinched and shook his head at the
last word. "But if you let me go right now, I can guarantee
that you'll get her back."

He blinked at her with pitiful resignation. A little squeak
came out of his mouth. They stood frozen for some time, long
enough for Fiona to try taking steps backward, toward the
doors to the outside.

"No, wait," he said, and she froze again.

Nervously, he dug his car keys out of his pocket, squatted
down, and placed them on the floor. He looked up at her
anxiously.

"Promise me you're not on his side," he said, his voice
cracking. "Don't play me for a fool. Don't do that to me."

"I promise," she said. "I'm going to find him, Mr. Fiddler,
and I'm going to bring him down. And you'll get Caroline
back."

Mr. Fiddler kicked the keys over to her. She thanked him
as she picked them up and then bolted for the door, leaving
the shivering man behind her.

chapter
26

At night, the Pit Viper's neighborhood was like a black hole. As Fiona had first driven into the city, everything had been illuminated beyond belief. Gaudy neon and jaundiced streetlights painted the night a radioactive orange. She'd forgotten that it was Halloween until she'd found herself crawling through downtown traffic, constantly being cut off by drunken twenty-somethings in stupid referential costumes (she'd been briefly tempted to run down a woman dressed as Slutty Morty). But though they grated on her nerves, the crowded streets and public events actually made her drive easier. She was still a little edgy behind the wheel, so the slow pace allowed her to take her time, and all the police were too busy looking for troublemaking partiers to notice a teenage girl who braked a little hard at red lights.

Once she was in Peter's industrial neighborhood, though, the night closed in and the hundreds of costumed drunks disappeared, leaving only empty streets walked by the occasional ragman or bag lady. The meager loading-dock lights and the occasional illuminated window did nothing to brighten the cold concrete drifting past her. Even protected by the Fiddler family's hatchback, she felt trapped and alone in a huge, dark world, like a cockroach crawling through Peter's speaker-strewn loft.

But somehow, miraculously, she came upon one of the "sounds" tags. The silver paint in which it was sprayed sparkled in her headlights, calling out to Fiona. She began following it toward the next one, and tag by tag made her way back to the Pit Viper's warehouse, like she had before.

As she approached Peter's place, she felt her nerves prickle. Two figures were hauling gear into a white van. At first pass, she recognized them—one was Perry, PM, huffing and puffing as he hauled an Orange head on his own.

The other was Vince, aka Swordfish, Horace's friend.

Disgust swept over her. Of course he was in on it. She didn't know how long, or how much he'd done so far. Hell, maybe he was just brainwashed, a mind-wiped servant of the *Canoris*. But given the way he'd threatened her earlier, she doubted it. He was probably just some wannabe gangster hungry for power. It was definitely him who had knocked her out and kept her from meeting with Filip, even if the voice she'd heard wasn't quite his—if he was willing to threaten her with violence, he was probably ready to barrel into her house and drug her.

She did a loop around the block, keeping her head low, and parked the car a few streets down. Then she crept back to the corner and watched the guys finish loading a round of speakers and boxes into the back.

"What's left?" asked Vince, cracking his neck.

"Just the rugs, that Marshall stack, aaand…oh, the *guitar*." PM sniggered.

Fiona felt a pang of relief mixed with panic. She'd made it just in time. Betty was still there—but not for long.

"He wants to keep the guitar?" asked Vince, just as amused.

"He wants to destroy it personally," said PM. "Thinks it'll give him...how'd he put it? *Residual energies.* Weirdo bullshit, I dunno. He just wants closure. Let him have his emo moment." The two laughed and headed up the stairs, their derision fading out of earshot.

Fiona bit into her cheek hard to keep from blowing her cover with a furious insult. She wouldn't let Peter have the satisfaction of harming her guitar. She'd smash Betty herself before letting him involve her in his twisted game.

Fiona crept over to the empty back of the truck and surveyed the Tetris board of amps, speakers, and monitors inside. Would she be able to sneak in and hide away in the truck, let it take her to their destination? Or should she wait for the guys and try to convince them—

Her gut curled into a fist. No, no way. She was sick of sneaking around, playing coy. She needed answers and needed them now. Time for the direct approach.

She grabbed a mini-amp that she remembered from the tuning session and tiptoed her way up the stairs with it at her side. Her arm quickly grew sore and then went numb, but it wasn't so heavy that she couldn't use it for her purposes, and just heavy enough that it would serve them.

The Pit Viper's loft was almost entirely empty now. All the blown-out pieces of equipment had been taken away, just like her poor manipulated friends, and tossed somewhere. Only the circle of shelves remained, and within them stood the two boys, talking about which part of their last haul they should tackle first. Fiona crept as quietly as she could over to one of the bookshelves and waited behind it, crouching.

"Ugh." She heard the sound of them lifting something. "You got it?"

"Yeah, I'm good. All right, let's get moving."

Vince breached the walls of the bookshelves, one end of a huge rolled-up rug sitting on his shoulder.

Fiona snapped, *"Hey!"* His head turned in a flash. Putting all her strength into her shoulder, she swung the mini-amp in a wide uppercut, smashing Vince in the side of the jaw. He went down hard, dropping his end of the rug and sending PM sprawling. As Fiona leaped over the downed rug, she saw the skinny hipster scrambling for a piece of shiny black metal in his waistband, but she brought the amp down onto PM's face with a hard crack, bouncing his skull off the ground and sending a glut of blood gushing out of his nose.

In an instant, Fiona dropped the amp and pulled the pistol from PM's waistband, doing her best imitation of her father back at the winery as she pointed it at PM's face. For a moment, she was terrified that there might be a safety on the gun that would totally fuck her in the moment of truth—but given how quickly Peter's little henchman held up his hands, he was obviously worried.

"Move and I blow you away," said Fiona.

PM spat a wad of blood with a tooth in it onto the floor. "I knew you were a bad idea," he coughed. "He never listens. *She gave me the apple.* Always with your fucking apple."

"Where are they?" she said, her voice cracking despite herself. "My friends. The ones he stole. I want them right now."

PM sneered. "You're shit out of luck, sweetheart," he said. "You don't know who you're dealing with here. They're under his control now, and once he drains them they'll be useless—"

"He wants me," said Fiona. "Doesn't he? Or my guitar, so he can destroy it. Either way, it's your ass if you don't show up, right, asshole?"

PM said nothing, but the way he exhaled told Fiona she'd hit the jackpot. She rose to her feet and backed away, keeping the gun pointed at PM. She tried to stop it from shaking, but it was so heavy that it wriggled in her grip.

"Get the guitar," she said. "Load it into the van, and then we go to where he's keeping them. Try anything and get a hole punched in you."

PM slowly climbed to his feet and shook his head. "You're not going to shoot me, babe, so don't—"

Fiona pointed the gun at the floor near him and squeezed the trigger.

A momentary fireball, a crack of noise that deafened her in the enclosed space. The floor at PM's side spat a plume of dust, and the henchman crouched with his hands up. The gun's recoil wasn't nearly as bad as she expected, but her wrist still sang after the kick.

She aimed the gun back on him, shaking even harder than before but newly resolved. "Get my guitar and get moving."

PM nodded at Vince. "Are we taking him? He's really hurt. He might die."

"He'll be fine," she said. She tightened her grip and raised the gun, keeping it steadily pointed at his face. "Next question gets answered with a bullet. Guitar. Now."

PM stared balefully at her for a moment, and then slowly walked over to where Betty sat in her case.

They drove out of the city in the opposite direction from Hamm and then out into the country. By the time they were off the highway, it was too late to worry about trick-or-treaters or drunk partiers, and though they did see the occasional costumed man or woman leaving a gas station or mini-mart, they went unnoticed, just another set of headlights and dashboard lamps racing through the quiet darkness. The nicer suburbs gave way to rundown and boarded-up little towns that had already been kind of miserable before everything had gone to hell in '08. Soon even those were devoured by shrubland and woods, with only the occasional roadside shack suggesting any nearby people.

Even as her muscles screamed and her arms went cold, Fiona kept the gun pointed at PM the whole time. She knew shooting him would probably cause a crash that would kill them both, but she repeatedly convinced herself that she'd do it if he tried anything; at this point, with Betty in her possession, she had settled on an entirely nihilistic worldview, one in which she'd go down taking out as many of Peter's cronies as possible. The boy's nose had stopped bleeding when she'd let him shove some tissues in his nostrils, but she could see a dull, concussed look in his eyes. She mentally prayed that PM wouldn't faint during the drive and send them hurtling into a ditch before she got a chance to either get to Peter or shoot him herself.

The silence in the car seemed endless and horrible. "How much longer?" she said. He didn't respond. "How much longer until we get there?"

"Let's just keep driving," he rambled in a nasal voice. "We can drive off into the night. I don't even care what you want to do later. Leave me by the side of the road, but take me away first."

"Shut up," she said.

"He's got your friends, and he's going to get you, too," said PM. "He'll turn you into something hollow, and then he'll give you to Udo, and Udo's going to make you do things, horrible things, in front of people who'll laugh and burn you with cigarettes—"

"*Shut up!*" she screamed. "What do you know? You're one of them. You're the one helping him."

"They took me from the mill."

Fiona couldn't help but gasp. PM must have heard her, because he let out a rattling laugh that had no smile behind it. "Yeah," he said. "I'm from Wright. You know that town, right?"

"Yeah," she finally whispered.

"I was there when he took everyone," he droned. "All I remember was that the set was incredible, and we were dancing so hard, it felt like we were all rolling or something… and then I come to in this house." He swallowed hard. "The house we're going to now. And he says to me, *You get to stay. I need someone to help me out with things. In return, you don't have to go the same way as your friends.* And then he showed them to me, all empty inside, ready to be rewritten. They looked like dead people you see in pictures, where they just seem like bags with nothing in them. So, I said yes, because I didn't want that. I was so scared. And when he gave me back my phone I saw that it had been two weeks." He shook his head. "Two weeks, just gone. Who knows what happened during them."

"That's enough," said Fiona. "Just drive."

"So I did what he told me to, and two months later, at a party he's spinning, I see my friend Chelsea," he said, "and she's all skinny and has a big split lip, and she's begging me for help, saying my buddies and I could do whatever we wanted to her—"

"I said enough!" Fiona shouted, but her cracking voice and high pitch betrayed her horror.

"That's where we're headed," mumbled PM. "That's what the Pit Viper does."

"His name is Peter," she said, almost involuntarily.

PM shook his head. "No, it's not. He's the Pit Viper. Trust me." Then he went silent again.

Finally, they turned onto a dirt road that led into the

woods. The whole world was blacker than pitch, the headlights almost swallowed by the darkness. Besides the occasional chipmunk darting across the path, they saw no signs of life. After about fifteen minutes of driving, Fiona began to worry he was just taking her to some far-off field to try and kill her… and then she saw the house.

Everything about the place was bad news out loud. The peeling paint, the blacked-out windows, the crisp white vans parked off to one side, the rusted-out propane cans scattered around the front yard, the mold-covered birdbath near the porch. Even the trees around it were bent and withered, not in a spooky autumnal way but in a sick and vine-choked way.

Fiona felt her skin crawl just looking at the house, knowing that in its silent language it told a story of pain and sadness and all the hideous truths her dad fought so hard to keep away from Hamm.

PM braked, stopped in the middle of the driveway, and turned off the headlights. After a few moments, the front door opened and a silhouette stepped out and motioned for PM to proceed. But the van remained motionless.

"Drive forward," said Fiona.

"No," said PM.

"Do it," she said, gesturing with the gun.

PM looked sullenly at the dashboard and shook his head. "Fucking shoot me if you want. I'm never going back in that house." A tear fell down his cheek. "Never again."

"Fine," she said, and climbed out of the passenger-side door.

As she turned, she saw the figure from the porch run toward her. "Perry," he yelled, "you're supposed to bring the van around the side, you know—"

She whipped up the pistol, her mind buzzing with the thought that this was it, the time she'd finally have to shoot someone.

Calvin Hokes slid to a halt on the muddy ground, his hands up and his mouth gaping. He wore a black hoodie and work gloves, and he had a faint sheen of sweat on his brow. "Holy— Fiona, what are you doing?" he gasped. "Jesus, where'd you get a gun? Put it down!"

"Where are they?" she snapped. The night air was cold, that and her shot nerves left her shivering all over. The gun danced in the air. "Where'd he take them all, Calvin?"

"Take who?" said Calvin.

"The... Everyone!" she yelped. "From the party! Does he have them? What's he doing to them?"

"Fiona, everyone's inside!" laughed Calvin, slowly lowering his hands. "They're all downstairs smoking pot and hanging out! This is the after-party! He's playing us his new album, *exclusively*!"

Fiona blinked repeatedly. No, it couldn't be. Out here? In this desolate place? But PM had told her. And, and her father...

"He took the club rats, Calvin," she gibbered. "From the old mill, back in the day, and now he's getting revenge—"

"I know!" said Calvin. "That's why he pulled this tonight! It's why I'm helping him. We talked about it, and he just wanted to scare our folks. It's supposed to remind them of how he felt when our dads beat him up. Did you know that? Our dads practically lynched the guy back in the day." He laughed. "It's called a *prank*, Fiona. You know, Halloween? We get the treat; our parents get the trick."

"No," said Fiona. The idea that it was all a joke made her head hurt. There was no way.

Calvin smiled and shook his head. "Is this about your relationship? He told me you two had had a falling out. It's none of my business, but still, this feels like...an overreaction." Fiona exhaled hard as all the fatigue and fear of the last twenty-four hours finally pressed down on her. Could it really have been a prank all along? She looked around—at the hijacked van, the gun in her grip, the truly horrified expression on Calvin's face—and realized that maybe, okay, maybe she'd been freaking out a little. She'd heard so many things from so many people—Peter, her friends, her father, Filip Moss—that she might have gotten caught up in her own head. What if there was no magic book or conspiracy? Maybe the tuning had all been some act to get her amazed and turned on. Maybe her last interaction with Peter had driven her crazy, and she'd gone off on a suspicious rampage when she should've just gone on Thorazine.

Could it have all been a psychotic fantasy? Had she been played? Had her gut been wrong?

"He's...he's not hurting you," mumbled Fiona.

"Hurting us?" laughed Calvin. "Jesus, Fiona, Peter's making a takeout call! He's buying us breakfast! Please, *please* stop pointing that gun at me!"

There. Hearing his real name from Calvin made it all the more horribly real.

What if she'd imagined it? Dear God, what if she was batshit crazy and had been reading into an elaborate prank? Her arm screamed in pain. She lowered the gun, its weight making her sway on her feet.

But as she ran through the blur of emotions and violence that she'd been through so recently, she kept feeling like there were hiccups in that plan, things that a prank couldn't explain.

"Calvin, what about your dad? I saw the Pit Viper hurt him."

"The thing about that is—" Calvin glanced at the car and winced. "Jesus, did you do that to Perry?"

Fiona looked over at the bloody driver, suddenly worried that her gullibility and mania might have landed her an assault charge.

Bam, collision. The world went white, and her teeth clicked so hard that one of her incisors chipped. The shock sent the gun tumbling from her hands. She lurched back, terribly aware of the jarring pain, and looked to Calvin. The boy landed a second punch on her cheekbone, this one dropping her to the cold, muddy ground. Then he was on top of her, and though she struggled with all her might, he carefully pinned her and plowed one last jab into her face, making her lie back with the taste of copper filling her mouth. He picked up the gun from next to her and shoved it in his waistband.

"Hush," said Calvin, in the voice that she'd heard in her house earlier that night.

chapter
27

One of his hands, larger than she had imagined them, grasped her wrists, and he dragged her across the lawn toward the house. Every time she tried to wrench away from him, his hand tightened, and he said, "Stop it, stop it."

The porch was a splintery mess dotted with rancid empty liquor bottles, and the front hallway of the house was rickety and water stained. He dragged her across the floor and down a sagging staircase into the cold air of a basement.

The smell of mold was overpowering, making her cough and choke. Rooms lined the basement hallway, each numbered and secured with heavy padlocks on the outside. Faintly, behind everything, there was a steady drone of sobs and moans. Through the veil of hair falling in her face and the spots in her battered vision, Fiona looked through an open door and saw Bill, the big man who had stood next to Udo, kneeling in front of a filthy cot with Keller on it.

Keller sat with his arms and legs bound with duct tape, but even if his limbs had been free, Fiona could see that he wouldn't have been able to do anything. Something was missing from her old friend—his will, his control. He was present, but barely. His eyes spun in his head and drool bubbled from the corner of his mouth as the man gripped his chin with one hand and thumbed pills into his mouth with the other.

Bill saw Calvin and stood, letting the half-conscious Keller tumble back to the cot. "What the hell are you doing?"

"I got this," said Calvin.

"Does he know?" asked Bill, nodding at the ceiling.

"Don't worry about him; he has to prepare for his big moment," said Calvin. "I don't want to bother him. It'll be fine. Just keep dosing them all. He'll be starting up any minute."

Another door stood open, waiting for them. Cal dragged Fiona in there, tossing her onto the cold concrete floor with a *thud*. She did her best to get to her hands and knees, but before she could, Calvin kicked her squarely in the stomach. Pain and nausea stabbed her core, and she collapsed with a grunt. Part of her was hurt and confused by Calvin's betrayal, but at the same time she wasn't the least bit surprised. She'd always known who Calvin Hokes was behind the smile, it had just been convenient and heartwarming to think otherwise. Should've listened to her gut.

Lying on her side, her swimming vision finally evening out, she saw that they weren't alone. Across the filthy cell, another boy knelt, hands and feet bound with duct tape and a canvas bag over his head.

Calvin turned and closed the door, and Fiona saw the mask hanging down his back, the smiling painted face of a clown. It was the same Halloween mask worn by the man who'd knocked her out.

"You...attacked me," she coughed. "You broke into my house and drugged me."

"Yeah, okay," he said, turning back to her with a wild light in his eyes. "You're right, I did, Fiona, but you know what, you were going to fuck this up for me. You'd done so well so far, keeping him distracted with your music practice. But then I overheard you talking to Filip Moss, and I knew, I knew you and that fucking shithead were going to get in the way and ruin this opportunity." He inhaled, smiling triumphantly. "He's down here, by the way. Filip, that fucking tattoo casualty. His plan was so obvious. They're all down here. And just like you, they're all *screwed*. It's just gonna be a lot simpler for them than it is for you, let me tell you. Your boyfriend gets them. But I get you. And I'm not going to stop with a simple mind-wipe like he does."

She tried to stand, but the pain in her jaw and the agony in her stomach just wouldn't let her move properly. "Calvin, please, we're not safe here—"

"Oh, I'm *fine*, Fiona," he said. "The Pit Viper's protecting me. He thinks I'm one of his people now, like Perry and that Vince kid. See, I've planned ahead. I've always planned ahead. That's your problem, Fiona. That's *everyone's* problem." Calvin shook as he tore off his hoodie and gloves. His teeth were chattering, but he kept smiling. "Our dads, they don't run those mill rats out of town before it's too late. Then they don't think about hiring the Pit Viper before it's too late, and then when he shows back up they don't do anything until it's too late." He laughed. "My dad, Jesus, my dad. Do you know how easy it was to make sure he didn't get involved and ruin all my plans? To send him charging after you like some asshole, with a tire iron in his hand? But he was like you. He was going to fuck everything up. So he had to go."

Fiona felt sick to her stomach, not just from Calvin's sharp kick but from the tone of his voice, the way his plan unfolded before her eyes. She wanted to scream and spit and cry out that she was right about him, she always had been. But she needed to get out of here first. "Calvin, just…just calm down. Please, just help me."

"No, Fiona, no no no," he said, shaking his head. "Again, you think I'm stupid like everyone else. I know. You're not my *friend*. I'm nice to you, I do you favors over and over, but never once does it mean anything for me. Never. Once. You just want *him*, because he has power and he's handsome and he's obsessed with you in a weird way. But he's an idiot, Fiona, with his book and his magic and his big plans for revenge on our dumb little town." He came in close to Fiona, clawing his hands in her face like he was getting ready to scratch her eyes out. "See, that was my original plan, too. Get you, take over the town council from our dads, get the book, and be the ruling party in Hamm. Control everyone in the town with the music, get them to do what we wanted. And then I realized, that's small potatoes, Fiona. You, our crummy town council? Forget that. I don't have to settle for that. I don't need to spend time meditating or tuning or building up strength, because I was *born* stronger than all of you. All I have to do is make things the way I want them. I took care of you; I took care of my dad. And once he's gotten rid of all the kids from Hamm and brought me into his circle, I'll take care of the Pit Viper. Then I'll have his book, and I can go after this Udo guy, the one running things. Someday, I'll take care of him." He pulled PM's gun from his waistband and cocked back the hammer with a deadly click. "But first, I have to take care of this."

Calvin yanked the hood from the kneeling figure's head. His twin brother, William, stared up at him, a gag in his mouth. Like Keller, he was incoherent, a human being without any control. He didn't even react when Calvin took off his mask, only swayed on his knees, barely conscious.

"My brother, everyone," said Calvin in a husky voice. He

placed the barrel of the gun to William's temple. "Give him a hand."

The door blasted open, making Calvin whirl and Fiona jump.

Cal raised the pistol, but Peter wrenched it out of his hands in a single swift motion. He tossed the gun aside, grabbed Calvin by the face, and bashed his skull hard against the wall. Then he let him go, and Calvin slumped to the floor with a moan.

Fiona stared at Peter in awe. He was shirtless, and his tattoos seemed to float and swim over the lines of his muscles. In the crook of his one arm was the *Canoris*, held to his body the way a priest might clutch a Bible. But it was the glowing in Peter's eyes, unblinking and more vibrant than any color she'd ever seen, that most shocked her. He'd never looked so powerful, so otherworldly and divine, as he did now. It was like the human was gone, and he was made of the music itself.

But then he looked down on Fiona, and the man resurfaced once more—the eyes were blue and human, the tattoos sweat-sheened, the book heavy in his grip. It brought Fiona back to the memories of him she'd held on to—the sound of his laugh, the warmth of his hands, the taste of his skin.

"You're just in time," he said softly and extended a hand to her. "Come on, Fiona. I've been waiting for you."

chapter
28

He led Fiona out of the room, through the basement, up the stairs of the house. Bill with the acne stood in the foyer, watching them ascend.

"I'm ready," Peter said to them. "Get your plugs in and wait outside. It shouldn't take too long."

"Got it," said Bill. He glanced at Fiona out of the corner of his eye and smirked. "I got that thing you were asking for out of the van. Waiting for you upstairs."

"Beautiful," said Peter.

Upstairs, they entered a room set up like the roof the night they had tuned together—the circle of speakers, the laptop and turntable, the master copy. This time, though, the space was unambiguously decorated for a ritual. The floor was chalked with concentric circles surrounding a triangle, each ring in the illustrated echo dotted with planets and notes that corresponded to the diagrams she remembered from the book.

At the center of the chalk design was Betty, laid carefully on the floor.

"What are you going to do?" she asked, slowly approaching

her guitar, feeling the humid cloud of power that surrounded them.

"Complete my symphony," said Peter. "The first step was controlling them, bringing everyone here. Now, I'll drain everything from them. I will wipe them clean and consume their minds for my own strength."

She sensed him coming up behind her, and then one of his hands gently clasped her shoulder. She closed her eyes and shuddered, all the times he'd touched her and the excitement he'd inspired in her flooding back in a single instant. For the first time in weeks, she felt safe.

"But I don't want to do it alone," he said. "One last chance, Fiona. Please, come with me. You could be so powerful. Play Betty while I spin. You'll get their strength, too, and then we'll be one. Admit it—this is where you belong. Away from them." Emotion crept into his voice. "With me."

Though it disgusted her to do so, Fiona considered the offer. She and Betty could take all the power from Hamm, all the youth and free will contained in those dank rooms downstairs, and then walk away with it. She'd always known she was destined to flee her hometown, but she'd refused to abandon it out of sentiment; this way, she could have both, all Hamm's wasted potential and none of its boundaries. And every night, she would lay beside her brilliant lover and feel how deeply they were connected.

She could be something unique, something the world had never known. Double platinum, in the flesh.

All it took was giving him what he wanted.

She opened her eyes.

"You know, my father isn't right about a lot of things," she said calmly. "But he was right about you."

The hand tightened and yanked. She went stumbling across the room, her back slamming hard into a wall.

Peter walked over to his soundboard, kicking Betty aside as he did so. He flipped on a switch; at once, the red demon eyes of every speaker in the room lit up and seemed to stare at Fiona.

"When I'm done," he said, "I'm going to burn your guitar." He pressed a button, and the music kicked in.

Sound pierced her mind, making her nerves jump and vibrate. Fiona fell to her knees, grasping her ears. The place surged with his sonic power, emitting a bone-shaking drone like a million down-tuned bass guitars plucked at once. Then he played another note, and another, each one filling Fiona with utter agony. Her stomach cramped. Her head ached. It felt as though a million pounds were weighing down on her, pushing her to the floor.

Peter lowered himself to his knees in the center of his symbol, ready to tune. He laid the *Canoris* before him, opened to a page with a threatening black triangle at its center. Looking at him now, Fiona saw him ablaze with power. His eyes glowed white. His tattoos seemed to jump and dance in the air around him like a halo of spider's legs. He was God here.

"You're going to witness something incredible," he said in a deep voice that came from a far distance. "All those minds down in the basement, absorbed at once…and you with your potential, in the middle of it all. It will be an epic tuning." He smiled. "I'm afraid you'll be ripped apart inside. A side effect of your talent with the *instrumentis*. I wish I was sorry."

The *instrumentis*.

Through the storm of noise raging around her, her mind registered a familiar black shape on the floor, rumbling around with the vibrations like a puck on an air hockey table.

All hope was lost. The Pit Viper would win. But if she was going to die here, she would die with Betty in her arms.

Fighting the music that seemed to beat her down from all sides, doing her best to ignore the hot blood she felt rushing out of her nose, Fiona crawled across the floor and grabbed Betty by the neck.

On the floor next to Peter, the *Codex Canoris* leaped. Its pages fluttered open to the back section, to the sheet music of the *instrumentis*.

Peter's gaze shot from the book to Fiona. For a moment, the energy surrounding him seemed to flicker and weaken as they both registered the response the book had shown her.

Fiona gritted her teeth. Her gut urged her forward. She knew what she had to do.

"Take me!" she screamed over the noise. "Use me! I'm the one you want!"

"You idiot, it doesn't work that way," scoffed the Pit Viper, his voice floating above the music. He did his best to sound snide, but she could hear his doubt, clear as day.

"How many like him have you dealt with?" she cried out to the *Canoris*—no, not to the flimsy book, to the thing that lurked behind it, to the collective of music that guided the hand that *wrote* the book. "How many people have just used you? How long has it been since someone played your final movement? Take me, and I'll play only for you!"

Peter growled and reached out to grab the *Canoris*. There was a crackle in the air, and he yanked his hand away again as though stung.

Fiona positioned the guitar in front of her. She could feel the book's influence spilling out of its ancient pages, moving away from Peter and toward her. Betty began humming like a live wire. She didn't need a cord to plug in; she and Fiona were the cable, the jack, the electricity, the amplifier. They were raw power, a live wire.

And Fiona played guitar.

The boards of the room stretched outward and then bent back in, rocked by thermobaric music. Peter screamed, his body bent as his power became Fiona's.

Fiona felt herself lifted off the ground, sensed Betty straining at her strap and yet drawing closer to her. For a moment, Fiona saw an awesome vision—of the room, the planet, the universe passing away beneath her, until she and Betty hung in a vast realm where a great and hungry being greeted her from a throne older than the stars.

Just like that, she was back in the house, crumbling to her knees. When the particles in the air settled, a deep silence fell over the room.

Fiona blinked as her guitar went limp at her side.

The smoke pouring out of the speakers around her emitted the trash fire smell of ozone. The *Codex Canoris* sat on the floor with a blackened ring around it as though it had burst into flames, but the book itself was unharmed. Peter's master copy bubbled as it melted, dripping slowly down the edges of the turntable on which it rested. A cool breeze blew over her face from the shattered window.

And Fiona felt…incredible.

Weakened physically, but empowered deep in her heart. She had been touched by something more permanent and powerful than any melody or rhythm.

Scanning the remains of the tuning room, Fiona realized that she was alone. A trail of blood led her out the door.

She found what was left of Peter crawling down the stairs, wheezing and coughing, hair white and burned in patches. His limbs were thin and gnarled, and his tattoos were leaking thin streams of blood that made ugly smears on the wood where he writhed and clawed. When he saw Fiona approaching, he turned and slithered pitifully away from her, a bony hand raised against her. One of his fingernails fell off and clattered to the floor.

"No," he gasped. "No, please, no more."

Tears stung her eyes as she watched the boy she'd fallen for cowering away from her. But the strength that now surged through her veins prevented her from breaking down. She was something else now, and the boy she'd loved was gone. Maybe he had been for a long time.

As Peter reached the bottom of the stairs, Fiona noticed them waiting, and froze, repulsed. Peter followed her gaze and moaned in dread.

The teens of Hamm closed in around him, sunken-eyed and aghast. With his power over them evaporated, they suddenly remembered having their minds violated, rewired, and controlled by the Pit Viper's music. Fiona watched the looks of rage and shame move over their gaunt faces as more and more of them filed out of the basement and joined the sweaty mob.

Caroline was the first one to scream, but then they all did at once, and leaped onto the desiccated DJ with swinging fists and spit-flecked mouths. Fiona put her head down and pushed her way through the mob, unable to watch them tear him apart.

On the porch, Filip Moss sat on a railing, talking to a hunched silhouette with his back to Fiona. "Filip," she called, and the other figure slowly turned around, making her stop in her tracks.

"Nice swing," hissed Vince, one hand clasped to the side of his jaw.

Fiona's heart leaped, and she took a hasty step back, but Filip held up a hand. "It's all right, Jones," he croaked weakly. "He's the one who let us out of the basement. Untied us and everything. He's been on our side the whole time, we just didn't know it."

Fiona eyed the boy warily, then turned back to Filip. "I take it your plan didn't work."

"Yeah." He laughed through split lips. "Calvin Hokes, man, he got me within seconds. Beat me up pretty good. Next thing I knew, I was here. How'd you get here?" He gave her a once-over and squinted. "Where'd you get that guitar?"

"Long story," said Fiona, eliciting a guffaw from Vince. "It doesn't matter. We need to help everyone. They'll be done soon."

"Done with what?" asked Filip.

One after another, the teenagers of Hamm stumbled zombielike out of the house and into the night air. Fiona, Filip, and Vince all helped them walk shakily across the lawn to the vans parked around the side of the building. Some of the kids thanked them profusely; some refused to look at them. Everyone seemed to be coming out of a coma—only now did they notice their hideous surroundings, their cold and thirst.

Only Fiona really knew what was happening. With Peter's hold over them gone, her friends were seeing clearly for the first time in months.

Caroline, Horace, and Keller all cried when they saw her, and she wept softly along with them. It was hard, being a responsible adult with tears running down her face, but somehow Fiona managed. Caroline and Horace tried to apologize, and she tried to apologize back, and eventually they all just cried more and hugged. It hurt too much to think about it right now. Maybe they'd talk later.

But the basement, labyrinthine as it was, could only hold so many people. Some were still missing. Tess Baron was gone, as was Ronald Schaffer. Amy Golden. Carter Mason.

Rita Alam.

Fiona checked five times, each round of the basement more frantic than the last. She asked her friends, but none of them had seen her since the party had started.

"But they brought her here," shouted Fiona as Keller shook his head. "They must have."

"We didn't see her," said Horace, tears coursing down his face.

"At the party, there was a guy," sobbed Caroline. "An older guy. He kept talking to her…after that, I don't remember. God, Fiona, there's so much I don't remember."

"*Think*, Caroline!" urged Fiona. "She can't just be gone!"

"Jones," said Vince, "she's not here. We'll figure it out—"

"*She has to be here!*" screamed Fiona. She ran for the basement stairs, but Vince intercepted her and held her tight. She fought against him for a few minutes, and then let him hold her as she burst into sobs.

William Hokes seemed relatively together, and he offered to drive one of the vans full of kids back to Hamm. Surprisingly, he asked about his brother. When Fiona tried to tell him what had happened, he held up his hand to stop her. "It doesn't matter what he did in there," said William, shaking his head. "I need to bring him home. My mom, you know? She loves Cal so much."

But no one could find Calvin Hokes. All that was left was a bloodstained mask.

Some of the other kids from the basement weren't too messed up to drive, and Fiona, Filip, and Vince organized groups to van people back to Hamm.

As the last of the transports, driven by Filip, rolled into the darkness, Vince sauntered off and came back with a gas can sloshing around in his hand. Fiona got his meaning quickly. "We're not going to call the cops or anything?" asked Fiona.

"You want to talk to the police about all this?" asked Vince. "Not me. I say we burn it down and never, ever, ever come back."

"But then Peter—the Pit Viper, he gets away with it," she said.

"He's not getting away with *anything*," snapped Vince, pointing at her. It was the most emotion she'd ever seen from him. "We shut him down. Any and all of his friends better *watch themselves*. They learned an important lesson today: our people are *not to be fucked with*."

Fiona should have flinched at his outburst, but the heart behind it didn't frighten her in the slightest. She began to understand what Vince was doing here, what he'd been doing the whole time.

"For you?" she asked. "What was it?"

Vince sighed, running his hand through his hair. "My brother, Mike," he said. "He was Geraldine Brookham's boyfriend. He gave her the dose that killed her."

"Jesus, Vince, I'm so sorry."

"And he knew that he should never go back to that

fucking mill, but he did it anyway. He felt so guilty about Geraldine. We all loved her, my mom and me and him. She was the bomb, you know? And he killed her. So he just wanted to die." He shook his head. "Mike, man, he was so cool. He was everything I wanted to be, and he just let them take him. And when I heard the rumors about the Pit Viper spinning the mill, and saw that Perry kid for the first time in years, I thought…" His voice cracked, and he swallowed hard and shook his head before continuing. "They never found him. He could still be out there. I have to know."

His honesty warmed Fiona. He was letting her see his pain, no frills, no defenses. She put a hand on his shoulder. "You did the right thing, Vince."

Vince nodded slowly and sniffed. "Yeah. Yeah, I did. That guy, the Pit Viper, kidnapped my brother. He fucked my entire life up." He raised the gas canister and unscrewed the cap. "So I'm going to wipe that piece of shit off the face of the earth, is my feeling."

"Let's do it," she said.

The house went up quickly, the old wood yielding to the flames in no time. They watched it burn from the lawn, the heat searing Fiona's face. She wanted to say goodbye to Peter, to the side of the person she'd known and cared for, but couldn't bring herself to do it. That his love had led her here, burning down a house after saving her brainwashed friends, poisoned all their time together in her mind.

She expected Vince to lead her to another white van, but instead he brought her to the Fiddlers' hatchback parked a half mile down the dirt road, one window broken and the busted dash dangling wires.

"Impressive," said Fiona.

"Not all Hamm kids are angels," mumbled Vince.

Once he'd re-hotwired the car, he drove them slowly back to the highway, the flaming skeleton of the house flickering in their rearview mirror.

Fiona watched Vince in the glow of the dashboard lights. Something still bothered her.

"If you were trying to avenge your brother," she asked, "why'd you let this happen to everyone?"

"Because of Udo," he said. "My brother didn't get found dead in a ditch. Plenty of his friends did, but not Mike. This fucking creep, the guy behind it all...I wasn't just gunning for the Pit Viper, I was going after *him*. Because if I find him, he can tell me what happened to my brother. But then there was this chick with her own plan fucking things up for me left and right, so I had to improvise." Vince looked at her face and visibly softened. "Okay, look, maybe it's shitty that I let the Pit Viper take everyone in town to get to Udo, but it was the only way. That DJ was just a puppet. I want to cut out the cancer, not just treat the symptoms, you know?"

Fiona nodded. "Don't worry, Vince," she said. "We will."

He glanced at her out of the corner of his eye. "Swordfish is fine," he mumbled.

chapter
29

November swept darkly over Hamm. It was soggy, not quite cold enough for snow but just bad enough to make the rain unbearable. Every lawn was sneaker-sucking quicksand. Every tree looked limp and bedraggled.

More than the landscape, though, the hearts of Hamm's residents were bruised and broken. The attempted kidnapping had left cracks in the veneer of the small town's spirit that might never heal.

The morning after Halloween, the teenagers of Hamm had returned home, strung out and weeping and begging forgiveness from their stunned parents. The adults had welcomed them back with open arms and kept them home for days, filling them with good food and stern advice.

Even though they'd only been gone a night, many of Hamm's teens spent their first week at home going through the symptoms of withdrawal. Somehow, over the course of a few hours, they'd gone from fresh-faced kids to ravaged junkies. Neighbors were trading remedies for shivering, vomiting, and extreme weight loss as though they were recipes for blueberry crumble. The local drugstore quickly ran out of hair dye being used to treat the mysterious white streaks so many of the teens now sported in their hair.

But the parents of Hamm didn't look too hard for an excuse. They went the easy route: drugs. Their kids had been sucked in by some dance-hall tweakers and had gotten forcefully hooked on Molly or smack or whatever substance they had read about most recently on Drudge Report. After all, the kids barely seemed to know what had happened themselves. And when doctors came back claiming that most of them had tested positive for Orbitin—a rare and discontinued seasickness drug that made the inner ear more sensitive to sound waves—the parents nodded, said thank you, and moved on as quickly and quietly as possible, taking care of their children with the same bewilderment and shame with which they had lost them.

Some families weren't so lucky. Edgar and Janelle Hokes were furious. Rumor was that Calvin had apparently contacted Janelle asking her to wire him some money, but even his twin brother didn't know whether or not that was true. Edgar Hokes, who now used a cane to walk and couldn't hear music of any kind without going into dizzy spells, had made several very public statements that Robert Jones should step down as the head of the town council. No one backed him up.

The Barons claimed Tess was actually at a rehab program in Los Angeles, though when he got drunk enough at the sports bar downtown, her father Dave would refer to Tess as "that no-good runaway bitch."

The Alams, Rita's parents, were beside themselves. They pleaded with anyone who would listen, and repeatedly went to the city to hand out flyers and speak with the police. When the Alams visited Hamm High, Rita's friends all avoided them out of embarrassment and guilt.

There was no sign of her. Rita had vanished into thin air.

But besides those few worrisome cases, Hamm did what it did best—it forcibly forgot. The parents scolded and nagged their teens for even speaking of this breach of their small town's sanctity. Younger siblings were told that their teenage brothers and sisters had been partying too hard. The town council began plans for the Hamm Holiday Festival, Christmas tree and all.

Robert Jones remained the town council's leader, though he was a tougher man than he once was. Even with his theft from the council members out in the open, no one thought they could run Hamm better than Robert. Most of the money had gone toward the victims' families and the town anyway. That was good enough for everyone.

Besides the Hokeses', no one messed with the Jones family. Not after what little their kids could tell them about their rescue.

By the second Monday of December, Hamm High had almost fully returned to normal. Now that they were over the hump of their withdrawal, most of the kidnapped kids acted as though nothing had happened. Everyone resumed the usual grind of gossip, homework, and weekend partying, though they did so with a strange, cowed innocence that was full of too much guilt to be truly pure.

But every so often, a couple of students would walk out to the far bleachers for a smoke or would try to use one of the music rooms to catch up on some homework. And they would look up, and stop, and apologize without expecting to. And then they'd turn and leave.

And later, with their friends, feeling a little uneasy but not knowing why, they'd whisper, "Dude, I ran into Fiona Jones today."

She was like a ghost. Everyone could swear they had a class with her, but no one knew. Sometimes, all you'd catch was a flash of the Ace of Spades floating over the cars in the parking lot, the soft harp-ish twang of scales being practiced on a Les Paul. She took the guitar everywhere now—"like a samurai of old," she explained to her teachers, which no one entirely understood.

But like a ghost, there was a pall over Fiona Jones. Her classmates couldn't remember exactly how she'd been tied to their recent ordeal, to the cold and horrible house they woke in with their hands covered in blood, only that she was. But they also seemed to understand that they owed her one. Without her, they might not have ever made it home to their familiar blankets and grateful parents. So they left her alone, and the seniors and juniors whispered to the sophomores to do the same. And she, for her part, seemed to like it that way.

Some kids talked about how she used to run with the rocker crowd, Horace Palmada and Doug Keller and that crew. When asked about Fiona, those kids would answer half-heartedly or dodge the question but would always make one thing clear: Fiona Jones was the real deal.

Horace Palmada, Caroline Fiddler's boyfriend, got especially grave if you mentioned her to him. "Fiona's on a different level," he would say, shaking his head. "I don't even want to know what she's up to." Then he would usually tack on, "We dated."

The only people Fiona was seen hanging out with were Filip Moss and Fish or Vincent or whatever that guy's name was. A few scandalous rumors spread about Fiona being polyamorous, but they died quickly; Fiona never came off

as flirtatious or even that warm to either of her rumored
boyfriends, and besides, the way those dudes looked, no one
wanted to be the one who got caught whispering about them
if they *were* dating her.

By Christmas break, even the freshmen had gotten the
story trickled down to them from their elders: There was
something weird with Fiona Jones. Something you didn't want
to mess with. Best to back off.

"You want to hear a story someone told me about you?"

"I don't know, do I?" asked Fiona.

She and Swordfish sat on the shag-carpeted floor of his
living room, discussing their next move. Filip had just left,
promising to send them some news stories he'd recently dug
up on a music forum. Swordfish was slumped against the
base of the couch, while Fiona sat cross-legged. In front of
them was spread their research materials: maps of nearby
towns, print-outs of the few news stories they could find
about the deaths of the original mill club rats. Everything was
heavily marked with red pen to indicate locations, patterns,
and obvious obstacles.

"You know my cousin Gabriella?" asked Swordfish. "She's
a year below us? Skinny girl, wears a lot of yellow."

Fiona nodded after a moment. "Yeah. Big smile?"

"Huge smile," he said. "She asked me about you. She was
like, 'Do you hang out with that girl?' And I said yeah. And
she was like, 'I heard she took over a biker gang by beating
the leader in a switchblade fight.' "

"A switchblade fight!" Fiona laughed. Swordfish joined
in, shrugging as if to say, *Right, but these kids, you know?* "I

wish I were that cool. Where'd she hear that?"

"Ah, around," he said. "It's just funny to me, because you were always Fiona Jones, this rock-and-roll chick whose dad ran things around here and who had the sweets for my boy Horace, right?"

"*Had the sweets?* Who says that anymore?"

"But now, you're this...figure," he said, ignoring her. "Like, everyone's a little afraid of you but also really respectful of you. You're a good *bad guy.* The...*avenging angel* of Hamm, if that's not too corny."

She smiled, pleased to hear it put that way. *Avenging angel.* Not bad, pretty metal. Rita would have thought that was cool. Would've called her that for weeks.

Rita, who should be here right now.

Slowly, Fiona's smile fell. "Tell her it's not like that. Tell her it's nothing to be proud of. It's all just horrible."

"I hear you," said Vince, nodding sagely. "Admit it, though, maybe you're something more, now. Something crazy. Everyone sees it." He stared at her again, doing nothing to hide it. "I definitely see it."

Hearing him say it was nice. Not beautiful or sublime or earth-rocking, but nice as hell. She'd grown to appreciate how straightforward he was, how he'd always been. His no-bullshit realism gave a sensation of being able to do whatever she wanted. Sometimes, she wondered if they would've made a good couple before all this...but no. The truth was, they had nothing to talk about besides this—the print-outs, the maps, the schemes. She was just looking for something to hold onto.

"Anything else?" she said, gathering up the papers.

"William Hokes stopped me in school today," said Swordfish. "He wants in."

"Oof," she said. "I don't know, dude. That guy's just such a bozo. What do you think?"

"I think he could be useful," said Swordfish. "Those jock types are assholes, but they have a weird Batman streak. Truth and justice, righting wrongs, all of that. I say for now, we keep him at arm's length, but we have him do some asking around for us. That way, we can cut him off if things get…messy."

She nodded. "Good call. But let's be honest, things are about to get messy really quickly."

Vince rubbed his forehead and sighed. "You got that right."

When Fiona got home, her mother clucked at her for her tardiness, but still served her a lamb chop with some wild rice and asparagus. Her dad was gone again, staying late at the office planning the Holiday Festival. Same as almost every night since she and her friends had returned. He still couldn't deal.

After dinner, she sat on her bed and wondered about William Hokes. She hoped his heart was in the right place, but she knew that no matter what he promised, part of him just wanted to find his brother. And while she understood that, she had to be ready to box him out when that side of things reared its ugly head. William might be surprisingly noble, like Vince suggested, but she couldn't be bothered to think about whether or not Calvin had been worth saving. That dude had shown her who he was, out loud, and it would be a mistake on her part to tell herself he'd changed.

And besides, she'd shown everyone that she wasn't the *best* judge of character.

Fiona sighed. Man, that stung. To doubt herself, to admit she'd been wrong. But she had to start thinking like Swordfish, living on the total honesty principle. It was what she admired in him—his ability to just tell it like it was. If Fiona was going to do that, she had to admit how taken she had once been by Peter.

And maybe *had once been* was a lie, too.

She thought about Peter every day. Static memories of the times they'd spent together haunted her every waking moment—the way he'd smiled at her, the way he'd believed in her. She wasn't sure she would ever be over him, but she definitely wanted to be. It would take time, and she'd have to work on it, but maybe she could forget him eventually. If she wanted to.

Vince was right about one thing, though: She'd become a bit of an outsider. She'd heard the rumors and whispers—people were freaked out by her. And that was a bummer, and a little lonely, but maybe it was for the best.

After all, did she really need a circle of friends when she had all the company she'd ever need, right here in her room?

Fiona knelt down, slid the black leather case out from under her bed, and opened it.

"Hey, guys," she said.

Atop Betty's black wooden body sat the *Codex Canoris*. Fiona had swiped the book as she'd splashed gasoline around the house, shielding her eyes from the sight of Peter's crushed corpse. After all, she'd only walked away from that house because the *Canoris* had transferred Peter's power to her and Betty. Both she and her guitar owed the book. And anyway, she wanted to learn what it had to teach her.

She'd been sitting with Betty and the *Canoris* all week, strengthening the connection between herself, her instrument, and the power behind the book. It wasn't all about hitting those jarring, ear-crushing worship notes. So much of the *musica instrumentis* was about lacing the arcane musical language through normal melodies, infecting common music with the resonant tones that resided within the depths of the yellowed pages.

It was taking a little while, but Fiona had all the time in the world, and anyway, it was worth it. She'd slowly learned that there were ways to position her hand, both physically and spiritually—yeah, her *spiritual hand*, as insane an idea as that was—which could easily meld magical sound with rock music. Now, when she played Betty, Fiona channeled emotion and madness into actual riffs, not just freestyle playing. With enough practice and dedication, her music would be able to seize minds, break hearts, and even drain the life out of those who stood in her way, just like Peter's had done.

Who knew? She might even start a band.

Fiona stared into the book and considered Vince's *avenging angel* comment. She sighed. It would be nice, she knew, to return to the life of Fiona Jones, the girl riding her bike through the cute small town. She'd spied Horace the other day at school and found herself nostalgic for what they'd had, the simple pleasure of giggling, hidden sex with a guy she thought was too terrific.

But maybe she'd stopped being that kind of girl long ago, when she'd first watched her father beat Peter on the side of the road. And maybe Peter had taught her, as she'd studied under him and had grown to love him, that someone with a gift like hers needed to do the things that others couldn't.

Every minute Rita was gone, Fiona's heart broke. She'd visited the Alams two days ago, and had promised Rita's teary-eyed parents that she'd get their daughter back if it killed Fiona in the process. That was her number one priority: find her friend. It would take skill, power, and balls, but Fiona had those in spades, and she'd put them to good use to right this wrong.

The obvious next stop was the benefactor, that greasy old creep she'd met in that horrible squat. The person who'd hurt those kids long ago, who'd made this whole twisted horror show possible.

Udo, she thought. *If you can hear me, run. Run to the hills. Run for your life.*

She played her guitar, filling the air with black-magic rock and roll.

Acknowledgments

Unending thanks to my mom and dad for their support, to my brother Quin for the endless icy runs along the overpass, to my sister Maria for always being there, to Lynn for being great, and to Arthur for the boops. Thank your all for teaching me to love more, every day.

Big thanks to the many friends who saw this book come about and kept me laughing: James McBride, Max Baehr, Abbie Walker, John Cheever, Jen Reese, Alex and Emily Wenner, Maddy Thaler, Jeramey Kraatz, Kim Kelly, Lily Domash, Matt Goldenberg, Ben Umanov, Luke Mecklenberg, Reed Bruemmer, JP Hooper, and Casey McIntyre for what she said at that airport food court.

A bowed head and clasped hands to Stacy Abrams, my intrepid editor at Entangled. Countless thanks to Tina Wexler, who cooled me down when I was fiery and stoked me up when I'd grown cold.

A raised fist for Melissa Harris, whose perseverance became my own. Melissa, I'm here if you need me.

To Azara. The stars, your eyes; the wind, my hand. I love you, I love you, I love you.

This book wouldn't exist without three people we've lost, so here's to them. The first is Nick Harris, who this thing is dedicated to, but screw it, I'll raise a thousand glasses in his name. The second is JP Nocera, the only man who died without any enemies and the patron saint of weirdo guitarists. He is sorely missed. And last but not certainly least is Mr. Lemmy Kilmister, who passed away during the writing of this book but gave us perhaps the greatest back catalog in the history of music. I leave you with his immortal words: "Don't you listen to a single word against rock and roll."

Seventh Born
by Monica Sanz

A Witchling Academy novel

Sera dreams of becoming a detective and finding her family. When the brooding yet handsome Professor Barrington offers to assist her if she becomes his assistant, Sera is thrust into a world where someone is raising the dead and burning seventhborns alive. As Sera and Barrington work together to find the killer, she'll discover that some secrets are best left buried...and fire isn't the only thing that makes a witch burn.

Echoes
by Alice Reeds

They wake on a deserted island. Fiona and Miles, high school enemies now stranded together. No memory of how they got there. Each step forward reveals the mystery behind the forces that abducted them. And soon, the most chilling discovery: something else is on the island. Something that won't let them leave alive.